"Because of you, my brother will never have a ranch or anything else to lose."

Shadow blinked back sudden tears. She hadn't cried since she was seventeen. She wouldn't cry now.

People in the diner were openly staring. She and Grey were clearly the stars of the town's reality show. Their waitress came to take their orders, but Grey waved her off. He waited until they were alone again. "I didn't...kill him, Shadow. You either believe me or you don't, which you obviously still don't."

"Neither does anyone else."

"If I had any way to prove myself to them, to you, I would." He paused, eyeing her with those sharp blue-green eyes. "Come on," he said. "You and I were a couple once. We even picked out baby names."

Shadow knew she'd just turned pale.

"Why did you come in here today?" Grey asked. "I doubt it was to have lunch with me."

"I—" She caught the pointed gaze of a woman in the booth across the aisle. "I have something to tell you. It's important."

"Fine. Let's take this outside."

Yet how would she find the words to tell him after all these years?

Dear Reader,

For Shadow Moran and Grey Wilson, the course of true love hasn't exactly run smooth. But does it ever? My own relationship had some ups and downs before we knew we were exactly right for each other. And many years later, we still are. Of course, we never had the kind of issues to deal with that my hero and heroine do.

Ten years ago, after a tragic accident, Shadow and Grey's relationship ended abruptly. Now she's back in their hometown of Barren, Kansas. Grey still loves her, but he already has his hands full trying to save his family's ranch from modern-day rustlers and seeking evidence to prove he's innocent in the long-ago death of Shadow's brother. Without that proof, she will never forgive him.

But when Grey learns he and Shadow have a nine-year-old daughter, things take yet another turn—and love for them seems even more impossible than it was before.

I've always loved reunion stories. I'm also partial to secret-baby books, and *Last Chance Cowboy* has both! If you haven't read the first Kansas Cowboys book about Blossom Kennedy and Logan Hunter, you can find a coupon in this book for *The Reluctant Rancher*. And then please join me again for the third book in this series—coming soon!—in which Logan's estranged brother, Sawyer, returns home to fall in love all over again with Olivia Wilson, Grey's sister.

See what I mean about reunion stories?

If you'd like to learn more about my books, please visit my website, leighriker.com, and sign up for my newsletter there.

Happy reading!

Leigh Riker

HEARTWARMING

Last Chance Cowboy

—

Leigh Riker

Recycling programs
for this product may
not exist in your area.

ISBN-13: 978-0-373-36838-9

Last Chance Cowboy

Copyright © 2017 by Leigh Riker

Printed in U.S.A.

www.Harlequin.com

Leigh Riker, like many dedicated readers, grew up with her nose in a book. This award-winning, *USA TODAY* bestselling author still can't imagine a better way to spend her time than to curl up with a good romance novel—unless it's to write one! She's a member of the Authors Guild, Novelists, Inc. and Romance Writers of America. When not writing, she's either in the garden, watching movies funny and sad, or traveling (for research purposes, of course). With added "help" from her mischievous cat, Daisy, she's now at home working on a new novel. She loves to hear from readers. You can find Leigh on her website, leighriker.com, on Facebook at leighrikerauthor and on Twitter, @lbrwriter.

Books by Leigh Riker

Harlequin Heartwarming

The Reluctant Rancher

Lost and Found Family
Man of the Family
If I Loved You

Harlequin Intrigue

Agent-in-Charge
Double Take

Harlequin Next

Change of Life

Red Dress Ink

Strapless

Visit the Author Profile page
at Harlequin.com for more titles.

With love for Linda and Kim,
Who are the daughters I always wanted
(My boys chose well!)

CHAPTER ONE

GREY WILSON WAS a mistake she wouldn't make again.

On what should have been a peaceful late morning in June, Shadow Moran peered out her office windows onto Main Street and felt another prickle of unease slide across her shoulder blades. She'd been having the same feelings for the past hour—no, since the night before—and for good reason. She had no doubts. As if she'd conjured him up after her midnight ruminations, Grey must be somewhere nearby.

In the past year, since her return to Barren and the Kansas plains where they'd grown up, she'd had an almost daily sense of him, even when he couldn't be seen. She'd been avoiding him, but she couldn't avoid him any longer. She'd made her decision just before dawn, and it was more than time. Ten years, in fact.

Now she just needed the courage to implement this first part of her plan at last.

After another quick scan of the area, Shadow spied him on the other side of the street. Sure enough, he'd just come out of the Cattlemen's Bank, the door swinging shut behind him. In spite of her decision and eternal misgivings, something deep inside her turned over. She should mind her own business. Literally. Her Mother Comfort Home Health Care Agency was still like a baby that had to be nurtured and fed and cared for 24/7.

Still, she turned from the window, then right back again.

Shadow watched Grey walk along the street then enter Annabelle's Diner before she scooted her desk chair back. Her stomach clenched with nerves, she flipped the Closed sign around on the door, locked it, then went across the street and down two blocks to the fifties-style diner at the corner of Main and Cottonwood.

At noon the place was already jumping.

Shadow halted just inside the door, taking in the swathes of chrome and Formica at the front counter and on the tables. They were all filled. Several people glanced at her before their curious gazes flicked away.

Frowning, Grey sat alone in the only four-person booth that might otherwise be empty, his long legs stretched out into the aisle as he studied his shined-up boots. His ever-present black Stetson was slung on a hook at the end of the booth. Ever the cowboy gentleman, he'd probably removed the hat as soon as he'd stepped inside.

As if he could sense her presence, too, he looked up and their gazes locked. In those ten years apart he'd only gotten more attractive, turned from a boy into a man in his prime. His glossy, light-brown hair still had sun streaks from the long hours he spent outdoors. His eyes were the same blue-green with dark lashes that she remembered. His broad shoulders strained the fabric of his coming-to-town, Western-style suit, but denim and leather were more his style, and Shadow detected a grim set to his mouth. Like his defeated posture, the suit looked all wrong.

Despite their differences, Shadow knew him well. She didn't bother to say hello or wait for an invitation to sit down. She slid into the seat opposite him. Along with the old gossip she'd stirred up as soon as she hit town, she'd been hearing fresh rumors for weeks about his financial troubles with Wilson Cattle, which must explain his visit to the bank. "What happened?"

Grey didn't pretend to misunderstand. "Nothing."

"Barney denied you a loan?"

His frown deepened. "What makes you think I need one?"

"People talk." And, in fact, it seemed everyone in the diner kept looking at them as if they wanted to say something now.

Grey fiddled with his fork. "Barney practically warned me not to darken his door again. You want to gloat, go ahead."

"No, I'd rather watch you eat a good hamburger. You look like you need one."

He groaned. "Don't make me think of beef right now."

She bit her lip so she wouldn't ask, *What will you do without that loan?*

As she knew all too well, farming—ranching, in his case—could be a tightrope walk over a huge, deep chasm. Yet for a long time, and until recently, Wilson Cattle had been a moneymaking operation, its thousands of acres and rich grassland studded with purebred Black Angus cows and prize-winning bulls. Shadow understood how important it was to Grey, but she had no love for his ranch or even the much smaller farm where she'd grown up.

As a girl, escaping her family's home had been a big part of her plans for her future. Now, Shadow would make a success of Mother Comfort and secure her independence—financial as well as emotional—from anyone else. She would never be poor again, and this was to be part one of the newer plan she'd formulated in the night. She should tell him what she'd come to say, then leave, let him digest the news on his own. But then, Grey had just had news of a different sort.

"Guess I'll have to tighten my belt another notch," Grey said at last, as if reading her mind. "I'll be downright skinny soon."

Shadow tried not to care. She stared at her shoes and lost her nerve, yet something drew her to stay. She hated to admit it was that look on his face and the hard line of his mouth.

She and Grey weren't together anymore, never would be again, but she had loved him once and her stubborn heart kept revisiting better times. Being home had only made that worse. More importantly, they shared a lifetime bond, one Grey didn't know about. This wasn't the right time to tell him after all.

As if her mouth wasn't connected to her brain, she said instead, "Maybe a bigger bank in Kansas City would grant you a loan."

"Been there, done that. No deal." He toyed with the fork again. "I think I'm a pretty good manager—better than that—or I was, until a few months ago. Then things started happening and keep on happening, and now this bank loan, and I can't help wondering if my dad was right to leave Wilson Cattle in my hands, even on a trial basis..."

"All is not lost," she said and tilted her head to look into his troubled eyes. Grey cracked a faint smile, as if he couldn't help himself. She'd always been able to talk him out of a bad mood after one of their many disagreements in the past. They'd been able to make each other laugh even at the worst times—until tragedy struck and they couldn't laugh, or love, any more.

"Now see what you've done." He waggled his eyebrows. "We always did make a good pair, Shadow."

"We did not." He gazed back at her, and

her pulse skipped a beat. "Grey. If we were going to hitch ourselves together like a couple of oxen, we'd have done so long ago. You know why we didn't."

Shifting her gaze, she stared at a point just over his shoulder. Maybe she shouldn't have come back to Barren, or stayed, or even walked across the street today. Ten years hadn't been long enough to quell her memories, including the good ones, and every time she saw him she also thought of what might have been. That is, before the other, worse memories flooded her mind.

As if he'd thought the same thing, Grey stopped smiling. His eyes were the color of dark jade now. "We live in the same town, Shadow. We see each other now and then… when you aren't trying to keep away from me like you did at my nephew's birthday party a few weeks ago. Or when you're not answering your phone. You knew I was going to call." He glanced toward the street. "Why give people something more to talk about?"

"I'm not the one who caused that—after what you did—"

"What your *brother* did."

She lowered her voice. "Because of you,

my *brother* will never have a ranch or any-thing else to lose." She blinked back a sud-den rush of tears. She hadn't cried since she was seventeen—ten years ago. She wouldn't cry now, but her voice trembled. "Jared doesn't have a *life*. There's nothing you could say, nothing you could do, to fix that. To bring him back," she added.

People were openly staring now. In one way, she and Grey were alike, the stars of Barren's own reality show. Their waitress came to take their orders, but Grey waved her off. "Give us a minute. Thanks." His voice stayed quiet, too, but his eyes were in-tense. He waited until they were alone again. "I didn't…kill him, Shadow. You either be-lieve me or you don't, which you obviously still don't."

"Neither does anyone else in this town."

Grey said, "If I had any way to prove my-self to them, to you, I would." He paused, watching her with those sharp blue-green eyes. "Come on," he said. "You and I *were* a couple once. We even picked out baby names. I still remember your favorite."

Shadow felt herself turn pale.

"Why did you come in here today, anyway?" Grey asked. "I doubt it was to have lunch with me."

"I—" She couldn't find the words. Shadow caught the pointed gaze of a woman in the booth across the aisle who'd been trying to control her two young children, then had given up to focus on Shadow and Grey. "I have something to tell you. It's—important." *Life-changing, really*, she wanted to say, but the words wouldn't come.

"Fine. Let's take this outside."

Yet, how would she phrase what she had to tell him after all these years? She hadn't thought this through carefully enough, and Grey was already hurting, worried about the fate of his ranch. In a show of compassion she wouldn't have considered last night, Shadow decided she couldn't blindside him after he'd already suffered such a blow today.

"I really can't stay. I have appointments this afternoon, and if I don't start now I'll be late. I'll be in my office all day tomorrow." By then, she'd know exactly what to say. "Come see me anytime."

"Shadow—"

She was already sliding toward the end of the booth when Grey said, "You're...okay, aren't you? Not sick or anything?"

"No, not sick," she said, standing to block the woman's view from the opposite booth.

"I'll be there. Tomorrow." Grey held up a hand. "Before you run off, I heard from Logan the other day. Did you get a call from Blossom?"

At the mention of their mutual friends, who'd recently become engaged, she turned back. "No, why? Is something wrong?"

Grey's gaze held hers. "She's going to ask you to be her maid of honor."

Shadow blinked. The change of topic had taken her by surprise and was almost welcome. "Really. I've never been in a wedding before."

He eyed her through those dark lashes, taking his time before he said, "You'd look real nice in a long white gown."

She swallowed. This hadn't gone as she'd hoped, and neither would trying to talk about something else. "White is for the bride. More likely, I'd have to wear a dress I wouldn't wear to my own funeral."

The last word hung in the air like a fresh reminder of everything that stood between them—a fresh reminder of Jared.

"Blossom has better taste than that," Grey

said, and Shadow winced. She'd only heard secondhand about bridesmaids' dresses.

"I shouldn't have said that. Blossom has every right to be happy without my mood spoiling things. She should pick somebody else."

"I'll leave you two to settle that," Grey said. "Fair warning, though—Logan's already asked me to be his best man." He held her gaze for another long moment, then added, "Which I am."

MOST PEOPLE SAID he had too much pride, and it was never easy for Grey to lose at anything. Especially with Shadow. Seeing her hadn't helped. That spill of jet-black hair, her dark brown eyes and chiseled cheekbones… He'd felt like the love-struck boy he'd been before everything fell apart. After her brother died, he'd come close to begging her to believe in him. But then, Grey had hesitated when he said, *I didn't…kill him*. He had his doubts about Jared's death. About himself.

And today his luck wasn't running very high. If he'd tried for more of their conversation in town, they might well have ended up in a nasty argument. Still wondering what she might say tomorrow, he drove home and down to the barn to find his new cowhand waiting for him, shifting his weight from one boot to the other in obvious impatience. Which came as no surprise.

"Glad I caught you. I was just headin' into town myself." Somewhere in his mid-twenties, Cody Jones had a shock of wheat-colored hair, close cut on the sides but longer on top. He still looked like a kid to Grey, who'd turned thirty this year, but Cody stood inches taller than Grey did, even at six feet. He had to look up into Cody's merry dark eyes, which never set well with Grey, who was now the sole person of authority at Wilson Cattle. "Thought I'd get my pay first."

"Sorry, you'll have to wait." After his morning appointment at the bank, he was sure about that. "We sold off those cattle last week, but the check hasn't cleared." He wouldn't mention the loan.

"Man, I thought trying to make a living on the circuit was tough. Five seasons as a bronc rider before I quit to hire on here, but winnin' prize money was way easier than this."

"And how much did you win?"

Cody flashed a grin. "Not enough."

"You know any riders who are earning good money?"

"Just the top guys, and they really rake it in. Private planes and all."

"There you go. Most don't ever reach that level. Being a top rodeo cowboy's not that easy, either—it's like winning the lottery."

Grey had tried rodeo, too, for a couple of years after college, so he could empathize with Cody. Still, Grey viewed him almost as the younger brother he'd never had. He'd given him advice before, taught him quite a bit already and wanted to believe that Cody would, sooner or later, be of real value to Wilson Cattle. Which reminded him to ask, "You feed the horses this morning?"

Cody had "forgotten" twice last week. He had a tendency to focus on himself instead of his work. Grey toyed with the idea of docking his pay for the double oversight, then discarded it. He lived up to his obligations.

Too bad he couldn't take that to the bank.

Before seeing Shadow, he'd made a quick stop at the local tack store to order a new saddle and buy some lesser supplies, but he'd come out empty-handed. His credit had been declined. Grey had been having a hard time paying the bills lately, which only compounded his growing sense of failure. A best man. Was he, really? If only he could find some way to prove to her, to everyone else—maybe most of all, to himself—that he was innocent in the death of Jared Moran. But what if he discovered just the opposite?

Cody's grin had stuck to his face. "Guess I can wait to go into town. Maybe on Saturday night I'll find a nice little buckle bunny to dance with. To be honest, that's what I miss most about the rodeo circuit."

"Good luck finding one in Barren." Grey noticed that halfway down the barn aisle, Cody had left a wheelbarrow full of steaming manure. The pungent aroma threatened to spread through the entire barn. Grey pointed. "Right now you'd better stop daydreaming and clean up that mess."

Cody's expression fell. "Thought you wanted me to mend fence today near the boundary with Logan's property. By the way, he's got a hole there, too."

Grey frowned. Two sections of fence breached at the same time? He wondered if that could be a coincidence.

"Can't be in both places at once," Cody added.

"First things first. The manure won't take long. Then get out there before those cows wander off the ranch."

Cody grumbled to himself but Grey had other things on his mind. He left Cody to the wheelbarrow and went on up to the house.

He wouldn't tell his dad about the loan just yet. A few years ago, after a long time spent as a single father, Everett Wilson had remarried, turned the operation over to Grey and moved to Dallas with his bride, as he still called Grey's stepmom, Liza. Grey was fully responsible here. He had to protect their mutual heritage or they'd end up with nothing. Yet those new holes in the fence nagged at him.

Maybe the loan he'd been denied, his cash flow issue and Shadow's blame weren't his only problems. He hoped tomorrow would be better.

As the sun began to set, Shadow pulled into her driveway. The house she'd recently purchased in Barren was her pride and joy. For the first time in her life, she had something all her own. At least, in thirty years it would be, considering her new mortgage. The house was another, necessary part of her plans for the future. But Shadow was still angry with herself for chickening out on telling Grey what she'd decided to tell him. And just when she needed to be alone, to rehearse what to say tomorrow, her mother was waiting for her on her front steps.

Shadow opened the garage door with her remote control, rolled inside then shut the door behind her. She went in through the kitchen and down the short hall to the entryway.

"Mama. What are you doing out there?"

Her mother blinked. "I came to see you. Didn't know I needed an excuse."

"I didn't say you did." What was wrong now? Through the screen door Shadow could see that her mother, in her late forties, looked somewhat worn today. Her dark hair hung in dull hanks around her face. What was wrong now?

Considering what had happened right after Jared died, she shouldn't feel bad for her remaining parent. Yet she still loved her mother, who'd lost her husband—Shadow's father—a year ago, who still looked lost herself, and showed up now and then to see Shadow as if she'd forgotten their rift. Shadow always had a hard time saying no to anything her mother needed and rarely did.

"Come inside," Shadow insisted.

"I'm fine right here," her mother said. "Actually, I came to tell you my water heater—yes, the one you bought me—leaked all over the floor last night." She added, "I don't know if it can be fixed, and I don't get my government check for another ten days."

Shadow forced herself to gentle her tone. They'd had this discussion before, but to Shadow's sorrow, nothing had changed. "Mama. How many times have I told you to sell that place?"

"It's my home."

Shadow suppressed a twinge of regret. Grey felt that way about his enormous ranch, which Shadow disliked as much as her family's small farm, the modest house with its now-sagging roof, the cramped rooms where her parents had fought late into the night over every dime.

She shook her head. "Five acres of dirt, a bunch of chickens and a house that's been falling down around your ears since I was in diapers." And someone in that house, she thought, had always been in diapers.

"I own my house, free and clear. How many people can say that?"

True enough. Shadow had her brandnew mortgage to pay, a strong motivation to succeed with Mother Comfort. She murmured, "At least Daddy left you something." Other than six children. Well, five now. For a time it had seemed her mother was pregnant every year. As the second oldest girl after her sister Jenna, Shadow had often helped with the youngest ones, giving bottles to Tanya and Cherry, wiping her little brother Derek's grimy hands and runny noses while her dad did…almost nothing to help.

"He was a good man," her mother said. "I loved your father."

Another casualty, Shadow thought, of a man who couldn't be counted on.

She took a deep breath. She didn't want to hurt her mother, but she needed to get through to her somehow. "Obviously, you can't keep that house up much longer, Mama. It's become harder and harder since Daddy died. The house is old. It needs too much work. How about I come out soon? We can get it ready to sell. That property's not worth much, but enough to give you a fresh start.

Away from all those memories." She didn't have to mention Jared.

"I'm staying." Her mother looked away. "We always did the best we could."

"I guess." But Shadow had gone to school with holes in her sneakers—they all had. The same shoes that pinched because they were two sizes too small. Shadow had felt like one of those women centuries ago with their feet bound till they couldn't walk. Now she had a serious obsession with shoes. They were her one indulgence. Everything else went into her plans for the future. Shadow looked down at her newest pair of flats. "You don't have to live that way now," she said. "Did you never consider what Daddy was doing to us then?" And that didn't come close to Shadow's last memory of him.

"He couldn't get good work."

"No, or if he did, it was because Everett Wilson hired him back again." She added, "I know you were in a difficult position, Mama." Shadow had been in one, herself. She'd had to make hard decisions, which reminded her now of Grey and their meeting tomorrow. "But when I actually *needed* Daddy—"

"He shouldn't have done that, but honey,

we'd just lost Jared! That was Grey Wilson's doing. You can't blame your father for feeling like he did. That boy killed our son and I'll never forgive him."

Shadow couldn't disagree. But this wasn't about Grey. It was Shadow her father had hurt then. "Yes, and after that, Daddy wasn't there for me." She almost hadn't come home for his funeral, yet she'd done so for her mother's sake. And stayed.

Her mother rose from the steps. "People make mistakes. Grey Wilson sure did, and you just ran off—"

"Because," Shadow said, fighting the urge to push her mother away when she also wanted to take her in her arms and comfort them both, "I had to." *Because, like Daddy, you wouldn't help me, either.*

As if she'd actually heard the unspoken words, her mother drew herself up. She stood barely over five feet, even when she squared her shoulders and stiffened her spine. Shadow had inherited her father's height, but she had to give her mother credit for the courage that had failed Shadow earlier. Or was that her mother's pride? Like Grey's. "Forget I was here," she said.

"Mama—"

She started down the steps. "I've made mistakes in my life, too. But at least," she threw back over her shoulder, "I never abandoned my own baby."

CHAPTER TWO

THE NEXT DAY at her desk, Shadow made a few calls, pored over several new applications for potential caregivers and mostly stared out the window again. She wasn't getting much done. When she finally saw Grey's pickup pull into a space in front of the agency, her anxiety ramped up another notch. Her mother's words yesterday had only made that worse, all the more because, in some ways, she was right. As Grey walked into her office, every muscle in Shadow's body tensed.

"Well?" he asked, sinking onto the chair in front of her desk. He wore a more familiar denim shirt, jeans and boots today. And, of course, the black Stetson, which he'd removed as soon as he opened the door. He balanced it on his knee.

Shadow pushed a pile of papers to one side and straightened the two ballpoint pens she always kept nearby. She folded her hands on the clean desktop but didn't look at him. She glanced at the phone, almost willing it to ring, creating a delay. "I don't know how to begin," she said at last.

"Just tell me. Whatever it is."

She made herself meet his gaze. "That would be best," she agreed, wondering, even fearing, how he might react. "Grey, something else happened ten years ago. Something other than Jared."

"Yeah," he said. "You and I broke up—not for the first time."

"For the last. And soon after Jared…died, I—" She cleared her throat, then rushed on, her heart a hard lump in her chest. She'd rehearsed these words but they stuck in her throat. "I discovered I was pregnant."

Grey blinked. For a long moment he said nothing. Shadow watched a dozen emotions flash across his face. He turned the black hat on his knee in a circle. "Pregnant," he repeated.

"Yes."

His mouth hardened. "And you never told me."

Shadow reached out a hand, but they didn't connect. Grey sat too far away from her across the expanse of her desk and he'd pushed deeper into his chair, creating even more distance between them. "You're right. I didn't. I take full responsibility, Grey."

"Well, that's something. Now," he murmured.

"I'm sorry. I know that sounds terribly inadequate, but at the time—because of Jared, too—I felt I couldn't tell you." She took a breath. "That was wrong of me."

"And it's still wrong. Ten years?" He shook his head. "I suppose you told your parents."

"Yes." Shadow had come home from school that day to find her father in his living room recliner, his "seat of business," he always claimed.

"The TV was on," she continued, "blaring some rerun of an old cowboy series. He watched the episodes over and over, like he was trying to relive his dreams of being a successful rancher. I could have recited the dialogue word for word, but I was too scared to even think. All day in class I'd dreaded telling him. It was only a week after Jared died."

"How did you know?"

"I'd had some physical signs but tried to ignore them. At first, I thought my body was just reacting to all the anxiety, the grief. Then I...was late again, and I bought a test." She remembered that night, locked in the bathroom while her youngest brother, Derek, banged at the door, saying it was his turn. "When my mother walked into the room and turned off the TV, my heart was beating like some ceremonial drum. I could hardly get the words out. 'Daddy, Mama, I'm pregnant.'"

The test didn't lie. At seventeen, Shadow had been about to become a mother.

Grey's mouth twisted. He still didn't look at her. "What did your father say?"

"His face got red and he gripped the arms of his chair—like he had to hold himself in place or he'd come after me. He stared me down. He guessed it was yours right away. I'll never forget those horrible days." Now she had added another, and inflicted it on Grey, too. Finally, he lifted his gaze, and Shadow refused to look away from his sharp, accusatory eyes.

"I told him you were the only boy I was seeing." Not that they'd been together anymore by the time she'd had that conversation with her parents. She hadn't had a chance to recover from their final fight, from Grey's rejection. How could she, after seeing Jared lying so still and pale in his coffin.

"And your mom?"

"She said nothing at first. Then it was just, 'Oh, Shadow,' and she started crying." Shadow swallowed. "My parents and I were alone in the room. I said a brief prayer of thanks that my sisters and Derek weren't around. I'd seen him wrestling in the yard with a friend—he still hangs out with Calvin Stern—on my way in, and my sisters were heading for the henhouse to collect eggs." The chickens' squawking had shattered the last of her nerves, as if even they blamed her for what had happened.

Grey worried the crease in his hat. "Then what?"

Shadow closed her eyes, remembering her dad leaning forward in his chair, pointing a finger at her. "He said he wouldn't have any more to do with *that family*, with you—" she sucked in a breath "—or anything belonging to you." Shadow laid a protective hand on her now-flat stomach. "My mom was staring at him. I was shaking so hard. Not any-*thing*, I said. Any*one*."

"Prodding the tiger," Grey muttered.

Her voice trembled, as it had then. "Daddy

slammed back in his chair again, aimed the remote at the TV and told me to get out."

"Your mother didn't say anything? Even then?"

"Not a word. You know she always sided with him."

Grey's voice was deadly quiet. "What did you do?"

"I stuffed some clothes in a backpack and left. I had a week's pay from my job at that fast-food restaurant. If Daddy thought I had betrayed him, he'd also betrayed me. So did my mom."

"Where did you go? You must have gotten help somewhere." He might have asked why she hadn't gone to him, found a way to get to his college in Texas—he'd already gone back for the fall semester by then. But Grey waited for her reply, and Shadow was thankful. She wanted to get the whole story out before she started trying to explain herself.

"To Doc's office."

"Doc?" Grey echoed. "What did *he* say?"

Shadow didn't meet his eyes. "'Well, young lady, what have you got to say for yourself?'" Remembering, she blushed. She'd sat up on Doc's cold metal table at his clinic in Barren and burst into tears. "I'd hitched a ride into town, then wandered along Main Street, my mind blank yet whirling at the same time— What should I do? Where would I go?—until, finally, I ended up at Doc's."

Cyrus Baxter had taken one look at her, swept out from behind the reception desk where he'd been studying a chart, passed his wife, Ida, who was talking on the phone, and ushered Shadow into the exam room, where she'd blurted out her earth-shattering news. In his late fifties then, his dark hair had been sprinkled with gray but his blue eyes were keen. Doc never wore a white coat; he believed his youngest patients found that intimidating.

"You never thought to come to me?" Grey asked now.

"Yes. I thought of finding you, instead, but after we broke up—after Jared—I couldn't."

In that moment she'd wished she hadn't gone to Doc, either, but still caught up in the fallout at home, and always a breath away from crying over losing Jared, she'd completely missed Doc's gentle tone of voice.

He'd given Shadow her vaccinations as a baby, treated her skinned knees and strep throats during childhood and offered her a birds-and-bees lecture when she entered puberty. Apparently that hadn't done much good, but he'd cupped her shoulders in both hands as he'd done many times before, and said, "None of that now, Shadow. Tears won't help."

"He knew you were the father," Shadow told Grey now, wincing at his pained expression when she spoke that last word. "His reaction was different than Daddy's, though. I explained that you'd already left, that even if you hadn't I could never go to you, not after what you'd done to Jared. But he interrupted me, said, 'I've known Grey since he was drinking milk from a bottle. He's never been in trouble before.' He said he did wonder what you were all doing together that night, why there was a gun. It's true that you and Jared didn't run in the same circles."

Shadow could feel the blood drain from her head toward her feet, as it had that other day. "Jared was defending my honor, I told Doc. I explained that he and Derek and Calvin Stern had gone to your ranch to teach you a lesson. And then…and then Doc told me he saw Jared. After. He saw his wounds. But even so, that we shouldn't jump to conclusions."

Shadow was barely holding back tears. Though she'd been grateful, earlier, for Grey's silence, grateful that he was letting her tell the story on her terms, part of her wished he would react. Show some emotion. She wiped her eyes.

"I wanted to believe him," she continued. "Wanted to believe you could be innocent and that we could be together again, get married and keep…our baby. I asked Doc if he though Derek and Calvin were lying about what happened, and he just told me to keep an open mind. And to talk to you—make a decision together."

"Why didn't you?" Grey pressed.

At first she didn't answer. She'd gone to Doc as a last resort, but she trusted his advice. So why hadn't she been able or willing to follow it? Shadow remembered hearing Ida, still on the phone in the outer room.

Doc's wife was the nosiest woman Shadow knew and her mother called Ida the town's best gossip. Suddenly, Shadow had been overcome with worry that she would walk in at any moment, that if Ida learned the truth, she'd broadcast it for sure, only adding to the scandal of Jared's death. That was when the enormity of the situation had hit her.

"I don't know," she told Grey, finally. "I was so overwhelmed. Doc took me in for the night and said we could discuss the… options in the morning. And then once everything was decided—" He'd told Shadow he would handle Ida.

Before Shadow realized how Grey might interpret that, she watched another emotion cross his face. He snatched the black Stetson from his knee, clamped it on his head then stood abruptly. "What did you do, Shadow?" He didn't wait for her answer.

"Grey—"

"No," he said, his hand already on the doorknob. He looked confused, conflicted. Overwhelmed. He had every right to be. "I need to think about this." He walked out, slamming the door behind him.

Shadow sank back in her chair, filled with regret. For ten years, only three other people had known about Ava—four, if she counted her deceased father. Her mother, her sister Jenna and Doc. Now Grey also knew her secret.

And she hadn't just shocked him. She'd hurt him more deeply than she'd ever imagined.

BACK AT WILSON CATTLE, Grey shook his head. Cody had failed to properly mend the broken fence yesterday—call him Mr. Reliable—and Grey propped both hands on his hips to study the gap that was still there, the few strands of barbed wire hanging where Cody had hastily twisted them together as a temporary fix. Lazy, he thought, and it hadn't worked. Grey had spent half the afternoon rounding up strays. Standing beside Logan Hunter, his friend and neighbor, he studied both sides of the property line.

"This fence was deliberately cut," Grey said, but he was having a hard time keeping his mind on that fact or even that Cody had let him down. He kept hearing Shadow's words. He'd had a *kid*, a child he'd never known about until now. He couldn't quite wrap his head around that. Couldn't believe she'd gone to Doc instead of him. Whatever decision she'd made, their baby was his business, not Doc's.

Logan ran a hand over the nape of his neck. "Deliberate, all right. Same as mine was. Not the usual teardown by some cow determined to get free."

"You missing any cattle? I mean, bison?"

Years ago Logan's grandfather Sam had

switched from raising beef, although Grey
still wondered why. The bison could be
mean critters, more aggressive than the
Angus breeding bulls Grey ran, any day. If
he needed proof, all he had to do was look
at Logan's grandfather, who'd been tossed
weeks ago by one of his bison and badly
broken his leg. His cast was off but he still
had a limp.

"I'll have to ask Willy or Tobias," Logan
said, referring to two of his cowboys. His
already deep-blue eyes had darkened. "I've
been too busy with the wedding plans to
count bison cows or ride fence. Darned if I
don't miss that."

Grey wanted to smile but couldn't. The
constant chore was nobody's favorite, and
to help his injured grandfather, Logan, who
was by profession a test pilot, had become
a temporary cowboy again—until he and
Blossom fell in love and the ranch gained
new appeal for him. Which only made Grey
think of Shadow. "You don't look unhappy.
The break from flying jets must agree with
you."

"Yeah, but I'll have to make some real
decisions soon. I've got applications in with

other aircraft manufacturers in Wichita, but there's not a lot of demand right now."

With his gloved hands, Grey retwisted some wires together, enough to keep his cows in until he could fix the fence himself.

"You'd quit?" he asked. "I thought you were just taking a short leave."

"We'll see. The ranch will always be home to Blossom and me, at least in part, depending on what I decide to do about flying for a living. Sam still needs help here."

Grey glanced at him. He and Logan had grown up together, although Logan was two years older and Grey had always seen him as an older brother—the way he looked after Cody now. "It'd be great if you could stay, Logan." He shook his head again. "I know I'll never leave this place." Not willingly, anyway. His stomach twisted at the thought of the loan Barney had denied him.

Logan frowned. "Why would you leave? Running Wilson Cattle is all you ever wanted to do, Grey. This ranch has been in your family even longer than the Circle H has been in mine."

His gut tightened. Grey's great-great-something-grandfather had bought this acreage right after the Civil War when land was cheap. As Logan knew, too, the old man was buried in the family plot just over the hill with the generations that had come after him. Grey had always wanted children who would inherit Wilson Cattle from him, but now... He had to steady his voice before he spoke.

"Yep. Wilson Cattle is in my blood, in my bones."

Logan clapped a hand on his shoulder. "Talk about old times. Remember when you and I—and my brother—scared ourselves crazy every Halloween in the graveyard? And rode all over both ranches, yelling like banshees, playing we were grown-up cowboys like your dad and Sam? Spooking the cattle? Pretending we were on some everlasting roundup?"

"Until we had to surrender our horses. Grounded," Grey said. "We gave my dad and your grandfather more gray hairs..." Clearing his throat, he squinted into the far distance, listening for the reassuring sounds from the Black Angus herd that would tell him everything was fine. He knew each shuffle of hooves, each calf's bleat or cow's bellow, though unlike Sam Hunter he didn't name the animals.

"Yeah," Logan said, "but I regret that I spent more time off the Circle H than on for too many years. Now, because of Blossom, that's finally changed. At least for now."

Grey envied them. Shadow's earlier words spun through his brain again like a McCormick reaper in a ripe hayfield. Years ago, he'd thought they were headed for the altar, like Logan and Blossom were now—until their last fight. Then Jared had died and Grey got blamed for it, at least in the court of public opinion. And sometimes within himself. All of which had prevented any reconciliation between him and Shadow. Logan had obviously picked up on his mood. Which of Doc's options had she taken? He hadn't let Shadow tell him what they were, or what she'd done.

"What's wrong, Grey? Except for this barbed wire."

"Plenty," he admitted, "but I'll get through it."

Logan dragged a hand through his dark hair. "Whatever you say stops here."

"I know, but…"

"If there's anything I can do—"

"Thanks. I'll let you know."

Logan punched his upper arm. "Someday that pride of yours is going to get you in real trouble."

Grey rubbed his biceps, as if Logan had actually hurt him. "I imagine it will." It already had, in town with Shadow today. He'd left her office shocked and mad at her for keeping their child from him all these years, afraid he'd say things he'd regret later.

He and Logan stood for a moment in silent companionship, two guys who were never comfortable expressing their deepest feelings. He guessed many men weren't, but with cowboys that went double. His pride definitely wouldn't let him tell his best friend about the bombshell Shadow had dropped on him. Not yet. He needed time to think, to decide how to react.

Logan scratched at a bug bite on his forearm. "The first truly warm weather—after all the rain—and the mosquitoes are already out."

"Whenever the wind's not blowing." The prairie breeze could be fierce, especially in spring, and in June it was still hanging on. When Grey's ancestors had settled here, the wind's relentless nature had driven some people mad. He was glad there was no wind today.

He surveyed his land once more. Wilson Cattle sat closer to the main road than Logan's adjoining Circle H did, and on what passed in the state for higher ground. It didn't have the Hunters' long driveway and was also near the crossroads—easy picking for modern-day mischief-makers? Someone with a pair of wire cutters might think opening a hole here and there was great fun. With proms and graduation coming up, this was high season for teenage pranksters.

He tipped his hat back, then resettled it, scanning the ranch to the horizon. Whatever happened next, he was not going to lose Wilson Cattle—which had become a real possibility.

What to do about Shadow was another matter.

BLOSSOM KENNEDY WAS the kind of person with whom Shadow had felt instantly comfortable as soon as they met. This was a first for her. She didn't let many people into her inner circle—she'd learned as a kid not to let others get close enough to see how she'd lived then—but she and Blossom had hit it off right away.

Shadow had no sooner watched Grey walk

out of her office than Blossom had called her cell phone. Still shaking, Shadow had let the call go to voice mail. Once she'd finally listened to the message, she'd known what to do, and she had driven out to the Circle H. She hated having to fib to Blossom, but at least she would do so to her face.

"About the wedding," she said. "I'm sorry, but I can't be your maid of honor." That role, and the responsibility it carried, seemed even more important to Shadow than if Blossom had simply asked her to be one of several bridesmaids.

"Of course you will." Sitting on the porch steps of the house she shared with Logan, Blossom pushed a stray russet curl off her forehead.

"Thanks for asking me, but..." And here came the thin lie she didn't want to tell. "I'm so busy—swamped—with the agency right now." Which wasn't exactly untrue. "I'm overbooked." There was no way, after she'd told Grey about their child, that she could stand up with him at a wedding. That he could want her to be there. As best man, he'd be close to her all day and yet they'd be so far apart. "I may have to hire more help." Even to her ears, that sounded weak.

"You'll be working that Saturday? Come on, it's not really the agency," Blossom said, as if she could see straight through Shadow. "I think this is about Grey. I told Logan this might be a problem."

Her insight didn't surprise Shadow. Blossom had seen her with Grey at the birthday party for Blossom's soon-to-be stepson. It had been no secret that Shadow had wanted to avoid him.

"I just talked to him in town," she admitted.

"I shouldn't pry. Logan told me you two broke up years ago for some awful reason, but I can see that Grey still loves you."

Shadow's heart turned over. "Which doesn't help. We always had a rocky relationship—on-again, off-again, with lots of drama—" And love, she thought. For a moment she couldn't go on, yet Blossom had a right to know at least part of the truth. "Then there was a shooting accident. The sheriff, the coroner, the forensics lab—no one could determine whose fault it was, exactly—though most people still think they know—and Grey was never charged. But I'd still lost him... Jared, I mean. He was my older brother, and of all the kids in my family, I was closest to him. I still miss him," she said.

"I'm sorry, Shadow. I didn't know."

She stared down at her shoes, soft loafers today from her ever-growing collection. "The town's still talking about that, more again since I came back to Barren." She sighed. "Now you know why I can't be in your wedding." Part of the reason.

Blossom sat back to rest her spine against the riser of the next step as she rubbed her pregnant stomach. Her coming baby had played a big part in helping Blossom turn her life around with Logan, and Shadow envied her that new start.

A brief silence fell. Shadow could see the disappointment in her brown eyes. Blossom didn't know that many people in Barren. Shadow was probably leaving her in the lurch.

She squeezed Blossom's hand, then got to her feet. "I'd better get going." As always, when she visited the Circle H, which was rare, she tried to avoid a glance toward Grey's neighboring ranch. Today, she couldn't. He was too much on her mind, the stunned look on his face when she'd told him about the pregnancy. Just over the slight hill between the two properties, she could glimpse the roof of his barn. She said weakly, "Tell Logan I said hey."

Blossom stood, too, wobbling to gain her balance until Shadow cupped a hand under her elbow to steady her. "Thanks. My center of gravity is off these days." She paused. "Please think about this, Shadow. I know it would be difficult for you with Grey in the wedding party, but there's no one else I'd rather have for my maid of honor even if I knew everyone in town and had lived here all my life."

Shadow had to bite her lip against another rush of tears. "That's sweet, Blossom. I'm honored." She moved toward her car. "Grateful," she added. "But really, I…can't."

She regretted having to say no, letting down her new friend. Now, all because of the tragedy from years ago, she'd hurt two people. Blossom and Grey.

CHAPTER THREE

IN THE DARK, on a slight rise above the lower pasture near the western boundary of his ranch, Grey trained his binoculars on the grass below and several hundred yards away. Earlier, on a hunch, he'd decided to keep watch tonight. Lying flat on his stomach, he doubted he could be seen behind this low scrub, but something was definitely going on. A few cows had skittered off, bawling, raising Grey's blood pressure and generating a surge of adrenaline. Then he heard the rumble of an approaching vehicle.

He muttered a curse as a big white truck towing a stock trailer rolled to a stop by the roadside. Trouble, all right.

He'd been expecting, even hoping, to see vandals. A couple of teenagers, maybe, out on a lark after prom or graduation at the local high school. Celebrating. Or rather, making mischief by knocking over mailboxes or cutting fence. Not this. What he suspected was about to happen would be far worse. And devastating to his bottom line— if he let it happen.

As he watched, the trailer's back gate opened. With a screech of metal on metal, the ramp rattled down. A wiry figure in dark clothing glanced around, then walked up to the fence Grey had fixed properly just before dusk. And snipped the wire.

"No, you don't," Grey said to himself, but the man was already through. He coiled up a rope then sent the loop sailing through the air with an audible hiss. Not bad form, but his first try missed. One of the Angus cows that had run off before took off again. "You won't," Grey said, but he didn't move. Not yet.

On his second throw, the man snagged a young heifer.

Grey grabbed his cell phone. When the sheriff's dispatcher answered, Grey said in a low tone, "Get me some help out here. Rustlers," then hung up.

The heifer, which had recently been weaned, was being herded to the van, protesting all the way. A cow, most likely its mother, bellowed in answer. The whole herd milled around, boxy dark shapes in the night caught between apparent concern for the younger cow and their instinctive need to flee. In the next pasture, Grey's best bull paced back and forth behind an uncut fence, eyeing the action, intent upon protecting his cows.

Grey reached for his rifle.

The sheriff would come, but his office in Barren was miles away. By the time he got here, the thieves would be gone.

Grey cocked the rifle. He wasn't close enough to be accurate with the weapon and didn't want to warn them, but if it came to shooting...he would. He would prefer to get hard proof of the theft, rather than scare them off, just as he wanted evidence to clear himself in Jared Moran's death—if things turned out his way. That meant waiting until the cows were on board before he made his move.

For a few moments longer, he eyeballed the three rustlers through the scope as they rounded up half a dozen cows and a few calves and drove them up the ramp. The men weren't subtle; they worked with speed yet didn't seem to care if anyone saw them. Then again, on this stretch of road that wasn't likely. The whole time Grey had been here, not a car or rancher's pickup had passed by. Most local people would be in bed at this time of night. Like Grey, they got up at dawn, if not before, worked hard all day then turned in early to get ready for the next.

The ramp screeched up again. The rear gate banged shut.

The physical evidence he'd wanted was now standing in the stock trailer. Over the noise from those kidnapped cattle, from farther away he could just hear an approaching car, coming fast. The sheriff's cruiser? But as he'd figured, not quick enough. Before Grey could move, the three men scrambled into the truck, slamming the front doors. The engine fired up, and the headlights pierced the darkness, illuminating the spiky grass along the newly broken fence line and the gravel at the edge of the road as if they were part of a stage set.

He'd waited too long. Aiming for the tires, Grey raised the rifle and fired. The bullet ricocheted off the rim of a rear wheel well, striking sparks. That, and the sound of the gunshot, sent the rest of the herd into a brief stampede.

Grey shot to his feet anyway, ready to shoot again. Needing a better position, he ran down the hill, hoping he wouldn't bust a leg in the dark. But like the sheriff, he didn't get there in time.

The rustlers blasted off into the night. Taking his cattle with them.

STANDING OUTSIDE A large chain bookstore halfway between her house in Barren and her sister's home in a Kansas City suburb, Shadow watched Jenna Moran Collins get out of a gleaming SUV on the opposite side of the lot—their distance from each other a metaphor for their prickly relationship—and shut the passenger door.

Shadow's heart sank. After her talks with Grey and her mother, she didn't expect this to be easy, either, and her mother's parting words had stuck in her mind.

At least I didn't abandon my own baby. That wasn't true, but it still stung. She'd tried so hard to do the right thing for Ava. Today would be no different.

Jenna walked toward her, tall and slim with their father's auburn hair and blue eyes. Wearing a stylish pair of dark pants and an expensive-looking patterned top, she had a smile on her face that, as usual lately, never reached her eyes.

Shadow led Jenna over to a metal bench, one of several lined up along the walkway of the strip mall anchored by the bookstore and an ice cream/candy shop. Whenever Shadow couldn't make it to the city, this made a convenient meeting place.

Jenna all but tapped an impatient foot on the sidewalk. She rooted through her designer handbag. "Why did you want to see me?"

Shadow abandoned the soft lead-in she'd rehearsed, as she'd failed to do with Grey before walking into the diner, and plunged right in. "I want to bring Ava home."

Jenna paled. *"Home?"*

Ten years ago Shadow had made some tough decisions—decisions she hadn't gotten to tell Grey about yet—and she and Ava had lived with Jenna and her husband for the two years before Shadow's move back to Barren. But now Grey knew about Ava, and Shadow could follow through with the rest of her plan. But Jenna kept shaking her head.

Shadow tried to soften her tone. "My business is doing pretty well, and I've even saved some money. I can never repay you for stepping in when I needed help the most, for taking us both in. You and David helped me move in to my house, and with the school year ending, you know there's no reason for her to keep staying with you—except that you want her to. I can't blame you for that. Ava just lights up a room, doesn't she?"

And only last night Shadow had gone into what would be her daughter's bedroom. She'd sat there, hoping Ava would like what she'd done with the space, dreaming of what it would be like when they were together again.

"She can't move right now." Jenna met Shadow's gaze. "Her summer break hasn't started yet."

"I know, and I realize we'll have to transition from your house to mine. That's why I wanted to talk to you first. Then I'll speak with Ava. I know she'll have some objections—"

Her sister's eyes filled with tears.

"Jenna, I love how good you are with her, I know you've become attached—"

"She's my only niece. This past year she's spent more time with me than with you."

Shadow tensed. This wasn't going well. "That couldn't be helped. I had to commute between Barren and Shawnee Mission. Building the agency, buying the house...all of that took time and effort, but you knew those were first steps toward me bringing Ava home. I didn't want to uproot her into yet another uncertain situation. But you knew I'd always planned for this. For us to be together in our own place again."

She couldn't wait for the chance to tuck Ava into bed each night, to know that in the morning she would be there, eager to start the day. With Shadow. But Jenna didn't agree.

"This is just such a...shock." She took a shaky breath. "Shadow, I love Ava. So much that I would adopt her if I could. No, I *want* to adopt her."

Shadow's pulse hitched. Why hadn't she seen that coming? She had no intention of giving up her child, and she'd thought Jenna understood that. Shadow had worked and worked toward bringing Ava home. To build the solid foundation she hadn't been able to provide her daughter for the first six years of her life, when Shadow had struggled just to pay rent on their tiny apartment. Jenna's statement terrified her. But then, Jenna also had her husband to consider. Had she talked to him?

Shadow doubted he would be as eager to adopt as Jenna was. He'd always liked being her first priority, and more than once Shadow had seen him turn away from Ava as if to cut out the competition. The infertility that had plagued her sister had never seemed to bother him as much, even though he'd agreed to all of the in vitro fertilizations they had tried without success. Would he really side with Jenna on this?

"What about David?"

Jenna's gaze flickered. "He's busy right now, planning for a conference in Chicago before he has to go on to his firm's branch in Salt Lake." She hesitated. "Dave's not in the best mood, anyway—he's worried about his chances to become partner—but as soon as he gets his trip arranged, we'll talk."

That news surprised Shadow. David had always portrayed himself as a legal star, the golden boy of his prestigious firm and a shoo-in to become partner. If he didn't make that, after all, his mood would probably get much worse. She wondered if he'd be willing to talk about adoption then. Not that Shadow intended to let things get that far.

"You're not being reasonable, Jen. David

has always wanted a child of his own. I remember his objections to you adopting in the first years of your marriage. I doubt he's changed his mind. And I certainly haven't changed mine. I understand how you must feel but Ava belongs with me."

Jenna lowered her voice with obvious effort. "Are you sure about that?"

The question pushed Shadow off balance. "Of course I am. It's not healthy for us to be apart so much. Without her, I'm just…adrift. I know Ava and I will need to make some readjustments, but I'm prepared to do that."

"You won't have to if she stays with me."

"Jenna, I'm not saying moving Ava will be easy, but it's the best thing for her. Not that our lives together were simple before. You know how we struggled until finally I felt so overwhelmed, and frightened for her welfare—"

"That you came to me."

And to be fair, Jenna hadn't hesitated to take them in. When one year had stretched into two, she'd been happy to let them stay. Then, a year ago, when their father died and Shadow had returned to Barren for his funeral, she'd found an opportunity she couldn't resist to open her agency there instead of paying Kansas City prices to rent an office. That had been the chance she'd needed to secure Ava's future. Ever since, she'd been juggling her job and her responsibility to Ava, working in Barren five days a week then spending the weekends with her at Jenna's house. Now it was time to end that, to be with her daughter every day. And oh, how Shadow had missed her. This past year had been very hard on both of them.

For a moment she let herself remember their everyday routine—getting Ava off to school, cozying up at bedtime to read her favorite book, sharing mother-daughter conversations and silly jokes. Kissing her good-night.

Still, she had to let Jenna know how grateful she was. "If it hadn't been for you and David, I don't know what I would have done."

The fact that Jenna, a year older than Shadow, had been, and still was, in far better financial shape couldn't be denied. Their spacious home in Shawnee Mission, an upscale community just outside Kansas City, had given Ava advantages Shadow couldn't supply then, especially the school in which

Ava had started first grade. Now Jenna stayed silent.

"I didn't want Ava to end up in poverty the way you and I grew up." Shadow drew a deep breath. "I wanted her to have something *better.*"

Jenna's mouth set in a hard line. "She still does."

Shadow was shaking. She'd never expected Jenna to be so unwilling to let Ava go, even to the point of bringing up adoption. "I'm in a different situation than I was before, and yes, that's thanks to you in large part. But Jenna, I'm her *mother*!"

Shadow tried to collect herself. This was going even worse than her moments with Grey at Annabelle's Diner and in her office. "We've talked about this before, Jen. Surely you knew we'd move out as soon as I was able to provide Ava with everything she needs. She's *my* first priority. She always has been. She always will be, and I used that time while we lived with you to improve things—for her benefit."

Shadow had worked two and sometimes three jobs, paid off her mountain of bills, saved every penny toward buying her house in a good neighborhood in Barren. After becoming a teen mother, she'd finally gotten her GED, and later completed courses to become an administrator at the same nursing home where she'd been an aide. As a supervisor, she'd developed the leadership skills needed to open Mother Comfort, all the while planning to be with her daughter in their own home.

"I have two bedrooms now," she said. "Ava won't have to share like we did when we had that first little apartment in the city." Shadow laid a hand on Jenna's arm and felt her flinch. "I don't want to hurt you, Jen. I don't want you to lose her, either," she said. "You can see Ava whenever you wish. That doesn't have to change. She can spend some weekends with you and David—the way I've been commuting this past year while I got the agency going. I know she loves you, too."

Jenna glanced at the sky. "Well, let's see. You love Ava. I love Ava. You love me. That's all very nice, Shadow. But the real question is—does she still love *you*?"

Shadow's breath caught. "I can't believe you said that."

"Haven't you noticed? She's become so resentful. While you were studying, working, she learned to rely on me. Most mornings I see her off on the school bus, and who takes her to soccer practice and the pediatrician when you can't be there?"

"That's not fair. I was home with her as much as I could be. Maybe I was wrong to wait even this long—"

"She didn't ask to come with me today. She didn't ask about you, Shadow. I don't think you realize what's happened here."

Shadow swallowed. It hurt to know that in recent months Ava had become closer to Jenna than to Shadow, and yes, she'd noticed that. Already her relationship with Ava had begun to change, not for the better.

Jenna did have a point. Ava hadn't understood why Shadow needed to be in Barren during the week this past year, only spending Friday night through Sunday in Shawnee Mission. The commute had worn her down, but Shadow had stuck to it. And several times, when Ava was sick, she'd closed the office to stay with her—which was only right. She'd gone to every parent-teacher conference, to her spring concert, arranged sleepovers with her friends. But in trying to do the best thing for her child, had she only made things worse?

Now she had Jenna and their relationship to deal with, too. And Grey.

GREY TOSSED HIS hat onto the sheriff's beige metal desk then sank down on a wooden chair across from him. "So that's what happened," he said.

Finn Donovan had listened patiently to Grey's report to his deputy about his missing cattle, offering a comment here and there or asking a question. Grey had first thought of the new chief law enforcement officer of Stewart County more as a typical hardworking cowboy—like Grey—rather than a cop. Finn wore no gold star on his chest, and on his lanky frame were a faded blue denim shirt and jeans, as if he'd just wandered in from some barn or pasture. He wore scuffed brown boots that had seen better days, but despite his casual look he had a mind as sharp as a spike of broken barbed wire.

He gazed at Grey.

"I gave Logan a call to follow up while you were signing your statement." He pointed toward the outer room, where Grey could hear the continual clack of computer keys and the constantly ringing phone. The air smelled of burned coffee. "His men tell him they've lost a few cows but not as many as you did. What does that say to you?"

"It isn't as easy for someone to pull up to the Circle H from the road as it is to pull up to my ranch and steal my means of making a living. You should have seen those guys. Slick as a whistle. Brazen."

"You saw them. Can't you add better descriptions?"

"Finn, it was pitch dark out there—no light to take photos. I was on the hill too far away to see much detail, even with binoculars."

"Yeah, and you should have waited for me. Instead of getting trigger-happy."

"I didn't hit anybody," Grey muttered. "They were already leaving when I took that one shot—trying to disable the truck. Missed their tire and off they went. I'm still kicking myself for waiting. Maybe I should have charged down that hill as soon as I saw them and taken them by surprise. Tried to get a look at their faces." He shook his head. "And here I thought I was dealing with high school kids on a spree."

"Keep a cool head, Grey. They might come back."

"I'll be ready."

Finn ran a hand through his unruly mop of dark hair. "That doesn't reassure me. I don't need somebody getting hurt. You said all your cattle were branded. Ear tags?"

"Yep."

"Get me a list of those numbers. I'll check around. Sometimes these cows show up pretty quick at auction. It's like fencing stolen jewelry. Fast money."

"Since Logan's missing a few head, too, maybe we can take turns posting a guard in the likely spots for those rustlers to cut fence again. I don't welcome having to send my new guy out to string wire every day."

"Who's the guy?" Finn liked to keep tabs on everyone in his county.

"Kid by the name of Cody Jones. Ex-rodeo wannabe."

Grey could all but see the sheriff adding him to a mental file. "Tell him to be careful. You, too." Finn stood up, retucked the tail of his shirt then started for the door. The interview was over. Grey picked up his hat and followed. The sheriff was a man of few words, but in the outer room he turned. "I'll be out to look at the damage sometime today. You didn't fix that fence already, did you?"

"No. I moved the herd to another graze. Again."

"Maybe we can lift an impression of those tires."

Grey adjusted his hat. "The ground was soft enough last night, but I didn't stumble around in the dark to see. If we're lucky, the tracks might still be there."

"I doubt we'll get any fingerprints, though." The corner of Finn's mouth kicked up. "Guess they'd be on the cows—or the truck. Which at the moment are gone."

"Don't I know it." Grey paused. Finn had moved to Barren about the same time Shadow came back to town. After a rip-roaring election campaign against the long-time sheriff who'd handled Jared Moran's case years ago, Finn hadn't held office more than six months. Maybe he could offer a fresh eye on the other subject that was bothering Grey to this day. "Since we're talking about crimes, here, I know Jared Moran's case was closed back in the day. But can it be reopened?"

"Not unless there's new evidence."

Grey explained his side of the event, then Finn said, "Let me review the file. It's somewhere in the archives but I've never read it. Then we'll see."

"Appreciate it."

A few minutes later, after he had said his neighborly goodbyes to Finn's deputies, the dispatcher and the sergeant at the front desk, Grey walked out to his truck with Finn.

"So," the sheriff said, a hand on the open door as Grey started to climb in. His hazel eyes looked as sharp as his mind was. "The other day I dropped in at the diner to get some takeout for lunch. Guess you didn't see me. You were with Shadow Moran."

Grey tensed, reminded of the classic TV show in which the disheveled but crafty detective wearing a trench coat always trapped the suspect at the last minute with some offhand yet leading statement that led to an arrest. "Yeah?"

Grey's personal life had long ago become common knowledge in Barren, usually with some reference to Shadow's brother. Except for his pride, he could accept that, but he didn't care to hear any more gossip about him and Shadow—especially after the shocking announcement she'd made.

He was still thinking about that.

"Thought you stuck to things like missing cattle and store break-ins or cowboys trashing the bars on Saturday nights."

Finn raised both hands, as if to say he was backing off. He glanced down the street toward the bank but didn't mention Grey's loan. Thanks to Barney Caldwell, Finn and probably everyone else in town knew about that.

With a wave, he drove off. If Finn came through, Grey's cattle might be returned before they got slaughtered, thousands of dollars' worth of assets back on his books. And maybe with some luck he hadn't had lately, Finn would find something in that file to justify reopening Jared's case. For ten years Grey had lived with the aftermath, but since Shadow's return, the unsolved murder seemed to be front-page news again—in other people's minds and in his. The small ranching community thrived on knowing what was going on with every resident, and Grey was still a high-profile topic. Unless he got to the bottom of Jared's death, and until he knew for sure he hadn't pulled that trigger, he'd be in the spotlight. And so much negative attention would do nothing to help bring Wilson Cattle back into the black.

And then there was Shadow's child. His child, the one he'd never been told about. He'd never even had a chance to be involved in whatever decision Shadow had made with Doc. It was a wonder that story wasn't all over Barren. Maybe it was, and he was the only one who hadn't heard it. He still felt crushed by the revelation. He doubted they could ever reconcile; that he should even want to now.

Grey glanced at the Mother Comfort Home Health Care Agency as he passed it on his right, and for a second he eased off the gas.

He saw Shadow's red Mustang parked in front and could glimpse her inside at her desk, sunlight slashing in disrupted lines across her through the half-open wooden blinds. He wasn't ready to talk to her yet. Wouldn't trust himself. His sense of shock, anger and even loss was too great.

Grey kept going.

CHAPTER FOUR

"You didn't get your water heater fixed, Mama?" Shadow stared at her mother, who was stacking dishes and pots on the drain board at the sink.

"I couldn't," she replied.

On her way to the local rehab facility to visit an elderly client this morning, Shadow had stopped at the farm. This wasn't something she did often, but after she'd last seen her mother, Shadow had put a check in the mail. Shadow couldn't stop her mother from staying at the ramshackle farm where she'd lived much of her life. And if Wanda was determined to stay, Shadow wouldn't see her without hot water. She didn't have an appointment with her client, and he wasn't expecting her, so she could stop in on him after this visit.

As she drove up the rutted driveway she'd tried not to notice the sorry state the place had fallen into—or rather, fallen deeper into.

The henhouse now listed to one side as if it might tumble down at any moment, and the hole that some other animal had dug between its floor and the ground underneath was still there, possibly weakening the structure even more.

Her parents' house looked no better now than the last time she'd come here. It was clean but that was all she could say about it. Even the curtain at the kitchen window—at one time a crisp, white dotted Swiss—now hung limply from the rod. The whole place depressed her.

Shadow sank onto a chair. "Why couldn't you get it fixed, Mama?"

Shadow expected her to say the heater needed to be replaced, as she'd feared, but her mother wiped her hands on a dishtowel and said, "I had bills to pay. I needed milk and bread. The electric was overdue."

Shadow picked at a spot on the red-and-white-checked vinyl tablecloth.

"What else did you do with the money I sent?"

Her mother sat across from her. "Derek needed help."

At the mention of her youngest, and now only, brother, Shadow's spirits dropped like a stone into a pond, creating ripples all through her body. "He's still living with you? I thought he was finally getting a place in town."

"That didn't work out. He's not ready to be on his own."

Shadow tried to control her voice. "Derek is twenty-five years old. He needs to support himself—" Hearing footsteps in the hall, she broke off.

Her brother strolled in and Shadow wondered if he'd been there awhile, listening, but she hadn't seen his car outside. She'd assumed he wasn't home.

Wearing faded jeans and a plaid shirt with the sleeves rolled up, Derek propped a shoulder against the doorframe. He crossed his feet at the ankles and grinned. "Thanks for the sisterly advice. I'll take that into account next time I look for a job."

Like their father, he was solidly built, though a darked scruff covered his cheeks and jaw. He'd also inherited their father's light-blue eyes. Shadow had always found Derek's eyes disconcerting, as if she might see straight into his brain and not like what she saw there. *He's my baby brother*, she had to remind herself.

Wringing her hands, her mother rushed

across the kitchen to pat Derek's arm. "You children shouldn't fight. We're family."

Shadow held her brother's gaze. "What did you need money for?"

He shrugged. "Things."

"I sent that check for Mama."

Her mother's mouth quivered. "Derek, Shadow. Please."

"I'm sorry, but I hate to see my little brother follow in Daddy's footsteps."

He smirked. "You mean without a *job*? I make my own decisions."

"Then you need to make better ones." Shadow rose. Could she have said that of herself years ago? Or even approached Jenna in a different way only yesterday? She'd never actually abandoned Ava, but they were still apart for now and Shadow ached to be with her. Maybe she could have handled things better. She picked up her bag with a trembling hand. "The next time Mama needs help, I'll drive her to the store. Pay right there for whatever she needs. I won't let another dime pass from her hands to yours. Are we clear, Derek?"

He shot Shadow a sullen look. He hadn't moved from the doorway. Shadow cautioned herself not to let this get any more out of hand than it already had. Derek wasn't a bad person, but he was still immature in many ways, with a mother who never held him to account. She often treated him as if he were five years old and had been pushed down on a playground.

It was as if Jared's shooting years ago had frozen Derek at fifteen and, shattered then, he had never finished growing up.

Despite their testy exchange, Shadow still wanted to somehow…save him, as if she could. But she needed to focus on Ava.

She pushed past Derek into the short hall that led to the front door. "I meant what I said about Mama. For now, until the water heater gets fixed, which I'll pay for, you'll have to take a few cold showers."

WITH A CUP of coffee in one hand and juggling a paper bag in the other, Jenna called up the stairs. If Ava didn't hurry, she'd miss the bus. With only a few days left in the school year, her niece's motivation seemed to be lacking, and on such a blue-sky day Jenna knew she must already be thinking of playing with her friends all day at camp. Or, at least, that's how it had been last summer and the summer before.

"Ava! The bus is turning the corner. Get a move on."

A moment later, footsteps clattered down the stairs. Ava streaked into the front hall wearing a pair of patterned leggings and a bright blue tunic, and Jenna pushed her lunch bag into her hands. She wore her dark hair in a ponytail. Her eyes shone with determination.

"Why can't I *buy* lunch? Like the other kids."

"Because this is healthier for you. As a treat, I packed the chocolate pudding you like," Jenna said in a tempting tone.

"I don't like chocolate anymore."

Ignoring the faint display of rebellion, Jenna kissed Ava's forehead. There had been worse changes of heart lately from Ava, times when even Jenna had wondered at the wisdom of trying to parent Shadow's child, even part-time—and part-time was the operative word now. Although Ava had always been a sweet girl, the preteen years were rapidly approaching.

"Don't be a goose. Have a good day."

"Last week," Ava announced. "Then I'll be a fourth grader."

To her that must mean impending independence, but to Jenna it meant pulling away. And she hadn't forgotten her talk with Shadow. In fact, that was all she'd thought about ever since.

The bus had stopped out front and Jenna stood in the doorway, watching the still-little girl she loved race toward it. Jenna waved at the driver. When she was satisfied that Ava was on the bus and safely in her seat, she turned back inside.

David stood there in his three-piece suit, briefcase in hand. Her husband shot a quick glance at the departing bus. Jenna wondered if he'd delayed leaving for the office to make sure he didn't run into Ava this morning. She looked up into his serious gray-blue eyes then noticed the set of his mouth.

They'd talked well into the night again last night, and this morning he seemed as weary as she felt. Jenna had tossed and turned for hours, replaying her conversation with Shadow and considering David's ambivalence, envisioning one emotional scene after another to come. All of them ended with Ava sitting in Shadow's red Mustang as she backed out of the driveway with Ava's suitcases in the trunk.

And Jenna's heart shattered.

Setting her cup on the entry hall table, she smoothed a hand over her husband's dark hair. He had it trimmed every two weeks at a high-end salon in Kansas City. In their suburban neighborhood Jenna used an equally pricey shop for her style, and she liked having nice things. She glanced down at her gray cashmere robe. She had no doubt he'd heard her exchange with Ava.

"What if she has to start school next fall in Barren instead of staying here?" she asked.

David eased away from her touch. "You know how I feel about that. Let's not talk it to death."

She followed him onto the porch. The morning air smelled sweet with the flowers that were beginning to bloom, not only in her yard but in others across their development. All around her were well-tended gardens and expensive homes like hers that were immaculate inside as well as out. No more falling-down house, no more chickens in the yard, even though having them was trendy now.

"I still can't believe Shadow wants to take Ava."

"Maybe three years with Ava was enough," David said. "I know how much you like having her here, but Shadow's right. She isn't ours. We don't have a legal leg to stand on— and I'm not sure I would want to if we did. I hope you won't bring up the idea to adopt again. Shadow would never agree. And where's the father? He has rights, too." He turned on the top step. Jenna had never told David about Grey Wilson. That had been for Shadow to share, and she'd remained silent. "Enough of this, Jen."

"But did she really think we wouldn't become this close to Ava?"

"She's a great kid, but she should be with her mother. *You* became too close." He continued down the steps.

Yes, maybe she had, but other than getting out of her parents' home years ago and making a new life for herself with David, the only thing she'd ever wanted was to be a mother. Nature had apparently decided that wasn't to be—at least, until Ava had come to stay. Jenna didn't want to lose her. She and David could provide far more than Shadow could, even now. Not that money made the difference. Ava was part of their family. It would break her heart to leave this house, her school, her friends…

Somehow, Jenna hoped to bring her lawyer husband around to her view.

There must be something they could do to keep Ava with them, at least for a while longer. Until she could help her niece accept the situation. Until Jenna got used to the idea of letting her go—if she ever could.

SHADOW GLANCED AT the sky. No wonder it looked so dark at the end of the day, the gathering clouds like an omen when only that morning the sun had been shining. She hadn't seen Grey since she'd told him about Ava, or at least a small part, and she'd just stepped out of her office when she ran into him on the sidewalk.

"I was coming to see you," he said. "I almost stopped yesterday but I wasn't ready to talk again. Now I am."

She held the bulky canvas envelope she carried closer. "I'm on my way to the bank. To make my weekly deposit."

He frowned. "You should do that every day." He cocked his head, viewing her from beneath the brim of his Stetson. "You shouldn't leave cash in your office every night. If I were a thief, I'd wait for Thursday when the receipts would be highest from the week before your deposit on Friday. I'd clean you out. Voice of experience." His scowl had deepened. "I got robbed."

Shadow squeezed the envelope even tighter, as if the agency was, indeed, at risk. "Robbed?"

"Rustlers cleaned out half a dozen head the other night. Took off before I could get a look at their faces—three of 'em."

She took another step. "I'm sorry to hear you've had more trouble—"

"I need to talk to you, Shadow." He looked around to make sure they were alone on the street. "Now. About…the baby."

She took a few more steps, her back to him, and sensed him following. "After I do my banking, I have to interview several new caregivers then drive out to the rehab center. Ned Sutherland had a stroke a few weeks ago and he's there now. I want to assess his situation." Since she'd stopped at her mother's house earlier and come back to town after her run-in with Derek, she hadn't gone to see Ned when she intended. She knew she was babbling now. "He may need our services."

"I see what you're doing. In a way I don't even blame you, but we're going to talk. It can be wherever you like, but we will talk. I won't be put off, Shadow."

"Then I guess you've done your thinking," she said.

She reached the main doors of the bank, leaving Grey to stand on the sidewalk, she assumed, but then he reached around from behind and caught the brass door pull, so close she could smell the soap he must have showered with that morning. "What happened after you went to Doc? And he gave you 'options'?"

"As I said, I spent the night at his house."

"Which option? You didn't—" for a moment he couldn't go on "—do something drastic?"

Shadow felt the blood drain from her face. That next morning, when she'd wakened at Doc's house, she'd known what to do. She'd already begun to love Ava. "No," she murmured, barely able to push out the words. "That choice might be right for some people but it wasn't for me."

She watched Grey relax. "Then, what option did you choose?"

Shadow hesitated. "I decided to give her up for adoption."

Another look of alarm crossed his features. "So, she's not…with you?"

Her heart skipped a beat. "Let me tell you what I did after I left Doc's then. You're right, I was trying to stall because I don't know how to say all this now, and you left my office before I could tell you." She looked around. "Can we talk in your truck? I hate to stand here like this where anyone could see us."

Grey nodded. He waited while she made her deposit then guided her to his silver pickup with a light hand at her lower back. Shadow felt his warmth through her summer dress. In that instant, she remembered other days and nights when they'd been inseparable, when she and Grey were in love, when she'd loved everything about him: his voice, his hands, his laughter, even the way he'd loved Wilson Cattle…because that told Shadow there was at least a different kind of family there, a different kind of home.

He sat against the driver's door while she pressed against the passenger side. And tried to think how to begin. The direct way seemed best.

"Doc and I discussed my choices that next day. He encouraged me to do what I thought best for her and for me, but he didn't pressure. You know he wouldn't." She studied the stores along Main Street, the bank, people passing by. "Please try to understand— I had no means of support, Grey, I hadn't finished high school, I didn't know how I could possibly care for a helpless baby when I could barely care for myself—Doc called his lawyer. We arranged a private adoption and I went to stay with the Merritts."

"Where? I don't recognize the name. Who were they?"

"A middle-aged couple, lovely people, who lived in Farrier. They still do. They agreed to pay all my expenses, the doctor there, the hospital…"

She told Grey about waking up there each morning, rolling over in bed in the sunny room she'd been given, feeling the baby kick against her palm. "When I saw a sonogram, I was able to make out fingers and toes and a snub nose. It was a little girl." Shadow laid a hand over her stomach. "'Good morning, Sunshine,' I always told her."

Grey's mouth tightened. "You should have called me."

"I still didn't feel I could. I'd left home, my family, you…all my friends behind. My parents hadn't changed their minds. The only people I saw were the Merritts and my obstetrician."

She kept her gaze on her lap. "I was so lonely, but for the first time in my life I didn't have to share a bed—except with the life growing inside me. She was so precious, but for her sake I knew I had to give her up." She paused. "Every morning Mrs. Merritt called up the stairs that breakfast was ready. She was a wonderful cook."

And every morning, still lying there for another few minutes, Shadow would cry softly into the blanket. Hormones, she'd thought. They were all over the place and she never knew which mood would come out next.

"They had no other children?"

"No, Mrs. Merritt was only forty but she couldn't have her own babies. Neither can my sister Jenna, and I know how that hurts. If I couldn't take care of my baby, I wanted to be happy that the Merritts would love and adore her."

"I'm glad they were kind to you," Grey said.

Shadow managed a smile. "Mrs. Merritt was so excited to have a baby. So was her husband. They couldn't seem to do enough for me. After breakfast, Mrs. Merritt and I always took a walk around the neighborhood. They live in a nice area with old but well-kept houses and big green lawns for children to play on."

They had really wanted her baby. Ava would have a good life with them, she'd told herself.

"What did they tell everyone else?"

"That I was their niece from upstate New York who'd come west because my pregnancy had worsened my lifetime asthma." Shadow lifted her gaze. "That was ten years ago and Kansas is pretty traditional, or was then. Now we could probably tell everyone the truth."

Shadow paused to steady her voice. She couldn't tell Grey that every day she'd thought that if Jared hadn't died, if she and Grey hadn't broken up and her father hadn't turned his back on her, maybe she and Grey would have woken each morning together, talked about their baby in low, happy tones. At times she'd yearned so much for that, she almost couldn't breathe, as if she really did have asthma.

But, instead, in the view of many, he had

killed her brother, and Shadow still had her own doubts. Was Grey innocent, as he claimed? Or guilty? Certainly she'd resented the fact that Grey had gone back to finish college as if nothing had happened, that he would take over his father's ranch...marry someone else. She was still surprised that he never had.

"So, after the baby was born..." His gaze flickered. "Where is she now?"

Shadow swallowed. "In school, staying at my sister Jenna's."

"You didn't give her up," he said, looking more than surprised.

"No," she murmured.

His mouth had that stubborn set she'd seen so many times before. "Then I want to see her," he said in a tone that didn't allow for her refusal.

"Grey, I'll need to talk to her first. We can't just show up and say, 'Hi, honey, this is your father.'"

He frowned. "I didn't exactly plan to do it that way."

She glanced at the darkening sky again. The thunderheads looked close enough to touch now. And a little frisson of doubt ran through her. If only Jared wasn't gone and she and Grey were still together. If only she could believe, like Blossom and Logan now, in happy endings and having the family she still yearned for.

With Ava home again, maybe she would. But that family didn't include Grey.

The first drops of rain began to fall. Soon the sky would open up, and unless she moved, they would still be here, eye to eye, at odds with each other.

Shadow said, "I've been planning to bring her back to Barren—but to introduce you that abruptly? No," she said again. "That's not in her best interest."

His voice was close to a growl. "I think it is. You've had nine years, Shadow. She's my daughter, too—and you've lied to me. All this time. No more."

CHAPTER FIVE

SHADOW HAD CUT short her work hours several days ago after she'd told Grey about Ava then gone to see Blossom. After talking with her mother and Derek, she'd meant to visit her client at the rehab center, but instead went back to the office. Then she'd told Grey about Doc and the Merritts and fallen even further behind. She needed to catch up. However, earlier today, she'd finally called Blossom to say she could be in the wedding if Blossom still wanted her. Even to avoid Grey, she couldn't disappoint Blossom. *How many true friends does a person have?* To be honest, she also felt guilty about him.

He was right. For too many years she'd kept Ava from Grey. The least she could do was stand with him while their mutual friends got married, a happy ending she couldn't picture for herself. Other than that she didn't know how to atone for what she'd done. To Ava, too.

Clearly, she'd made mistakes. Had it been easier to go about her life with Ava in Kansas City and Shawnee Mission rather than face Grey? If she'd never come back to Barren, would she ever have told him? She'd always planned to—at some point—but the opportunity never seemed to arise, and she'd tried to tell herself maybe that was for the best, that Grey had his own life without her. Now she knew that had been another error on her part. What if he'd simply run into Ava somewhere? She couldn't risk that.

Today, as the next step before he met her, she was going to see Ava. She wouldn't mention Grey just yet, although Ava had asked about her father over the years. Shadow had always kept it vague, telling Ava he couldn't be part of their lives but that, of course, he loved her. Another reason to feel guilty now.

But first, after dealing with the morning emails and texts at the office, she had an appointment at the rehabilitation center to finally check on Ned Sutherland, the elderly rancher who had suffered a stroke. Shadow had provided a caregiver for him before that and he would probably need one again.

"You're doing well, Mr. Sutherland. When do you expect to go home?"

For a moment, he didn't answer. Their visit had been punctuated by long silences and the obvious frustration she saw in his weathered face. His speech halting, Ned covered his first stumbling attempt to speak with a discreet cough.

"I…go…prob'ly next…week." His mouth leaned a little to the right and he gripped his weak hand in his lap with the other. The staff here had done their work, though. They'd gotten him on his feet and walking again, although he seemed to prefer staying in his room. That wasn't good. He needed cheering up.

Shadow had found him sitting by the window, his bony shoulders slumped, looking out toward the babbling brook on the lush green property. Several rough wooden benches were arranged along the bank for patients to enjoy the view and listen to the rushing water. For a man who'd spent most of his life outdoors on a horse or a tractor, like Logan's grandfather Sam—like Grey— Ned's enforced confinement had likely been more than difficult.

"You'll be back in the saddle before you know it," Shadow said, leaning down to pat his joined hands. He had bowed his head over them, the circle of bare scalp at his crown, which was normally covered by his hat, appearing larger than before. In the past months, the rest of his hair had gone from gray to snowy white. She bent her knees to peer into his weary dark eyes. "I'm sorry I missed seeing your granddaughter today, but please tell her I said hi."

"I...will." He blinked up at her. "Nice place...but I'm pretty homesick."

"I don't blame you." When she straightened, Shadow glanced down and saw the well-broken-in boots on his feet. Those he hadn't left behind. Putting the bouquet of yellow freesias she'd brought for him in a pretty blue vase on his nightstand, she said, "Enjoy those magazines. Keep your chin up, Mr. Sutherland. I'll check on you again the next time I'm here."

"Hope I...won't be." Then he grinned.

"I hope you won't be, too." Shadow silently applauded his show of spirit. A good sign, yet she knew that once he left here he would still need care. "In that case, I'll visit you at home."

"Look...forward to that." His mouth twisted. He'd probably taxed his strength and needed to rest. "Good...girl, Shadow."

He gave her a wink before she stepped out into the hallway. Still smiling, she headed for the large reception area with lush sofas and deep-cushioned chairs arranged around a flagstone fireplace and, across the room, a big aquarium filled with colorful fish. Oriental area rugs centered the spaces.

Shadow would speak to his granddaughter soon about his in-home care. She had a lot of older clients like Ned Sutherland, including Sam Hunter, who'd been thrown by that bison cow on the Circle H. Shadow had hired Blossom then as a temporary caregiver— and now she was planning to marry Logan. Shadow was determined to put on her best face for the wedding.

On her way past the reception desk, Shadow spotted another acquaintance, Bertrand O'Neill, who she hadn't seen in a while. Bertie sat in a wheelchair holding a large package on his lap. That must be everything he'd brought with him to rehab weeks ago. She laid a hand on his shoulder. "Going home today?"

"Yes, ma'am." He beamed at her. "How you doin', Shadow? How's your mama and daddy? And all those brothers and sisters?"

Shadow tensed. Bertie's memory wasn't

the best these days. He'd clearly lost his sense of time and events while he was here. "My father died last year," she reminded him in as gentle a tone as she could manage. "My mother's doing okay."

She bypassed any update on her siblings. One brother was dead, of course, and she had nothing right now to say about Derek. The youngest Morans—Cherry at twenty-one and Tanya at twenty-two—were away at college. Which left Shadow. And Jenna. She didn't want to think about that right now.

Next to Bertie, a tall, dark-haired man was talking to the receptionist. He pulled out his wallet and handed over a credit card. Then he turned toward Shadow. His brown eyes lit up before he smiled.

"Jack Hancock." Or should she call him Jacques? For a while, after Shadow had hired him to replace Blossom as Sam's caregiver at the Circle H—which hadn't proved necessary because Blossom never left, after all—he'd insisted on referring to himself by the French version of his name. "I thought you'd left town."

"Left and came back," he said. Just like Shadow. "Uncle Bertie needs me."

"Yes, he does." Somewhere along the

way, Jack had lost his faux French accent. "Is there anything I can do to make things easier?"

"Nothing except to find me a job. But then, I'd have no one to watch Bertie."

"That's what my agency is for." Shadow rummaged in her bag for a business card in case he or Bertie had misplaced the one she'd given them before.

Jack took it, then retrieved his credit card from the clerk at the desk, signed the rehab center's copy and gripped the handle of his uncle's wheelchair. He pushed Bertie toward the exit. "He's anxious to sleep in his own bed tonight. Eat some of my home cooking again." Jack was a chef and a good one. "We'll be fine," he said.

"You'll call me if the situation changes?"

"Sure will. Bertie's stay here cost more than the finest hotel in KC. Don't know how we'll balance the budget this month if I don't get work. I've been looking, but nothing has turned up."

"You want a job as a cook?" she asked.

"Cook, wrangler, whatever. I'm a jack-of-all-trades, you might say."

"Let me know once you find something, and I'll see what I can do for Bertie."

AFTER SHE LEFT Bertie and Jack at the rehab center, Shadow stopped by her office to re-read Jack's file. Weeks ago, Logan Hunter had given him a good reference as far as Jack's cooking and household skills went, but there had been an unpleasant incident at the Circle H involving two ranch hands and Jack had abruptly quit. If he found a job now and needed care for Bertie, she would step in.

With a growing anticipation that tightened her stomach and made her heart beat faster, she drove to the same strip mall where she'd met Jenna. Seeing Ava in midweek had been a rare occurrence this past year, and Ava's sunny smile always made Shadow ache with love and longing. The very sight of her little girl set her world right on its axis again, every time, yet their previous weekend hadn't gone that well and Shadow couldn't seem to block out Jenna's words. *She didn't even ask about you*.

Shadow wasn't smiling as she crossed the parking lot outside the bookstore. At the other end of the row of shops was the candy and ice cream store. Taking a moment to school her features into a more pleasant expression, she watched Ava, who had just gotten out of Jenna's car. Ava squared her shoulders as if she was about to face some punishment rather than enjoy an hour with Shadow, and she fought back another quick surge of guilt. In the past year they hadn't spent nearly enough time together—which was what she hoped to begin to correct now.

At her approach, Shadow finally smiled. Ava had the same slight frame and long legs as Shadow had had at her age, the same height. In the photographs taken with her sisters and brothers years ago, Shadow had looked painfully skinny and angular, but at nine Ava was better cared for. And not only because she lived at Jenna and David's house. Though Shadow knew this past year must have been tough on her daughter, Ava didn't lack for love and attention. Shadow had made sure of that, even when she couldn't be with her all the time.

But once Ava moved to Barren to be with Shadow, they would cuddle up each night at bedtime, as they used to do, and Shadow would read Ava a book. At the memory of her favorite story years ago about a cowgirl named Janie, Shadow ached with longing. Ava must have outgrown that by now, but they could share another book written for children more her age. And did Ava still have the little pony that had been her best "stuffie" ever since she was born? Shadow hadn't seen it in a while.

As Ava neared her, Shadow focused on her with another lurch of her heart.

Ava had inherited Shadow's dark hair with the brown lowlights that gave it depth... and Grey's blue-green eyes. To see her now, with a growing frown and a stiffness in her posture, made Shadow ache in a very different way.

"Hi, baby." She tried to draw her close, but Ava stepped back.

Her gaze focused on the pavement between them. "Hi."

Shadow glanced over her daughter's head at Jenna, still seated in her flashy new SUV, holding her cell phone to her ear. Was she deliberately prolonging a call to avoid speaking with her again?

"We won't be too long," Shadow called out. "Meet you back here."

Jenna hung up. "Ava has a birthday party," she told Shadow. "As soon as I buy the gift, we'll have to leave."

Shadow didn't answer. She mentally readjusted her plans for the day. There wouldn't be time to take Ava to the clothing store and let her pick out some new summer outfits unless they didn't stop at the ice cream shop.

Jenna knew she'd observe their time limit, yet in the months since Shadow had opened her agency in Barren and begun to commute between there and Kansas City, her meetings with Jenna had become more and more uncomfortable. Shadow was never quite sure of her sister's current mind-set or mood, and lately she hadn't been able to reestablish their connection during her weekends in Shawnee Mission, either. The same was true of her relationship with Ava.

She reached again for her daughter's hand, this time catching her fingers. "How does an ice cream cone sound? With caramel syrup and lots of sprinkles?"

Ava loved anything with sugar in it, and the warm afternoon should have tempted her to indulge, but she hung back. "I have to say bye first." Pulling free from Shadow's hand, she hurried across the tarmac to Jenna. Shadow stood back while they exchanged kisses and hugs, and murmured words Shadow couldn't hear. Jenna had been good to Ava, she couldn't deny that, and she was grateful for it, but their growing closeness made Shadow question her choice to leave Ava in Shawnee Mission for this long. Shadow needed to take a harder look at herself. How could she have let things get to this point? Jenna sent her a warning look. "We need to talk again, Shadow."

"Yes, we do. But right now, as you said, the clock is ticking." She started to walk away. "Come on, Ava. Let's pig out."

Shadow didn't look back but Ava kept glancing at Jenna until she'd backed the SUV out of its parking space and pulled away, turning onto the nearby street. Ava looked up at Shadow with what appeared to be tears in her eyes.

"Where have you been?"

The question stung. True, Shadow had been gone a lot this past year, but she'd explained the situation to Ava many times. She'd thought her daughter had adjusted to her weekend stays and nightly phone calls during the week. She'd repeatedly promised that was only temporary, but clearly Ava was still hurting.

"Ava, I know you're not happy with me right now—"

"Uncle David went away."

Caught off guard, Shadow took a breath. "You mean on his business trip?"

"I guess. I don't know where."

Shadow tensed. She had never cared for David Collins, who didn't seem to care for her, either, and his inability to show Ava much affection, although partially offset by Jenna's love, made Shadow all the more determined to bring her daughter home for good.

She gave her a quick hug. "I'm sure he'll be home soon."

For another long moment Ava seemed to think that over, then her face brightened and she was once more a little girl who simply wanted a treat. "Can we get ice cream now?"

"You bet. A double scoop."

They were in line at the counter of the small shop done in cheerful red and white with candy canes everywhere, when Ava asked, "How come I don't see you except on Saturdays and Sundays?"

"And Friday evenings." Shadow swallowed that lump of guilt. Jenna had warned her. Shadow and Ava had been inseparable for the first six years of her daughter's life and their partial separation had been harder on Ava than she'd expected it to be. Hard on Shadow, too. That had to change.

The clerk handed Ava's chocolate cone across the counter. She wasn't a baby or toddler anymore, or even the six-year-old she'd been when she and Shadow moved in with Jenna and David. Ava's resentment would only worsen over time unless… Shadow needed to broach the subject carefully. After that, she could let Grey meet Ava.

They took their ice cream cones outside to a shady spot under some trees. Shadow watched Ava for another moment, trying to choose the right words to say.

"Sweetie," she tried again. "I can't always be at Aunt Jenna's when I need to work during the week. I want to make sure we have everything you need…and you know about the new house. It's ready now." The announcement she'd once hoped would bring a big smile to Ava's face fell flat. Ava licked her cone. "I only saw that house once."

Shadow had driven her to Barren on the day of the closing, and Ava had seemed excited, but in the last few months, while Shadow unpacked and organized before she brought Ava home, Ava had lost her enthusiasm. In the meantime Jenna had redecorated Ava's bedroom in the Shawnee Mission house, and Ava had stopped asking when she would move in with Shadow.

"I know you like staying at Aunt Jenna's, but—"

"I want to live there. All the time. Why can't we stay there?"

"Didn't we always plan to move into the new house? Our house?" She tried to lighten the mood. "Remember when we lived in that tiny apartment where we had to share a bedroom? Staying at Aunt Jenna's was only meant to be for a while. Now it's time to move on."

"That's why you bought me *ice cream*?" Ava's mouth turned down. "I didn't even want to come today. I'm supposed to spend the night at Kaitlyn's house and watch movies. Her mom doesn't care how late we stay up." She dumped the rest of her cone into the nearby trash can. "I'll miss the birthday party. I can't go with you!"

"Wait. I didn't mean this minute, Ava."

She voiced Jenna's concern. "School isn't even out for the summer. How could I move?

I'd miss the end-of-year field trip and my class picnic and all my friends!" She jumped up from the bench they'd shared. "I *won't* go with you!"

In that same moment Jenna's car swung back into the parking lot. Ava's eyes brightened. Before Shadow could say another word, she'd bolted and was running across the pavement to her aunt's SUV. She didn't look back.

LYING ON THE bed Aunt Jenna had bought her, shut in her upstairs room at the house she loved in Shawnee Mission, Ava curled around the stuffed horse in her arms and held on tighter. Stormy was hers, now and forever. Someone—she couldn't remember who—had given him to Ava when she was a baby. Well, she wasn't a baby anymore, and *no one* could tell her to get rid of Stormy. She wouldn't leave him behind. The adults, meaning her *mother*, shouldn't be able to make Ava move to Barren as if she was still small enough, light enough, to just carry around or tuck into a stroller.

Barren was little, and mostly rural, and even its name sounded weird to Ava. She preferred Kansas City. It was big and busy and full of fun things to do. She'd never spent more than a few hours at a time in Barren and that hadn't been often.

The only thing she liked about it were the ranches everywhere with horses eating grass in pretty green fields. What else did Barren have? There was no movie theater, no shopping mall other than the outdoor one with the ice cream shop where her mom had told her they were leaving Aunt Jenna's house for good. Ava wished she'd said no to that cone with sprinkles and caramel.

Wiping a tear from her face, she picked up her cell phone—a hand-me-down from Aunt Jenna this year so she could call for a ride home after soccer practice—then put it down again. How could she call Kaitlyn? Tell her she was practically being kidnapped?

I won't leave this house. I'll lock my door and stay right here.

She didn't think Aunt Jenna would mind.

Ava wasn't as sure about Uncle David. He still wasn't home from his trip, but he never had much to say to her, anyway.

After arranging Stormy on the pillows, she scooted off the bed then padded down the stairs on bare feet. This couldn't happen. She needed help.

Her aunt was in the big, high-ceilinged family room that was usually sunny in the late afternoon. But the blinds were drawn over the wide windows that looked out onto the new swimming pool and Ava frowned.

"Aunt Jenna?"

She had the TV on, staring at the screen. Images danced across it, looking dimmer than they should because some light still leaked through the blinds. It took a moment for Ava to realize she was watching something they'd seen a hundred times. *Finding Nemo*. Once, that had been her favorite with her mom.

Her aunt started. "Ava. Hi, sweetie." She flicked the remote to shut off the sound, and Ava's frown darkened. Her mother used that nickname and she didn't want to think about her right now.

"I like it here," she said. "I don't want to move."

"Oh." When Aunt Jenna turned her head, Ava saw tears in her eyes as she patted the cushion beside her. "Let's talk about that."

"Why can't I stay with you?"

Her aunt sighed. "I wish you could."

She leaned against Jenna's side. "Just tell my mom."

"Ava, when you moved in with us, your mother needed a place to stay—a place that would be better for you than the apartment. I know you like your school here. You have your friends, but..."

Ava watched the tears streak down her face. She laid her head on Aunt Jenna's shoulder and felt her shake. "I didn't mean to make you feel bad. Just because I do," she added.

"Your mother has a home for you now. You'll be closer to your grandmother there, and you won't have to move again."

Ava tensed. "Live in Barren for the rest of my life?"

Aunt Jenna looked into Ava's eyes and seemed to pull herself together. She planted a soft kiss on Ava's forehead, pulled back and smiled. "That's a bit dramatic, isn't it?"

The smile seemed fake. "You didn't like it there. You left."

"So did your mom. Now she's home—and she needs you there with her."

"I don't even know my grandmother," she said.

"You have a point." This time her aunt's

smile looked real. "I can't change that, but I've told your mother we need to talk again. I'll see what I can do."

CHAPTER SIX

GREY HAD WAITED until tonight to call his father. As the legal owner of the ranch, Everett Wilson had a right to know about the loan Grey had been denied, about the rustlers too, and Grey gave him a full report, mentally holding his breath the whole time. When he'd finished, his dad asked to hear more about the missing cattle.

"No suspects?"

Grey settled deeper into the leather chair at the desk in the ranch office. Their father/son relationship had often been difficult. His parents' divorce when he was eleven had made that worse. He and his older sister, Olivia, had grown up hearing angry words in person or by phone. Their mother had demanded allegiance, which Grey had balked at, preferring to spend as much time with his dad as possible, but Olivia remained closer to their mom. She still barely spoke to their dad. But

Grey had been given the ranch to manage. To prove himself.

"No suspects," he said at last, staring at his boots, which were propped on the broad desktop and still bore the dirt of the day's work. So did his shirt and jeans. He could use a shower and clean clothes, then some much-needed sleep. "I went over every inch of ground with Finn Donovan."

"Tire tracks?"

"Yeah, but Finn tells me they're standard issue for that truck's model—if I even got that right. He made some casts. He'll try to get a better read from the lab but it doesn't look promising."

"Tell him to try harder."

"I've got a man on watch here. Finn's going to send out a cruiser on regular patrol, see if they can spot any suspicious activity—or even that truck on the road again somewhere looking for more easy pickings."

His dad scoffed. Grey could almost see him running a hand through his thick but graying hair, the glint in the eyes Grey had inherited from him. "I'm not sure Finn Donovan is up to the job. I didn't vote for him. As far as I'm concerned, the man hasn't settled in at this point. No wonder a couple of broken-down cowpokes—if that's who they are—are out stealing an honest man's cattle."

"We don't know who they are yet." Grey lowered his legs from the desk.

"I've put my trust in you. I don't have another son to leave that ranch to. You need to get a handle on this, Grey."

This was his biggest fear: not merely disappointing his father when he'd handed over Wilson Cattle to Grey, but running the ranch, and their legacy, into the ground even before he became the official owner.

He leaned on his elbows on the desk. The scarred but still-solid piece was an heirloom. Every stick of furniture in the house, every bale of hay in the barn, every horse and cow and bull that roamed these acres, were his to preserve, to hand on one day to the children he didn't have yet. To defend.

"I was doing fine—for three years—until the other night."

No, he thought, until he started losing money, Barney denied him the loan, and then Shadow had told him about the baby. Hearing about her parents' reaction, her visit to Doc's office, her decision to give up their child for adoption…he didn't know what had changed her mind, though he was grateful she had, but Grey was still angry that he'd missed out on nine years of his daughter's life. In some ways, it seemed worse that she'd been so close, within reach, all this time instead of with some anonymous family. Yet he'd been denied any chance to know her. He and Shadow would talk about that soon.

In the background his father cleared his throat. "I'd hate to see you fail, Grey."

"I won't," he said.

"Beyond the ranch's survival, this town needs to know that we Wilsons are decent, God-fearing people...not murderers. You know that's still some people's opinion."

For some time after his father hung up, Grey sat and listened to the tick of the old grandfather clock in the corner. He pulled out his handkerchief and swiped at the dust on his boots. *Jared Moran.* He'd carried the past around for years like a heavy yoke with two water buckets dangling from his shoulders, forever weighing him down.

He needed to prove to his father, the town of Barren and himself that he was worthy of Wilson Cattle. And, for Grey, that he wasn't responsible for Jared's death. *If* he wasn't.

He wondered what Finn Donovan had found in the file.

THE NEXT MORNING, when Grey marched into the sheriff's office, the old case was far from his mind. The present had taken center stage.

Barren was the Stewart County seat, and Finn's headquarters occupied a small one-story building next to the town's community complex, where the mayor, the senior center and the school board also had their offices. Grey shut the door from the parking area behind him, inhaling the aroma of fresh coffee in the air.

As he'd told his father, he'd already met Finn to inspect the initial crime scene, and they'd gone over that list of ear-tag numbers with his foreman. The sheriff had promised to send deputies to scour the auction places within county borders. Unless Grey's cattle had already been trailered to Montana or Idaho, the Dakotas or Wyoming, he might get lucky.

Not so.

"I lost a dozen more cattle last night," he announced to the dispatcher, the desk sergeant and anyone else who happened to be around this early in the day. After he'd talked with his father, he'd felt tempted to take the watch on the hill instead of sending one of his ranch hands. He should have trusted his instincts. "Finn here?"

"The sheriff is on the phone. I'll page him."

Grey cooled his heels until the receptionist told him he could go in, then pushed through the swinging half door that separated the waiting area and front desk from the offices behind. There was an empty holding cell back there, too, and he wished the right someone were in that cell this morning.

"Finn, something else has to be done—"

He broke off. The sheriff was on the phone again. It nestled in the crook of his neck, and Finn held up a finger. At the unspoken command, Grey could hear his pulse pumping in his ears. He kept both hands braced on the desktop until, with a sigh, Finn hung up. "Now see what you've done. That was the mayor."

"Sorry to interrupt, but this is important."

Finn half smiled. "More important than the security detail at the county fair this summer?"

Grey didn't smile back. "For the first time in my life I won't be going to any fair. We've always sent cattle to be judged, but the way things are going I won't have any cows left."

Finn waved him toward a chair. "Sit down. Please."

"I may not have a ranch by then," Grey went on, knowing he must sound like a raving lunatic. "Somebody cleaned out six of my best cows last night, five calves, and—would you believe?—a prize-winning bull that cost thousands."

Finn pulled a pad out from under a stack of file folders and a paper cup of coffee that sat on top of his messy desk then rifled through a drawer for a pen. "Let's write up your statement."

"Again," Grey said. "What are you doing to find these guys?"

"Everything that can be done, but there's not much to go on."

"A bunch of extra patrols won't cut it. Obviously."

Finn sighed. "Those tire tracks didn't exactly light up the state forensics lab, either. There must be hundreds of trucks like that with those same tires."

"I was about to call you anyway—ask about expanding the search for that truck even farther—when I got up this morning to a brief note from my new man telling me all those cattle were gone."

"Cody Jones."

"Yep."

Finn's pen poised over the pad. "Twelve head of cattle, you say. The thieves must have cut the fence again."

"That's what Cody said. But he claims he never saw the truck or those men—if they were even the same ones." Grey ran a hand through his already rumpled hair. Before his first cup of coffee, he'd seen Cody's note tacked to the kitchen door, then dressed in haste and left the house with his temper flying. "When I talked to him at the barn he insisted that he saw nothing."

"Fell asleep on the job, did he?"

"That's how it looks to me." On his way into town Grey had thought again of letting Cody go but he was already short-handed, and he had a soft spot for the kid. Keeping watch was a lonely business; it could be hard for anyone to stay awake. "He says he'd spent the early part of the night before his watch having a few beers in town."

"What kind of man did you hire? You should consider assigning another hand to the job. I'm sorry about all this, Grey." Finn twirled the pen between his fingers. "I'll contact the other departments in the area, and I've already talked to the sheriff over in Farrier. Let's see what turns up."

"That's it?"

"For now."

Grey studied him for a long moment, but in his view that wasn't all. And he remembered the original purpose of his trip to town before he'd learned about his missing cattle. He took a breath. "Did you get a chance to look at the case file on Jared Moran?"

Finn shook his head. "Grey, I did—but I found nothing to justify reopening the case."

Grey's jaw set. "Then I guess it's up to me."

"I wouldn't advise that," Finn said. "I'm law enforcement here. If I could see any benefit to using the scarce resources I have to dig up the past, I would. But I can't. You shouldn't either. From what I read, you're in the clear—you and everyone else involved— without further evidence to go on. Stick to watching out for your cattle, okay?"

Grey tried to tamp down his disappointment. Then he realized that Finn hadn't once looked him straight in the eye since he'd barged into his office. Was there something Finn wouldn't tell him? He waited until the sheriff finally glanced up. "Sorry about the old case. And I'd like to do better about these thieves. I will. But there's something else, outside my job, Grey, that I'd like to ask you about."

"What's that?"

"Some*one*, actually," Finn said. "Shadow."

Grey propped his hat on one knee, then switched it to the other. This wasn't the first time Finn had tried to probe their relationship. Or, rather, nonrelationship.

He came to attention in the hard-backed chair. "Shadow and I have a long history. I imagine you've picked up on that from people here in town. So, yeah, we used to have a thing. Then we broke up. She left Barren for reasons of her own and didn't come home for ten years."

Finn's gaze shifted. "She's a fine person, Grey. Smart, pretty… I'd like to ask her to have dinner with me."

Grey plucked his hat from his knee, plunked it on his head and stood. "I can't speak for Shadow. I wouldn't if I could. She makes her own decisions." One of them had been to leave years ago, another was to never tell him about their child. He still wasn't sure how to reconcile that. "I don't need to know about anything between you and her," he said and headed for the door. "Good luck."

AFTER LEAVING FINN'S OFFICE, Grey decided to finish the rest of his errands another time. He'd spend this afternoon working at Wilson Cattle before his night watch. He opened the driver's-side door of his truck and looked at the sleek sedan parked behind him and the rusted-out Chevy Nova with the peeling roof in front. Grey's silver pickup was wedged in like a cow being funneled, nose to tail with the others in the herd, down a chute into a feedlot. There couldn't be two inches of space in which to jockey his way out of his parking spot. He'd just resettled his hat on his head when someone bumped his shoulder and he turned.

Grey had recognized that rusty Chevy. Derek Moran stood there, puffed up like a bantam rooster on the sidewalk in front of the Barren Cattlemen's Bank.

Derek grinned. "Looks like you're caught between a rock and a hard place, Wilson. Wonder what the owner of that Mercedes will say when he comes out of one of these stores loaded with shopping bags and finds his shiny front bumper all dented in."

"There's no one parked in front of you, Moran. Move your car."

"I don't think I will."

Grey tried to hold on to his temper. Tall, though not as tall as Grey, and strong, Derek had never been Grey's favorite person, even when Grey and Shadow were dating. But he was still Shadow's youngest brother, and Grey always tried to remember that. Grey slanted him a look. Derek wore a straw cowboy hat, a striped denim shirt and jeans.

"You out job hunting this morning?"

Derek's grin stayed in place. "Nothing seems to suit my talents."

Grey stared at the pavement. The kid sounded just like his old man. Shadow's dad had worked for Grey's father off and on for a number of years, always quitting on some trumped-up excuse or because of an imagined offense, then coming back again when he got close to losing his house and postage-stamp-sized farm. The sad routine had made Grey's dad furious.

"Your sister worries about you. You have to start somewhere, Derek."

"For minimum wage?"

"If that's what it takes, yeah. Maybe you should adjust your expectations."

Derek's light-blue eyes cooled. "Seems to me you haven't changed yours one bit."

Grey blinked. For an instant he couldn't think what Derek had meant, but then he knew. He and Derek rarely had any other topic to discuss. Plus, he remembered what Finn had said. "I'm not going to talk with you about Shadow."

Derek stepped closer, into his face. "I'm going to tell you this one time, Mr. Big Deal Rancher. Stay away from my sister. She left here years ago—best thing she ever did— and frankly, I wish she hadn't come home again. That can only mean more trouble from you." He added, "A wonder people in this town didn't ride you out on a rail."

Grey's jaw clenched. He entertained the idea of punching Derek, then thought better of it. Derek had been just fifteen when Jared got shot, and Grey wouldn't get anywhere with him now. Derek might be well on his way to becoming a flawed man like his father, but Grey hoped there was still a chance for him. And he'd always tried to cut Derek some slack. The kid had been there the night Jared died, and Grey couldn't blame him for standing up for his big sister today, even playing the tough guy, though that didn't sit well with Grey.

"Message received," he said anyway. He turned from Derek to his truck's open door. "Now move that Chevy—before I move it for you."

CHAPTER SEVEN

LATER THAT AFTERNOON, Grey drove over to the Circle H, needing someone to talk to, someone he trusted. He and Logan stood at the corral fence, where he started with Finn Donovan's refusal to reopen the Jared Moran case.

"Sorry to hear that, Grey. I know you were hoping for a different result."

What had he expected Logan to say? He couldn't change the sheriff's decision. The past few days had been one long frustration. "Then, for good measure, I had to run into Shadow's brother." He related the parking incident. "I hate to think like this, but I swear he's turning into the spitting image of his dad."

Logan rubbed the back of his neck. "Derek didn't have a good role model, that's for sure. It's a sorry tale," he said. "Like Jared's death. Wish I'd been here for you when all that happened, Grey." Logan had been in the air force then.

"Nothing else you can do now, either. Except to keep being my friend," Grey said. "I know you've taken heat for that more than once."

He started to peel away from the fence. "Better get on home. We had a sick cow earlier—one of my best breeders—with a weak calf at her side that may not survive. When my men and I weren't seeing to that pair, we were branding other calves. I doubt they'll want to stand watch tonight, looking for rustlers." He half smiled. "Besides, they're still hazing Cody. He gets all the dirty jobs." Of which there were many on a ranch. At least he hadn't forgotten to feed the horses that morning, but Grey remembered Finn's statement earlier. *What kind of man did you hire?* Was Cody just a careless kid or could he be hiding a more sinister side? Grey changed his mind. "I'll take watch myself if I have to."

"Tobias and Willy will keep watch here," Logan said. "Sure hope we come up with some clue—or even better, an actual sighting. That white truck couldn't just disappear."

"Unless it's not local. Maybe Finn can expand the search to other counties, too—even the rest of the state. See what turns up."

He had one booted foot still on the fence rail when Logan said, "Before you go, come inside for a cold beer. We can strategize."

Grey was about to say yes—he'd worked up a thirst branding with his men all day—when he glanced down the long driveway to the road and saw Blossom's shiny new car turn in. Logan had bought it for her as an engagement gift to replace her old tan sedan.

As the car neared, he saw there were two people inside. When they got closer, he realized the other person was Shadow. He didn't see her red Mustang anywhere, and he hadn't seen her since she'd told him about going to Doc and then that she'd changed her mind about putting the baby up for adoption. Also, to Grey's relief, he'd heard she'd changed her mind about the wedding and agreed to be Blossom's maid of honor, after all. He didn't want their friends to be pawns in his chess game with Shadow.

Logan waved at the approaching car. "Blossom and Shadow drove to Wichita today to shop for a wedding dress."

"Guess we'll hear all about it," Grey commented.

You'd look real nice in a long white gown.

Logan raised a brow. "I'm told I can't see it before the ceremony."

"That's supposed to be bad luck." Grey knew little about weddings, but his sister had told him about the superstition years ago when she was making preparations to marry Logan. Now they were divorced and Logan was about to wed again, which had left Olivia as a single mother to their seven-year-old son. She and Logan shared custody.

As soon as Blossom's car stopped, Shadow flung open her door. Obviously she'd seen Grey. Her chin set, she started toward the rear of the house where she must have left her car, but Logan caught her arm. "Hold on. You don't say hello before you take off? There are people who want to hear about that shopping trip."

Joining them, Blossom beamed. "I found it!" She made a zipping motion across her lips. "And that's all I'm going to say."

Shadow eased her arm from Logan's light grasp. "Before I spill the beans—because, Logan, you won't be disappointed, her gown is absolutely gorgeous—I'm going home."

"Grey and I were just going to have a drink. Join us."

"Thanks, but I have to... I need to..." She ran out of steam. Grey knew Shadow wouldn't invent some lame excuse just to get away from him, and she didn't.

"Don't mind me," he said.

Logan had walked off with Blossom, and at the back door he guided her into the kitchen. "You two stay there for a minute." He grinned over his shoulder. "You can practice being nice to each other for the wedding, which—like this house—will be a stress-free zone. Another warning—so will our weekend with the wedding party in Kansas City. Hope neither of you have forgotten about that. We need you there—and Shadow has to pick a dress, too."

Grey almost groaned. The bridal party was supposed to spend a few days in KC to firm up some of the plans and the time was fast approaching. He imagined Shadow wasn't looking forward to that, either. Their last talk hadn't gone that well, and Grey still had questions. For a start.

The door shut behind Logan, leaving Grey alone with Shadow. She avoided his gaze. "What did I get myself into here? A whole *weekend*? When Blossom asked me, I thought it would be just the two of us again, like going to Wichita for her dress today. Why do we all need to go to Kansas City when the ceremony's going to be here?"

"Logan says we have to get tuxedoes fitted. There'll be some kind of cake tasting, too, and he and I are supposed to rent a wooden dance floor for the reception." He couldn't resist adding, "Imagine us all dancing under the cottonwoods with lights strung through the trees." But that didn't seem to appeal to Shadow.

Grey studied her. Beautiful, he thought, even prettier than ten years ago. Her face was more refined, and she had a stronger sense of herself. He recognized her expression as if he were looking in a mirror. He knew her every smile and frown like the back of his hand. "What's wrong? Other than the trip?"

She turned away. "Nothing. I guess I'll see you in Kansas City."

From the kitchen Grey heard the refrigerator door open then close. Several bottles clinked onto the table. A cupboard door banged shut. Blossom was probably preparing snacks to go with the drinks.

He tracked Shadow toward the Mustang. There was definitely something bothering her, other than the prospect of a weekend away with him. Grey realized what that was. No wonder she didn't want to talk. "Shadow, I asked to see her. When?"

She briefly pressed her lips together. "I've planned to bring her to Barren. Unfortunately, my nine-year-old daughter doesn't agree and neither does my sister. I don't quite know what to do about the impasse…"

"Or me?" he asked, and in that instant made up his mind. Jared's death wasn't the only issue between them. "I have a right to see her, Shadow. Make it happen."

As if she'd been expecting that, her eyes grew moist. They glistened, their deep brown turning as dark as black onyx before she turned away again, fishing in her bag for her car keys. "I told you that's not a good idea just now. I can't bring her home just like that, either. She needs to be prepared and Jenna might dig in her heels," Shadow said. "It's not as if she has any legal right. She's not a guardian, but I know I'll be damaging our relationship—mine and Ava's—maybe irrevocably. I don't want to do that. I don't want to upset my child. And as far as you're concerned, Jenna hasn't forgotten about Jared, either."

"Neither have I. You think it wasn't hard for me, too, being accused of something I didn't do?" *Probably didn't do*, he thought. He resettled his Stetson. "And if you haven't noticed, the second you hit town again, all of that came back.

"I know," she said.

"Just this morning two people went out of their way in front of the bank to avoid me. They didn't say a word, but they didn't have to." His mouth tightened. "And Derek recently gave me an ultimatum to keep away from you. People here don't forget, Shadow—just like Jenna. They can see me every day, doing my job, keeping my nose clean, and still they wonder…who really killed Jared? I don't know how to stop all that except to find the truth myself."

"I understand that. I hope you do."

Grey kept one hand on her door. That car with its bright-red paint job seemed to shriek at him. *Stop. Go away.* He'd be darned if he would. "That's all you can say? Then I have another question. What made you decide, after arranging for that adoption, to keep the baby, after all?"

He'd startled her enough that at first she didn't react. Then she looked over his shoulder at the house as if hoping to be rescued. Her voice quavered. "I always wished things could be different. That this wasn't how it was supposed to be, and every day I felt more disloyal to Mrs. Merritt." She hesitated. "Every morning, lying there with the baby, alone for those few minutes together in that sunny room, I kept thinking—what if we hadn't broken up and Jared didn't die? And I thought…" She removed his hand from her door latch. "I always thought of *you*."

Grey was so surprised, even stunned, that he couldn't say a word. He wanted to pull her close, hold her, draw her in for a kiss that might heal them both. Instead, he watched her get into her car and heard the engine start, but he didn't move.

What could he say to that?

He was still standing there when she drove off in a cloud of dust that nearly choked him. Grey looked after her, aching. And he knew that she must be hurting, too.

SHADOW FLEW ALONG the country road toward town, paying little attention to the speed limit. She passed the local ranches in a blur, driving from the Circle H toward town with her hands clammy on the wheel. On such straight roads, she found it hard to rein in her Mustang. The classic red beauty wanted to run.

So did Shadow. She couldn't get home fast enough.

Why had she let Grey see so deeply into her soul? Just as she'd gotten a fresh look into his. Remembering that lonely time before Ava was born, she'd wanted to cry out for him when he wasn't there. Now that he was, how would they find the common ground they needed for Ava's sake? She was no longer alone in making those choices. And Grey would be right to blame her for some of the decisions she had made. Without him.

The flashing red lights behind her came out of nowhere. So did the siren.

Worried about Grey, regretting that she'd bared herself to him emotionally, she reacted in slow motion. Saw the sheriff's car in her rearview mirror. Saw him motion her to pull over. And yet it was another half mile down the two-lane before she pulled to the side of the road, put on her flashers and sighed. Finn

Donovan. She slapped the steering wheel with the heel of her hand as he strode from his cruiser to her car.

He shook his head. "Shadow Moran."

"Yes, sir."

"I clocked you doing eighty-five. This is a fifty-five mile per hour zone."

"Guilty as charged."

Finn quirked an eyebrow. His dark hair gleamed in the late-afternoon sun that slanted across the road. "No excuses?"

"None." She was still trembling from her confrontation with Grey. "Write me the ticket, okay?"

He cocked his head, barely suppressing a smile. "Maybe I need to impound this car," he said. "Let you spend the night in a cell downtown."

Shadow knew what he really meant. Pushing aside her concerns for Grey, if not for Ava, she tried to relax. With every day that dragged on without her, she missed her daughter even more. She needed a laugh. "Maybe you'd like to drive this classic car around town. That really why you stopped me?"

"No, ma'am. You *were* speeding." He brandished his citation pad like some trophy won at a high school sports banquet. Since Finn was relatively new in town, she hadn't known him in what people called his glory days. Finn had been a star quarterback somewhere in Indiana, and rumor had it the wall of shelves in his living room here was loaded with awards. Shadow hadn't seen them or his house, yet she and Finn kept meeting up in the most unlikely places. Where had he been hiding? There wasn't a bush or tree in sight, an outcropping of rock. They both surveyed the pancake-flat plains. The wind was picking up, a spring curse every year. By now, it should have become a milder, summer breeze.

"I spied you from near the Wilsons' place. Obviously you didn't see me."

No, she'd been lost in her thoughts. The wedding trip to Kansas City, Grey, the adoption she hadn't gone through with, Ava...

She tried to capture a strand of hair that swept across her face. "So. Just write me up and I'll be on my way. You'll have your quota for this month—everyone says you have one—and you're welcome. I'm happy to support the town of Barren and Stewart County."

He grinned. "You've got a lot of chili pepper in you, Shadow."

She half smiled in spite of her grim mood. "Watch it, Finn."

"That's Sheriff Donovan to you." He looked mildly affronted for a moment before he said, "But instead of giving you a ticket, I'd rather take you to dinner tonight."

Shadow swiped at her hair again, trying to hold it back against the wind. "That's an abuse of your power as an officer of the law. It's—"

"A pretty good idea." His eyes twinkled with mischief, tempting her to set aside her problems. "Come on, why not?" he said. "Bet you don't have anything better to do."

"How would you know that?"

"Because neither do I," he said, his mouth suddenly turned down like a pouting boy who'd been caught stealing cookies from a jar. "Take pity. I'm isolated by this very badge—" he pointed at his chest, where Shadow saw no badge "—and being in such a position of power, as you said, gets lonely."

She clapped her still-clammy hands. "Bravo, that was an award-winning performance."

"You'll never know I'm serious if you don't say yes. It's only dinner."

At last Shadow tucked the wayward strand of hair behind one ear. With only a brief spurt of what might be guilt, she took Finn's challenge. Besides, in spite of the tension she'd carried with her from the Circle H, her stomach was already growling. By tomorrow morning it would be all over town that she and the sheriff had been sighted at Annabelle's Diner, the only place for a dinner date in Barren. The café down the street served only breakfast and lunch.

But at the moment she didn't care about other people's gossip. She needed to escape the persistent memories of Grey and her concern for Ava, the newer image of Grey standing, speechless, in the driveway after she'd all but admitted that her feelings for him hadn't died with Jared.

It's only dinner. A few hours of conversation, some shared laughter and she'd be home. Shadow wouldn't think of Finn's invitation as a date.

Just as she wouldn't allow herself to think again of Grey tonight.

CHAPTER EIGHT

AT HER MOTHER'S kitchen table, Shadow reread the notice from the county tax assessor's office. Her heart sank all over again.

After she'd driven the rest of the way home yesterday, the months she'd spent with the Merritts during her pregnancy, always knowing that Ava would be theirs, had kept playing in her mind like an old, bittersweet tune made new again since she'd told Grey that the adoption hadn't gone through. And with Ava to consider, she wasn't ready for another relationship—with Grey or with Finn.

As soon as she'd gotten home, Shadow had called the sheriff's office and left a message.

Sorry, I won't be able to do dinner, after all.

She had to put Ava's well-being first. And that would mean spending every spare moment with her once she moved back to Barren. Baking cookies. Shopping for those new summer clothes. Sharing good-night kisses in Ava's new room, which was waiting for her. Shadow had always started with a kiss on top of her head then the tip of her nose and on both cheeks before she finished with a light peck on Ava's lips. That had been their nightly ritual. It would be again.

Shadow held up the notice. "When did this come?"

Her mother stood at the sink, looking out the window as if to check the yard for children playing, even though they were all grown and mostly gone. Or else she was watching the ever-present flock of chickens squabble by the henhouse. Her tone was one of defeat. "Yesterday."

Shadow didn't believe her; her mother had probably kept this notice for some time, afraid to tell her. She'd taken a hard line with Mama and with Derek the last time she was here. She always hoped there wouldn't be a next time or more trouble, but there always was.

"This says it's the final notice." Shadow gentled her voice. "Mama, they're going to take your house from you for unpaid property taxes." The home where she'd insisted on staying. "Why didn't you call me?"

Her mother turned from the window. "I didn't want to ask for more help."

Shadow glanced at the figures in front of her again. She knew all about issues that never disappeared and her talk with Grey at the Circle H had only reminded her of that. "Apparently you haven't paid taxes for four years." The total amount was staggering for someone who had few resources.

Her mother's mouth set. "Where was I going to get the money? It's not as if Derek has been able to help—though I know he tries—and before your daddy died and the bills came to me to deal with, I didn't know about the taxes. I still do the best I can, Shadow. Keeping up this farm is hard enough without my daughter scolding me."

Shadow envisioned the yard outside. *Farm* was a loose word for the property. The chickens were the only "crop" now, producing enough eggs, her mother had told her, to pay for groceries. "I'm not scolding. I'm trying to understand." She added in a softer tone, "I don't mean to sound harsh, but honestly, Mama—did you think the problem would just go away?"

Her mother half smiled. "I kind of hoped it would."

"So the notices kept coming and you kept ignoring them."

Her mother looked toward the hallway, perhaps hoping Derek would appear again, making this two against one. Shadow reached out to take her hands. "Nothing is going to make this farm a going concern. I know you wish otherwise, but it really never was."

"I have nowhere else to go." Tears filled her eyes. "And what about my chickens? I don't want to sell them."

"I know that, but I doubt you'll have any choice. That's sad, but—"

"Not like *Wilson Cattle*," her mother muttered. "Thousands of acres, all those cows everywhere. That big house. I know that's what attracted you in the first place. You thought Grey Wilson was your ticket out."

Shadow flinched. "That's not true." But it had been said before.

"You wanted to get away from us," her mother went on, "and this place."

Shadow squeezed her hands. "Mama, this isn't about me and Grey. Or even what happened with Jared. What are you going to do?"

But her mother refused to leave the topic. "Grey Wilson started all this when he killed Jared."

Shadow sighed. Once her mother brought up her brother's death, Shadow wouldn't get anywhere with her.

"What if he finds out about Ava?" she went on. "She has his eyes, Shadow. When I first saw that baby, she broke my heart."

And her mother rarely saw Ava now. Shadow wondered if that could change when she brought Ava home. She wanted her daughter to know her grandmother. She wanted Ava to feel closer to her. Maybe Shadow could forgive her mother at last and repair their relationship, too. If she couldn't have the family she'd always hoped for with Grey, maybe she and her mother could work on this one.

"Grey already knows. I told him."

"Has he seen her"

"Not yet."

"What happens when he does?"

Shadow took a deep breath. "Right now I have to think of Ava and what's best for her. She needs me."

"Are you sure about that?"

Considering their last meeting at the ice

cream store and Ava's resentment, Shadow wasn't so sure anymore. But if Ava stayed with Jenna and David much longer, everything would become even more complicated. Shadow had to make amends with her, which meant bringing Ava to Barren, where they could not only be together but also talk things out. She couldn't wait to hold her daughter again, to let Ava know how much she loved her. And then she would decide the best time for Grey to meet his daughter.

"You were the one who said I abandoned her, which I never did, but you made me think. I've tried to make the best choices for her. That's what I'm doing now." Shadow released her mother's hands. "First, let's figure out what we're going to do about this house."

"I'm staying. I don't care if Finn Donovan shows up to throw me out."

Shadow suppressed a twinge of guilt over her refusal to have dinner with him. "He probably will."

"Then your daddy's shotgun is still in the front closet. Derek knows how to use it and so do I." Both of her brothers had been hunters and their game birds had fed the family many times. Shadow had once bagged a pheasant herself for Thanksgiving dinner. She wasn't a bad shot, either. But the handgun Jared had taken with him to defend her honor that night was another matter; that had only led to tragedy. And where had he gotten it?

Shadow held her mother's gaze. "Using that shotgun would only mean free lodging for you in the county jail. And you still wouldn't be able to keep this house."

Her mother began to fret. "What will I do? Where would I go? David won't have me in Shawnee Mission, and I won't create friction between him and Jenna. Cherry and Tanya are living in dorms at school. And what about Derek? I won't see him become homeless."

Shadow didn't mince words. "I'll do what I can for Derek because he's my brother and for your sake, Mama." She smoothed a hand over the final notice on the table. "We'll figure out your living situation—somehow. You're always welcome for a few nights at my place, but Ava will have the second bedroom soon. You need to begin sorting and packing—I can help you with that. If we wait, there'll be no choice." She breathed in deeply. "Let's get started."

GREY RODE INTO the barnyard with Finn Donovan. With a light touch he reined Big Red to a stop at the barn. His horse, a sorrel that stood nearly sixteen hands high, lived up to its name, which had been the nickname of the great racehorse Secretariat.

He heard Finn sigh in relief. The sheriff wasn't comfortable on a horse, even though Grey had picked the most placid gelding in the barn for him. Together they'd ridden to and from a corner of Wilson Cattle to inspect the latest broken fence where, despite posting a nightly watch, Grey had lost more stock.

He dismounted then reached for Finn's reins. "I'll put these guys inside. Cody can unsaddle then cool them down before he rides out to repair that fence. By now, he should be an expert."

"Better him than me," Finn murmured, climbing down with a groan from the bay gelding he'd ridden, however reluctantly. They could have gone cross-country on the Gators or even most of the way in Grey's pickup, until the ground became too rough and rutted, so he had to admit he'd caved in to the urge to make Finn sweat. He'd heard about him and Shadow.

Finn wiped a hand over his brow. "I hope that's the end of my punishment."

Walking between both horses with the reins in hand, Grey led them into the barn's dark interior, inhaling the familiar scents of hay and grain. To Grey, there weren't any better smells on Earth, and this most recent loss of cattle reminded him that he might lose the whole ranch.

Several horses were slurping water from their buckets, a sound Grey also liked. He hooked Red and Finn's horse to the crossties, one behind the other in the aisle, then turned around to see the sheriff still standing by the first stall door, as if he didn't want to come any farther.

"I haven't ridden since I was a kid, and then it was pony rides at the Indiana State Fair. Or on a merry-go-round. My experience is limited."

"You live in Kansas long enough, in a community like Barren where most of us are ranchers, you'll learn to ride and love it. Might even get a horse or two. Pretty good company," Grey said.

"So you say." Finn came down the aisle to the horse he'd borrowed. He stroked a tentative hand down the gelding's nose. "Sorry, big guy. Nothing personal."

"This horse took care of you as if you were a baby." As he might care for Grey's child, the one he hadn't yet seen.

Finn said abruptly, "Grey. I hope you'll stop holding it against me that I asked Shadow out to dinner. She stood me up." He shook his head. "My ego's still wounded."

Grey fought an urge to gloat. He didn't want to antagonize Finn; he was counting on him to find the rustlers—if not to work with Grey on Jared's case. In addition, he hoped they might become friends.

"I told you. That's your business with her." Not that he had to like it.

He looked around for Cody, who didn't seem to be in either the barn or the nearby tack room. Goofing off again? He hoped not, but Grey couldn't fault him. All the feed and water buckets were clean and filled. Cody hadn't needed a reminder.

"So, where do we stand?" Grey asked. "I need to find out who's been stealing my cattle. My livelihood and the legacy of this ranch depend on that."

"I'll put out another BOLO alert for that white truck."

Grey patted the two horses' rumps then crossed his arms. "Most rustlers these days show up in a big semi, but that truck and trailer are pretty modest by comparison. I'm thinking those guys may be amateurs, even though they seem to know their way around the cows."

Finn agreed. "I think so, too. I didn't get the chance to tell you while I was trying to stay on that horse, but I've talked with my counterparts in neighboring counties. None of them has reported anything close to what's happened here at Wilson Cattle."

"I know this sounds paranoid, but what if this is personal?" Certainly Grey had enemies in town. He doubted any of them had turned into cattle rustlers, but he couldn't dismiss the notion. "What if my missing cattle are someone's payback for Jared Moran?"

"If that's so, why wait until now?" Finn frowned. "In the case file—yeah, I took a second look—what's there doesn't show you in the best light, Grey." He tilted his head to study him. "From what I read, you had a motive to kill Jared Moran."

"Sure, we'd had words before—more than once. A few shoving matches. He didn't like me dating his sister. I didn't like him butting in. But that didn't mean I wanted to kill him. That night he was on this property. Trespassing. Carrying a gun."

"And you'd just broken his sister's heart."

"That gave *him* a motive, not me. Because of Shadow, Jared came loaded for bear."

"Giving *you* the opportunity to blow him away."

"That would have been in self-defense," Grey said. "But that's not how it was."

Finn ticked off the points. "Motive and opportunity, possibly for both of you. Two out of three. Which leaves the weapon. What about that gun? Did Jared really bring one? Or was it the gun that should have been in your dad's safe but wasn't?"

Grey's pulse jumped. "I don't know where that other gun went. I told the sheriff then. All I know is, it wasn't the gun that killed Jared. Maybe my dad had sold it. If he had, he wouldn't have mentioned it to me. Gun collecting is a hobby of his. The guns come and go. And nobody knows who really pulled that trigger." Which, after all these years, was still a problem for Grey, one he meant to find the answer to. "Jared brought that gun with him," Grey insisted. His mouth hardened. "We were boys, Finn—hotheaded, the four of us—including Derek Moran. He and his friend Calvin Stern were there, too. Why don't you talk to them again?"

Finn ran a hand through his hair. "On what basis? The case is still closed, Grey. Sure would have helped," Finn said, looking almost sympathetic, "if the weapon had ever been found...but without the gun itself we can't make a match to the bullet that killed Jared. Somebody knows where that gun— whichever one it was—disappeared to."

Was Finn accusing him of knowing where it was? Of having used it on Jared that night? The missing weapon was a critical piece of the puzzle. If Finn wouldn't cooperate, or couldn't, Grey would have a talk with Calvin Stern.

JENNA PERCHED ON the end of the sofa in her family room, wanting to talk, while David continued to read the newspaper. He'd come home last night from his extended business trip, but he'd had little to say about his meetings or even Salt Lake City, where his firm had a branch office. There'd been a time, several years ago, when he'd tested the waters with her about a move to Utah, but Jenna had argued then that they had to think about Ava.

Now Shadow was living in Barren and wanted Ava back. "Are you too tired for me to ask you something, honey?"

For a full minute he kept on reading the business section of the *Wall Street Journal*. The only words they'd exchanged since he'd gotten back had been about his suggestion to move some stocks in their portfolio to better balance the trusts they'd set up. They did this every few months, so Jenna hadn't thought much of it. "Dave? Did you hear what I said?"

"I heard you." He turned a page, rattling the paper as he refolded it in the precise way he always did.

Jenna was getting a bad feeling. She decided to just plunge in. "Shadow still wants to take Ava from us."

"Yes," he said, "I know." He didn't even look up.

He was reading the editorial pages now.

She took a breath. "I've said I want Ava to stay. *She* wants to stay."

He glanced at her. "Your sister has done the best she could since Ava was born. Maybe she should have gone through with that private adoption, but she chose to keep Ava and that was her right." His eyes were cool. "I also know that wasn't easy for her. She and Ava had a hard time, and when Shadow came to us for help we stepped up to the plate. Temporarily, Jenna. If Shadow is ready to take her home now, to the new house, then it's best—and time—for that to happen."

"I still want to adopt her."

He blinked. "Shadow will never sign away her parental rights. I know *you* want to be a mother, Jenna, and I wish you could be, but we tried. And failed, more times than I care to remember. I'm done."

Jenna sat there, stunned. She could tell by the set of David's features that he'd already thought this through, anticipated what she might suggest and removed himself from the equation.

"I'm sorry, more sorry than I can say." Tossing the paper aside, he rose from his favorite chair. "I didn't want to have this discussion tonight, either, but I suppose we must."

Her heart had begun to bang against her ribs. "What discussion?"

He stood over her. "You can call this my

midlife crisis, an indulgent fantasy or whatever…" His gaze softened as he seemed to consider what to say next. "But since our last attempt at in-vitro fertilization, frankly, I've realized that this preoccupation with having a child by any means possible, including your notion to adopt Ava, has damaged our marriage—at least, for me. Every morning I just want to get out of this house and not come back."

He hadn't unpacked last night, she realized. David was always meticulous about that, and the lapse had troubled her, but she'd assumed he was merely exhausted.

"Salt Lake is a more dynamic place, and I'm ready for a change."

Jenna reeled back, numb with shock. He hadn't changed from his suit to more casual slacks and a polo shirt, his usual choice when he came home. She wondered if his bags were all standing in the hall upstairs, ready to be taken to the car. "You mean you're leaving? Is this really about my wanting to have a child, about Ava? Or because you got passed over for the partnership?"

He didn't disagree, but she had obviously stunned him. "I'll have a second chance to prove myself in Utah. I've been distracted by the situation here," he said. "But no, that's not why I want a divorce. I'm disappointed, yes, but that's not the reason."

"Divorce?" she echoed. "Is there someone else? In Salt Lake?"

"No one." He shook his head as if she were slow to understand. "We had some good years, Jenna. Maybe I've done this clumsily, and I apologize for that, too, but please don't make this harder than it has to be." He walked past her and left the room. "You should think about how to make yourself happy—not through Ava or me. If I were you, I'd drive her home to Shadow tonight." He paused. "Then maybe Ava would be happier, too."

CHAPTER NINE

SHADOW RANG JENNA'S front doorbell again. No one had answered the first time and she wondered if she'd misunderstood her sister on the phone. Their conversation had been brief, but that wasn't unusual, and even though Jenna's voice had sounded oddly thin to Shadow, she had said she'd be home all day. Shadow could come over anytime. Maybe Jenna was in the backyard, sunning by the new pool she and David had put in last summer.

Jenna had claimed the gorgeous pool was for Ava, another point in what seemed to be an ongoing war for the girl's loyalty. Shadow had neither the money nor the space in her small rear yard for such an amenity, and she didn't like the idea of competing for Ava's affection with material things. She buzzed once more, in case Jenna had gone upstairs and didn't hear the first two rings.

Still no response.

She had to begin to to mend her rift with Ava. And she hoped to get her sister's help with that. Certainly Jenna would come to see what was best for Ava. After that, Grey could finally meet her.

Frowning, she walked around to the backyard but saw no one there, either. Then, as she came to the front again, intending to send Jenna a text, the door opened. "Shadow." The same reedy tone she'd heard earlier that morning brought Shadow up short. When she peered inside, the hallway looked so dark she could barely make out her sister's form.

It was easier to see that her face appeared to be dead white, a striking contrast to the room's dim light, and her usually well-styled hair straggled around her face. "Jen. Are you sick?"

She shrugged one shoulder. "Heartsick." She waved a hand. "Come in. I have something to tell you."

Shadow's pulse tripped in maternal alarm. "Ava's all right, isn't she?"

"Of course. After she left for school, I went back to bed and tried to sleep…"

Shadow touched the back of her hand to her sister's forehead. No fever. She hadn't heard a cough or sneeze. *Heartsick*, she'd said. What could be wrong? "Why didn't you call me if you don't feel well? Or say something when I phoned this morning? I would have come sooner."

Jenna turned back into the slate-tiled entry and, to Shadow's surprise, she was barefoot—she hadn't seen Jenna without shoes since they were girls. She walked into the vaulted family room that looked out onto the pool. By this time of day, Jenna would normally be dressed, usually in a perfectly matched outfit, and wearing makeup even if she didn't intend to leave the house. The wide glass patio doors had been fully opened, leaving seamless access between house and outdoors.

Ava must love this. Really, her child had spent the past three years surrounded by luxury, not to mention Jenna's constant, loving attention. Shadow couldn't argue with that, and at times she felt even guiltier for wanting to take Ava from what must seem to her a perfect place. Shadow couldn't disagree; she'd enjoyed the time she'd spent here, too. But it wasn't her house and Ava belonged with Shadow. She heard the pump come on and water gently lapped against the pool's concrete apron, occasionally splashing onto the expensive patio. An Italian craftsman had laid the custom tiles. The water's crystal-clear surface sparkled in the sun.

When Jenna collapsed onto the nearest chair, Shadow noticed she was still wearing her cashmere robe. Now she was weeping into her hand.

"David left me."

For a moment Shadow was speechless. She and Jenna had grown up with parents who rarely agreed on anything except forcing Shadow's decision to leave home at seventeen.

"You and David? I've never seen you say a mean word to each other." As if this couldn't be true. Maybe she'd been right and he had put his foot down about Jenna's wish to adopt Ava. Shadow wouldn't raise that issue.

Eyes closed, Jenna dropped her head against the seat back. Tears trickled down her cheeks. "In the past year or so we've fought a lot. Then last night—" She took a shaky breath, the words tumbling out. "He's moving to Salt Lake to his company branch office."

"A girlfriend there?"

"I don't think so. That's not David," Jenna

murmured with a rueful smile. "He's all about becoming partner, but he didn't make it recently, and I'm guessing when they offered it to someone else, he fell apart. Now he hopes to prove himself in Utah, and apparently I'm in his way." She added, "Ava, too, he said, or words to that effect."

Shadow had guessed David would be against an adoption. Yet to make such an announcement then leave Jenna to sweep up the pieces? No wonder she looked like the shocked victim of some accident.

She was half sobbing. "My hopes to become a mother, and all those in-vitro attempts, were the breaking point for him, he said. Or maybe that was just his excuse. But he's not coming back, Shadow." On the last words, Jenna's voice broke again. "I spent all last night going over our finances, and, of course, I had to marry a lawyer. Who knows what kind of settlement he'll try for?"

"You misjudged him, that's all. You trusted him."

"Guilty," she said, removing her hand from her forehead to give Shadow a grim smile. "I'm just waiting to be sentenced."

Her attempt at dark humor made tears well in Shadow's eyes, too. Jenna's voice sounded thick. Of all their sisters, she and Jenna had always been closest to each other, and Shadow's heart hurt for her. "Stop beating yourself up. We'll figure this out." She sat beside Jenna in the oversize chair and gathered her into her arms. Her sister's last bit of strength seemed to dissolve and she clung to Shadow, openly sobbing now.

"Shh, it'll be okay."

"How—how did you manage back then? After Grey shot Jared? When you learned you were pregnant? Mama and Daddy didn't help you at all. You must have felt totally alone in the world. I know I do right now."

"I did, at first. But then I had Ava. We had each other," she said. And that was why she'd come to see Jenna, but Shadow wouldn't bring that up now, just as she'd been unable to tell Grey that they had a child that day at the diner after he'd lost his loan.

"It's the last day of school." Jenna glanced at the mantel clock then toward the front door. "She should be home by now, but she's probably at the bus stop talking with her friends." Jenna straightened. "I don't know how—or if—I can stay in this house. If I'll be able to afford the mortgage."

"I understand how you feel. We had so

little as kids, Jen. We never knew where our next meal was coming from or a new pair of shoes." Shadow glanced down at her latest purchase, a pair of rope-soled wedges she already loved. "You had a right to enjoy your freedom from worry. But let's not panic. David will work out a settlement with you, your assets will get divided and you'll be fine." *Eventually*, she thought, but there was no need to remind Jenna that she was in for some even rougher times before her life settled down again.

Jenna had bigger problems than Shadow— uncertainty about her future among them— and worse, her heart was broken. Her spirit, too, at the moment. "I'm worried about you, though. You shouldn't be alone here. Why don't I go upstairs to pack a few things for you and Ava? You can stay with me as long as you want."

"You have two bedrooms. Where would we all sleep?"

Shadow had thought the same thing about her mother's situation, offering the spare room for a few nights. She squeezed her sister's hand. Right now, Jenna was even more desperate. "You must have forgotten how we all used to bunk together as girls. Ava can have the room I've done for her. You and I can share my king." She tried a small joke, hoping to cheer her. "That is, if you don't steal all the covers."

"No, Shadow. I want to be in my own house—for now."

She passed a hand over Jenna's uncombed hair to smooth it, to let her know she was there for her. Jenna clasped her hand and squeezed, then Shadow planted a kiss on her cheek. They didn't need more words. When she rose, she heard the click of the front door opening before it closed again.

Ava bounded into the room. When she saw Shadow, she stopped.

"What are you doing here? It's not Friday."

"I came to see Aunt Jenna—and you." Shadow went toward her for a hug, but Ava tossed her backpack into the hall closet then spun around to Shadow, her blue-green eyes angry.

"Ava, I heard what you said last time, at the ice cream store. I haven't been around enough. I'm sorry. That's why I came— to spend more time with you.And we can talk. Maybe you could put on a swimsuit and show me what you've learned in the pool. I'll borrow one from Jenna."

"It's not your pool."

"You can tell me all about school," Shadow continued, as if she hadn't heard the slight.

"Shadow doesn't know about your end-of-year field day," Jenna said. When Ava had come in, school papers trailing from her backpack and fluttering to the entry-hall floor, Jenna had quickly dried her eyes, running a hand through her unkempt hair.

"She doesn't want to know." Ava studied Jenna then frowned. "Why are you still in your robe?"

"I'm not feeling well today," Jenna said.

"You're sick?"

"Just a bit under the weather." She managed a smile. "Don't worry."

Shadow said nothing. She had to face the truth: her sister had a better relationship with Ava than she did. Shadow's fault, mostly because of the agency this past year. Her throat tightened. "Ava…"

The girl turned and stomped up the stairs.

Jenna murmured, "Oh, Shadow."

"Yes. I know." For another moment she stayed in the hallway, afraid Jenna would see her unshed tears and start to cry all over again. She had stepped back into the family room when the sun suddenly struck light off the swimming pool right into her eyes. Shadow blinked at the starburst.

With Jenna in this condition, exhausted from crying and wrapped up in her problems with David, how could Shadow leave Ava here? Ava had only started to take swimming lessons a few months ago. What if she slipped on the patio, fell into the water and Jenna wasn't around to see or to help? Jenna wasn't herself at the moment, and who knew how long she'd be in this state? Shadow didn't want her sister to be burdened with having to care for Ava. Jenna needed time for herself.

This wasn't the beginning Shadow had hoped for to repair her relationship with Ava, but she didn't see another option. She marched into the hall and followed Ava up the stairs.

Now she knew for sure that Jenna hadn't lied.

Ava really didn't want anything to do with her.

AVA HEARD THE knock on her bedroom door. Her throat tightened.

"Come in," she finally called, already dreading what her mother might have to say.

She walked in and took a look around. Her mom had only seen her room once since Ava and Aunt Jenna had redecorated a few weeks ago, painting the walls a soft blue and taping up boy-band posters and one of Tim McGraw in a cowboy hat that announced his new country tour. Sometimes she pretended he was her father. There were a few framed awards from school. Everything else was green and white and that same shade of blue. Aunt Jenna had let her pick all the colors.

Ava sat on her white spindle bed studying some papers in her lap. One of them was her report card.

"I'm in fourth grade," she announced. "I forgot to show Aunt Jenna."

Her mom tried a smile. "I can't believe how fast this has happened. I still think of you in kindergarten. Or even as a baby."

"Well I'm not. I'm almost ten," Ava said.

When her mother eased down onto the bed beside her, Ava shifted away. "I understand how you feel, sweetie, but sometimes things happen that even adults can't cope with very well. Your aunt Jenna feels that way today. She's going to be okay, but at times we have to make decisions that might be hard to understand."

"You think I'm a baby but I'm not. I heard her crying. I saw Uncle David put his bags in the car then drive away. Are they getting a divorce?"

"I think so, yes." Her mother cleared her throat. She gestured toward the closet. "Why don't you pick out a few things you really like to wear? I'll help you pack and we can buy new summer things tomorrow."

Ava glanced up. "Why?"

"I'm taking you home with me," she said, as if that was obvious. "I wasn't going to do this today, not so soon, but I think it's best."

Ava disagreed. "I already said I don't want to go with you."

Her mother craned her neck to look at the pool outside. The sun bounced off it and sent bright, wavering reflections onto Ava's ceiling.

"You have to come with me, Ava. You can't stay here." She made her voice tempting. "We can make pizza tonight."

Ava loved pizza, but all she could think of was when she'd had to pack up before, when she was six, to move here from Kansas City. And of leaving her best friend. "Do you have pets at your house?"

"No, but it's *our* house. Do you think we should we get one?"

"A dog," Ava said, picking at a spot on her knee. "Everybody should have a dog but Uncle David says he's allergic. I'd name my dog Shrek." She thought for a moment. "Or maybe Anna, if it was a girl. Like in *Frozen*." She didn't need to explain. She'd watched that movie with her mom and Aunt Jenna a dozen times. "Would you really buy a dog?"

She was testing her mother.

"I might. I hadn't thought about getting a pet. With Mother Comfort I rarely get home before seven o'clock, which wouldn't be fair to an animal unless we adopted an older one that didn't need much activity, a dog or cat that might be content to lie around, keep us company and be there for you. We can talk about that."

She stood to open the closet door. Her mom's agency had a weird name that somehow made Ava feel left out. "Bring pajamas and things to wear to camp," her mother said. "I can sign you up for something at the community center."

Ava didn't like that idea, but she got off the bed and padded barefoot over to the closet.

Frowning, she caught her mother staring at her feet. Ava's toenails were half painted, some a shiny bright green, others with the enamel flaked off and almost gone. For her and her friends, it was a fashion statement.

Her mother didn't seem to agree.

HOPING TO FIND answers about Jared Moran's death, or at least some clue, Grey parked his truck in front of the hardware store. He couldn't rely on Finn. After their talk yesterday, Grey doubted he'd ever question Shadow's brother again, or his friend.

But for ten years Grey had felt isolated by blame, from others and within himself. It had only gotten worse since Shadow came home and he'd learned he had a child. He couldn't remain in this limbo if he was to build a relationship with his daughter, Jared's niece. Grey hoped to meet her soon—as an innocent man. How could he enter her life if he was really guilty of murder?

Grey passed the window displays filled with garden tools and sacks of fertilizer and grub-control products and opened the door to the upstairs apartments. One was rented to Derek's friend Calvin Stern.

Grey knocked on his door. Calvin answered, blinking against the rush of light from the stairwell, though it was far less bright in here than outdoors at noon. Seeing Grey on the step, he recoiled.

"What do you want?"

"I have a few questions. I hope you might be able to shed some light." Clearly, he remembered Grey, who didn't explain the purpose of his visit before Calvin shrugged one shoulder, inviting him in. Either he had nothing to hide or he was too wasted to care.

Calvin looked as if he'd had a long, hard night. Which didn't surprise Grey. He and Derek Moran had twin reputations for partying, if not much else. Grey suppressed a twinge of sadness. Derek might give him the business now and then, as he had over the parking incident, but he was still Shadow's little brother. Grey tried to keep that in mind. He and Shadow already had enough tug and pull between them. But Derek made Grey even more grateful for his only sister. Olivia could frustrate him at times, but Grey loved her with all his heart.

Still, at least Calvin was trying to make something of his life. After Jared's death, he'd enlisted in the army. He'd come back to Barren only months ago, when he'd been discharged, and Grey had heard he was now working part-time at the hardware store downstairs.

Once Grey was inside the apartment, Calvin thrust out his unshaven jaw. "I didn't have anything to do with that fight at Rowdy's bar last night, Wilson. You're not Finn Donovan's deputy now, are you?"

"No." He didn't care how he and Derek spent their nights—except for that one night when Jared had died. "I'm here on my own."

Grey took in the small living area, which contained a couch and matching chair, the upholstery worn but unstained, a scarred wooden coffee table littered with bottles and a pizza box, and a shabby rug in faded primary colors on the floor. He reminded himself that Calvin, like Derek, was still in his midtwenties, not that long out of high school. Long enough, though. "Let's clear up a few things," he said. "About Jared Moran."

Calvin had lost his deer-in-the-headlights expression, presumably since Grey had put him at ease about had happened at Rowdy's. He met Grey's gaze head-on. "Have a seat."

Grey remained standing. "I need to refresh my mind, maybe get another take on that night. Cal, you were there when he got shot."

Calvin's eyes flashed, yet they didn't meet Grey's gaze. "When *you* shot him!"

"Nobody has proved that."

"The sheriff said the gun was like the one your father owned."

"If so, where is it? My dad said his pistol had already been missing from the gun safe in his office for months. Jared *brought* a gun with him. The only other people there that night were you and Derek. One of you must know what happened." *And who really pulled the trigger.*

Calvin tensed. "I gave my statement. So did Derek."

Grey could guess how Derek had related the incident to make himself look blameless. "I won't ever forget the scuffle over that gun. When Jared came at me, Derek tried to stop him—but, if my memory's right, you stepped back. You must have had a better view of what went on."

"You bet I got out of the way. Scared," Calvin said. "I was shaking in my boots. Three guys fighting over a loaded weapon?"

"You must have seen everything from that different angle."

"I saw the three of you wrestling for control of the gun. Then it just went off—*bang*—and Jared fell. It all happened fast. In a second or two, just like I told the sheriff at the time."

"Then afterward, what? The gun disappeared. Someone knows where it went that night. And why it's never been found."

Calvin shifted his stance, stuffing his hands in the pockets of his low-slung jeans. "I couldn't say. Never liked guns, even when my daddy took me out hunting. I always ended up behind the biggest tree trunk I could find. I've been a disappointment to him all my life." He shrugged again. "I hate the sound of gunfire—yeah, even though I was in the army. Worked a desk. So don't look at me. I never touched that gun."

It seemed pointless to go on with that line of questioning. Grey had gotten nowhere, and for a moment he regretted even coming to the apartment. Then another topic crossed his mind, more recent but as much of a mystery to him. "While I'm here, I've been missing some Angus cattle. More than two dozen head. The truck and stock trailer the rustlers are using to haul them in is a white Ford

F-150. Extended cab. Kansas plates," he said. "I'm not accusing you—"

Calvin's face, always an indoor kind of pale, had turned ashen. The dark cowlick on the crown of his head stood up.

"White, you say? Must be dozens of them in Stewart County alone." Echoing Grey's own thought, Calvin glanced toward the street. "Can't help you. My car's a used Kia sedan. It's parked in front of the café right now." He grinned, but the too-quick expression fell flat. "Least, I think it is. I don't remember driving home last night, to tell the truth."

Grey hadn't asked Calvin about his car. He'd answered too fast.

"That's what I'm looking for. Truth." Grey added, "Know anyone who does drive a white truck? Someone who could handle a bunch of frightened cattle?" He looked directly at Calvin. "Maybe you saw something at Rowdy's."

Calvin laughed. "Good thing you're not a lawman. Your technique needs work." Before Grey could react, Calvin grasped his shoulder and pushed him toward the door. "I've told you what I know. Now go. Don't come back."

Grey went. He wasn't about to get into a fight with Calvin Stern. Most likely, he had been involved at Rowdy's last night, but that was his business—and Finn's. Grey still thought Calvin knew more than he'd let on about Jared and the gun.

He'd had that lingering unease in his eyes, as if Grey had come too close to the truth he needed. And not the truth about the white truck. Or a bar fight.

CHAPTER TEN

BY THE TIME she got home, Shadow felt limp. Ava had continued to balk at leaving Jenna's house in Shawnee Mission, and after they got underway, she'd begun to cry, which broke Shadow's heart. She was tearing Ava from the home she'd known for the past few years, even as Shadow felt sure this was the right thing to do. Several times she'd checked the rearview mirror, trying to show Ava she understood her tears, but that had only made her cry harder. Shadow had a lot to make up for.

Because they'd left at rush hour, the drive had taken extra time. As she drove into Barren, Shadow breathed a sigh of relief. Home, she thought, amazed. In the year she'd been back, living here only during the week, she'd never called this town home. But she was making that life for herself—for Ava—and with the new house, they would have roots.

Shadow's mother met them at the door.

After their packing session at the farm yesterday, Shadow had invited her for dinner tonight, but she had forgotten to call her from Jenna's house to say that wasn't a good plan, after all.

"What's happened?" Wanda asked, her gaze darting to Ava.

"Later, Mama." Shadow went down the hall to the second bedroom. Ava followed, carrying her backpack stuffed with the wadded-up clothes she'd thrown in with angry reluctance.

"This will be your room, sweetie," Shadow told her. "Can you get your other bag from the car?"

"I guess." With a look at them that seemed to wonder what she wasn't supposed to hear, she left the room.

Her mother leaned in, lowering her voice. "Except for her eyes, that child is the spitting image of you at her age," she said. "Now you've brought her here. To Barren."

"I couldn't leave her with Jenna. This is just sooner than I planned to bring her home." Quickly Shadow told her about David. "You can imagine how distraught Jenna is. I hated to leave her, but she wouldn't budge. That house is still a comfort to her. She needs the privacy and time to figure out her next move."

"You don't think she'd try to harm herself?"

"No," Shadow said. "But she'll need to do some hard thinking. The future doesn't look very bright to her right now."

"She doesn't even have a job to fall back on," her mother pointed out.

"I know." At twenty Jenna had married David without completing college, but at least, unlike Shadow back then, she'd finished high school. "At times I've wished she'd never gotten that admin job at his firm. She was so young—"

"I think your daddy and I met David twice—once at their wedding—and he didn't want us there. I still don't like him."

"Mama, we all have fences to repair."

"I'm not sure I'm up to that—with certain people." Then she brightened. "I forgot to tell you. Derek's taking good care of my hens tonight," she said with pride.

"If he remembers to feed them," Shadow couldn't help saying.

"I've asked him to pay special attention to Little Addie and Beulah. They haven't been eating. They'll likely miss me. They may be feeling poorly."

Shadow sighed. Her mother sounded more worried about her flock than her troubled daughter. "We need to make dinner. I promised Ava homemade pizza."

As Ava came back into the room, lugging her second suitcase, Shadow's mother slipped out into the hall. "Too much change," she said as she started toward the kitchen. "I hope you have bacon for that pizza."

Ava dropped her suitcase on the floor. "Is that Grandma? Does she live with you?"

"No," Shadow said. "She's visiting. You two will have a chance to get to know each other better."

Ava continued to survey the room. The first thing Shadow had done after she moved into the house was to decorate this space for her.

The walls were light—blush pink, the paint chip had read—and the familiar white and black accents were everywhere. Stick-on decals of familiar, whimsical Hello Kitty characters adorned the walls and the quilt pattern on the bed. Even a throw pillow on a chair and the pencil cup on the student desk in the corner displayed the popular logo. Shadow had meant this as a surprise, but now she realized she'd made a mistake.

Her spirits plummeted. Remembering the posters of Tim McGraw and boy bands in Ava's room at Jenna's house, she knew she'd misjudged this situation. Somehow, Shadow had missed Ava's change of taste, of interests. How many other, much more significant, changes had she failed to see?

"Why is there Hello Kitty everywhere?" Ava said. "I'm tired of that."

Shadow's throat closed. "We can repaint. Choose a theme you do want."

But Ava shook her head. "I'm not staying that long."

A strange silence had settled over the house that had so briefly been Shadow's lone refuge. Bringing Ava here was what she'd yearned for, planned for, but this wasn't how she'd envisioned it.

Ava was searching for something in her backpack, and Shadow's heart melted when she pulled out the stuffed pony that had been a baby gift. She'd slept with it every night. Did she still? Shadow had wondered about that, but something squeezed painfully in her chest when she realized she hadn't known.

"You still like horses?" Shadow asked gently.

Ava nodded. "Aunt Jenna said maybe I could take lessons to see how I liked riding and then we could talk about leasing a horse...but I don't think that will happen now." The brown pony had a slight tear in the fabric near its black tail and the stuffing showed through. "I'll keep Stormy always. I would never let him go."

She held the pony tighter, her hair sliding over her cheeks to hide her expression. "A mother should never leave her child," she said. "Even for a little while."

Shadow weakened, as if all the stuffing had come out of her instead of Stormy. There would be no good-night kisses to Ava's nose and cheeks tonight. Her daughter wouldn't let Shadow hold her close. What had she done to this child whose well-being had been her main priority since Ava was born? Had she made the right choices? Or done damage to her child's spirit that could never be repaired?

Shadow had always tried to take responsibility for her actions. The only person she'd ever blamed for anything was Grey and she wasn't as sure about his responsibility in Jared's death anymore, either.

AFTER LEAVING CALVIN Stern's place, Grey had stopped across the street at Mother Comfort, where a makeshift sign informed him that Shadow was gone for the day.

Grey had gone back to his truck. He'd considered calling her, then thought better of it. Instead, he'd gone home to do afternoon chores before he headed to Shadow's in the early evening. He was certain he'd found a weak spot in his old case. He wanted to share that with her, maybe convince her she'd been wrong about him years ago and there was still something more to be learned. He also wanted to see her again. Maybe he could urge Finn to talk to Calvin now, ask better questions, and Grey would get somewhere in his search for answers about Jared.

When no one answered Shadow's door, he hit the bell again. While he waited, he studied the neighborhood. He hadn't been to her house before, but he liked the rows of neat yet simple homes, the well-kept lawns and flower beds. Except for Shadow's property. She hadn't planted any marigolds or geraniums in spring and no summer perennials had popped through the now-warm earth. The grass needed mowing.

He wished, because of her difficult childhood, that she could have grown up here instead, that he'd always been welcome.

Finally, the door was flung open. To his surprise, Wanda Moran stood there, but she wasn't glowering, as he might have expected when she saw him. Instead, she looked shocked. Still, he imagined she'd checked him out through the security peephole. Squaring her shoulders, she blocked the entrance, and Grey tried not to be too obvious about glancing past her. He hoped to see Shadow there, but Wanda appeared to be alone.

Grey removed his hat. "Mrs. Moran. Long time."

Her gaze seemed to say, *not long enough*. She took him in, from his everyday straw cowboy hat to the tips of his scuffed Tony Llama boots. He should have worn his go-to-town pair, polished to a high sheen, and his black Stetson. Not that better clothes would have made her like him.

Grey felt like the teenage kid he'd once been, coming to call on his girlfriend.

"Is Shadow home?"

"She may be." Wanda fidgeted with a dish towel in her hands. She didn't invite him in.

Grey removed his hat. "I have something she needs to hear."

I doubt that. She didn't say so; she didn't have to. Her opinion of him was written across her face, and she hadn't moved half an inch from her spot in the doorway. Grey stared right back.

Ten years faded away, and he could almost hear the wail of sirens on that dark night, see the whirling strobe of red ambulance lights in front of his house and the prone body of Jared Moran, blood seeping from underneath him. So still that Grey, his ears ringing from the gunshot, had known Jared was dead before he hit the ground.

"You can leave a message," Wanda said. "I'll try to see that she gets it."

No, she wouldn't. Like him, she hadn't forgotten—how could they?—and, like Shadow so far, she wasn't ready to forgive. He'd have to drive into town again tomorrow and hope to find Shadow in her office.

Grey had turned to go back down the few short steps to the sidewalk when he heard other voices behind Wanda. Somewhere from the center of the small house, he made out Shadow's tone. So she was home.

"Mama?" she called. "Who's here?"

Wanda didn't answer. She made a jerky move to close the door, but before she could manage it, an unseen hand stopped the motion. Shadow peered over her mother's shoulder and turned pale.

"I need to talk to you," he said, twisting his hat in his hands. "This won't take long. Would you come outside? I know I should have called first, but I only want to—"

She stepped in front of Wanda, but her mother stayed put in the doorway. He'd been afraid of this. From her mother, she must still hear diatribes against Grey, and he couldn't blame Wanda Moran for how she felt. If he'd had any doubts about that, Wanda had just dispelled them. "Five minutes, that's all I need."

"Is this about the wedding party trip to Kansas City?"

"Nope," he admitted, which only made Shadow's features tighten. Her face had no color and her lips were pressed tightly together as she suddenly spun around at the sound of footsteps behind her.

Wanda placed a hand over her heart. "I told you, Shadow. This would happen."

"Oh, Grey," she said.

Half hidden by Shadow's body, a little girl gazed up at him. Her eyes were wary, and she had Shadow's dark hair. The stubborn tilt of her chin could have come from his father…and so could the color of her eyes, the exact blue-green of Grey's. Actually, the chin was his, too. Every ounce of blood, and all of his strength, seemed to leak from him in that moment as if he were Jared Moran, gut shot and going down for the last time.

"Shadow," he managed. The reality of this—his child—raced through his mind. He'd wanted to meet her, but hadn't been prepared for the shock of actually seeing her in person. It was even more stunning than when Shadow had told him about her.

Shadow reached out a hand, but their little girl darted forward, coming to stand right in front of him. She wore a Shawnee Mission Elementary School T-shirt and denim shorts, her feet bare. She had his mother's toes.

Shadow cleared her throat. Wanda had disappeared. *I told you, Shadow.* She didn't resent Grey, even hate him, solely because of Jared. Wanda resented him for this child, the permanent connection between Grey and Shadow.

Shadow laid a hand on the girl's shoulder. "Grey, this is…obviously—"

"Ava." He didn't even need to think about it. "I should have known." That name had been their first choice. He'd even remembered that day at the diner. "We always talked about that, certain that someday we'd… I've never forgotten."

Ava gave him a curious look. "You know my mom?"

Grey could hardly speak. His breath seemed to be locked in his lungs. His eyes met Shadow's above their daughter's head, and held.

"I thought I did," he said.

SHADOW WATCHED GREY'S truck pull away from the curb. He hadn't said another word before spinning and clattering down the steps. She'd expected him to burn rubber, but he didn't. He used his blinker before pulling out, eased onto the street and then rolled slowly toward the corner. Way under the speed limit. Oh, yes, she should have known. He was angry. No, far worse, he was hurt. And she hadn't been able to say a word.

He'd said over and over that he wanted to meet Ava. But Shadow had stalled, wanting to prepare her first. She'd never expected him to just show up at her door. And on the very day she'd finally brought Ava home.

"Who was that man?" Ava asked, standing beside her.

Heart aching, Shadow turned. *Not now*, she thought. *Not yet and not this way.* Her voice shook. "Someone I used to know," she murmured. "Go help your grandmother, sweetie. You can tell her what you like on your pizza."

But her mother appeared from the kitchen, her eyes on Shadow, then Ava. For the first time since Ava had walked into the house, her mother addressed her directly, with a soft look that Shadow hadn't seen in a long time. "Go, darling," she said. "I'll be right there to help."

The subtle order galvanized Ava, who didn't seem to know what to think of her grandmother, never mind Grey. Without a backward look, she went off to the kitchen, and Shadow thought, *Can this family get any more broken*? The answer was yes, which seemed to be her fault again. She'd hoped to work up to this, yet she should have guessed something like this might happen. Grey could be impatient, and he hadn't liked being put off before. Why had he decided to come tonight?

Now, he had finally met his daughter. Shadow wanted to crawl into a hole and stay there, licking her fresh guilt like a mortal wound. She kept seeing his expression, that stunned and angry and injured look, even worse than when he'd first learned about Ava. She remembered Ava's questions about her father over the years, and Shadow's own wish that she could simply go to him, let him know. And yet each time she'd thought of their painful breakup, and of Jared. And that had stopped her.

"You were right, Mama," she said around the lump in her throat. "I should have told him sooner. I almost did."

"Well, he knows now."

"Yes," she agreed. "I should have let him see her. I just couldn't figure out how to tell Ava first." All along he'd had a right to know, even with Jared's death between them. And yet she'd kept Ava from him. How differently things might have worked out if she'd told him sooner. How many times had she yearned to tell him about the Merritts, about not going through with the adoption, about all of Ava's milestones?

If she and Grey hadn't broken up, still loved each other as they did once, they would have been married for nearly a decade by now. They would have raised Ava together, two parents instead of one. But living at Wilson Cattle, no matter what her mother had implied, was not an option for Shadow. The ranch was another obstacle because of what had happened to her brother there. No, even when part of her had longed for a relationship with Grey, it hadn't seemed possible. At least not then. But now…

Leaving her mother behind, she went down the hall to her room.

Shadow moved a pile of fresh laundry off the bed then sat down there and took her laptop from the nightstand. Still seeing Grey's face—that handsome face with its strong planes and angles, the firm mouth that knew how to kiss so well—and the way he'd left so abruptly, as if he couldn't trust his own reaction. She didn't look up but sensed her mother in the doorway. "Mama, I need to be alone. I have to go over a few things for work." Her business couldn't sustain her tonight, though.

But her mother didn't take the hint to leave. "I already called in an order for our pizza. Won't be homemade tonight. I've told Ava we'll make one another time." She took a seat on the other side of the bed. "I doubt you're that concerned about work, Shadow."

As if to prove her mother wrong, she pulled up Jack Hancock's old application on the screen. If she tried to talk about Grey right now, she wouldn't be able to control her emotions. "I've been trying to think of a job for someone. You remember Bertie?"

"Bertrand O'Neill? I thought he was in rehab."

"He's home again—doing better, actually, than he has in years—but his nephew needs to earn some money for them. Not all of Bertie's hospital bills will be covered, Jack said, and I'm sure more will turn up after his stay in rehab. He doesn't have the savings left to pay them." She scrolled through the list of Jack's work experience, mostly, as he'd said, as a chef or bartender. "I'd like to help them. I have a few contacts. I'll call—"

"If his nephew is taking care of Bertie, how would getting a job help? Where would Jack find the time? Bertie would be alone."

Her mother was right—Shadow and Jack

had talked about that, too. She knew she was merely masking her worries about Grey and Ava with a far less critical issue, but it was the only way she could cope at the moment. "Hmm. How would you like to make some money? A job might help you, too, Mama."

She frowned. "The only thing I know how to do is care for my children—and you've all but said I didn't do a good job of that." She paused. "These days, taking care means my hens. They're my girls, too."

Shadow wasn't sure she appreciated being lumped in with the chickens, but her mother was devoted to them. Was it possible she loved her children as much? *We did the best we could*. Her mom had said that more than once in different ways. And despite her tendency years ago to cater to Shadow's father, she'd been a pretty decent parent. Shadow remembered childhood illnesses, hers and the other kids', remembered her mother sitting up with them all night. Maybe it was time to acknowledge that, to set aside at least some of her resentment. "I think you'd do fine, Mama. Many of the people I place as temporary caregivers have less experience by far—take Blossom, for example. She turned up at my office, desperate for work, and did a great job for Sam Hunter.

"As long as the care consists of light housekeeping, making meals, being there for someone, I'd say you're more than qualified. You wouldn't need a nursing degree to be Bertie's assistant. What if I ask him and Jack about having you there while he's at work?"

She paused to let that sink in. Shadow didn't mention the still-looming eviction notice on her mother's farm. "Let me make a few calls about a job for Jack before the pizza gets here."

Going to bat for Jack and Bertie wasn't far removed from her normal order of business with the agency, and she welcomed what she had to admit was a distraction.

Not that she could really keep her mind on business. And off Grey.

CHAPTER ELEVEN

IN A RED HAZE, Grey drove home at dusk from Shadow's house without seeing the road or registering when he passed through the archway to Wilson Cattle. He parked his truck by the back door then went down to the barn, not even wondering if Cody had fed the horses tonight. Grey's head spun with thoughts of Shadow, of *Ava*. He hoped a ride might take the edge off his tangled feelings, the emotions he normally avoided. Tonight he couldn't tamp them down.

With the swift, smooth motions of a lifetime's practice, he tacked up Big Red, using the saddle he'd owned since he was a teenager—a gift from his father the year he and Shadow started going steady. Guiding the horse down the aisle and out into the fading sunlight, he swung into the saddle then nudged Red into a lope from the barnyard toward the nearby pasture gate. He still wondered if the expensive saddle had been a bribe of sorts. His dad had tried to discourage his two-year relationship with Shadow, citing their youth and hoping to refocus Grey's attention on the ranch well before Jared was killed.

Grey leaned over to open the gate. *Ava.* He couldn't believe that quick, hard punch to his heart at seeing her for the first time. It was one thing to hear about a child he'd never known he had, another to actually see her, the color of her hair and eyes, the sweet, if guarded, expression on her face. *Nine years*, he thought. *Way too long.*

He rode through the gate then closed it again. A narrow trail led from Wilson Cattle across the hill between the two ranches to the Circle H. It was the same ride he'd made many times; once, years ago, he'd done it with Logan in the dark and rain to save Grey's then-three-year-old nephew—Logan's son—who'd been sick and trapped at the Circle H during a flood. Right now, he just didn't want to be alone. He hoped Logan was home.

Grey left Red tied to a tree near the kitchen door. As he climbed the back steps, he noticed the sorrel gelding had ignored a clump of rich, green grass to sidle over to

Blossom's newly thriving herb garden and nibble a plant. He seemed to like basil.

"Grey, move that animal to a safer spot." Blossom had opened the door. She stood, hands on her hips. She had a faint smile on her lips to show she was teasing. "I've spent most of this spring and now early summer getting that garden going again. More important, Red will get a bellyache."

"Sorry, ma'am." With a tip of his hat and a rueful smile that threatened to crumble, he went back down the stairs to shift Red to a spot halfway across the yard. He hoped the sapling proved stout enough to hold his quarter horse or he'd be walking home tonight. If freed, Red would take off and aim straight for his stall and tonight's unfinished dinner, putting the perfect cap on Grey's day. Which was why he hadn't simply ground-tied him this time by dropping the reins, his more usual practice.

On the porch again, he asked, "Logan around?"

"He's in the family room. Watching a ball game with Sam." Blossom held the door wide. "Come on in. What can I get you?"

"Coffee, if there's any left."

"I keep a pot on all day. Logan just got

back. He and Sam were gone all afternoon to check some baby bison near your place. With their wandering ways several of them had drifted on to federal land with their mothers to graze, so they had a mini-roundup."

Grey kissed her cheek on his way by. "You're looking mighty…pregnant there, Mrs. Almost-Hunter." Maybe he could stick to such simple, even happy, subjects. They could discuss the upcoming wedding and he'd try not to think of Shadow. Even though she was part of it. And the weekend in Kansas City was coming up fast.

"Get your hands off my wife." With a lazy smile Logan sauntered into the kitchen, his gaze not on Grey but on Blossom. Grey quickly removed his hand from her shoulder. "Haven't seen you in a while. Any more word on those missing cattle?"

"Nope."

Grey told him about his talk with Calvin Stern, and that he'd taken the lead in his own investigation because Finn didn't seem that interested in Jared's old case. Grey finished, "My gut feeling is Calvin might know more than he let on, but I didn't get far with him."

Blossom peered into Grey's eyes. "Is that all? We always love to have you come visit, and you're more than welcome to stay for supper, but you don't look right to me."

He dropped onto a kitchen chair. Logan pulled out the one opposite and Blossom, as if to give them space, went back to the stove. Something simmered there that smelled like heaven, yet Grey had no appetite, which was a rarity for him that proved one thing: he was a basket case tonight.

"Blossom's white bean chili," Logan said with a nod at the stove. "Homemade biscuits and house-churned butter. Something about this baby that's coming has made her into a domestic goddess."

"Be careful, mister. Or there'll be no more of your favorite chicken curry in this house." At the stove, Blossom smiled over her shoulder to show she was teasing. "There's salad, too," she told Grey, "and enough strawberry-rhubarb pie from last night for everyone."

"Did I hear something about pie?" Sam called from the other room. He limped to the doorway, eyed Grey and said, "You look like ten miles of bad road."

"Sam, dinner will be ready soon," Blossom cut in. "I'll call you when we're ready. Maybe you could let us know what the score is then."

Sam took another look at Grey. "I know what the score is—but I can take a hint."

Blossom watched him until he went, grumbling, back to the family room, her eyes still full of concern. Grey suddenly wished he'd stayed home. The last thing he wanted was to intrude on her obvious happiness with Logan. Spoil things.

"Are you sure you wouldn't rather have something stronger than coffee?" she asked.

Logan's gaze had sharpened, too. "Might as well spill it, Wilson. She'll get it out of you sooner or later."

Grey set aside his coffee spoon, hoping his hand didn't shake. *I have a beautiful little girl I never knew about. I met her tonight for the first time. Go figure.* He hadn't expected to feel angry again, but he couldn't seem to snuff the feeling out. "No, I was just lonesome over there," he said with a gesture toward Wilson Cattle. "Had some news today, but I'll make sense of it on my own."

"Pride," Logan murmured.

Grey hadn't forgotten their talk the day after the first cattle went missing. But he had learned years ago to keep his emotions under wraps. He'd felt torn between his parents for most of his life, and often the only way to keep the peace had been to stay quiet and not get involved. Maybe he'd come over tonight just to see Blossom smile, to watch her and Logan tease each other in the kind of normal relationship he could only yearn for. As if…he couldn't imagine how he and Shadow would ever come to any agreement now.

He wanted to turn his back on her, but because of Ava he couldn't. He wanted to forget about Shadow's silky dark hair and liquid, deep brown eyes, how her warm smile always lit him up inside. He'd always thought she would make a great mother, a perfect wife. Tonight neither of them had been smiling.

Blossom stirred the chili then took a seat at the table. She leaned her chin on her hands and stared at him until Grey squirmed.

"Shadow," he said, studying the table-cloth. "Seems I never learn my lesson with her."

Blossom laid a hand over his. "I've heard about Jared Moran. I don't pretend to know all of what went wrong between you years ago, but time does heal, as they say."

He snorted at the platitude. "You think?"

"I'm not trying to make light of whatever is going on, Grey, but I have to assume something bad—as well as new—has cropped up."

Grey shrugged. "Old and new," he said under his breath. Then, before the thought crossed his mind, he heard himself say the words. "We have a child—a little girl. She's already nine years old."

"And you didn't know until now?" Blossom asked.

"Tonight."

"A daughter?" Logan shook his head in disbelief. "You and Shadow?"

Grey nodded. "I'd never seen her before. I stopped by Shadow's house—unannounced—and she was there. Ava," he added, saying her name out loud for the first time. His throat stung and he pushed back from the table.

"Hey, wasn't that the name you guys always talked about?" Logan asked.

"Yeah." He stood up. "Thanks, but I can't stay for dinner."

"Grey," Blossom said, half rising from her chair.

"Just wanted to catch you up about Calvin Stern."

Blossom and Logan gazed at each other

as if to say, *what just happened here*? "Grey, wait," Logan said. So did Blossom.

He ignored their pleas, as Red had earlier ignored the grass in the yard in favor of Blossom's basil.

Ava had floored him, the way she'd looked at him, assessed him—and likely wondered who he was.

He hadn't wondered about her. He'd known right away.

Ten years too late.

Doc, Shadow's sister Jenna and Wanda Moran had all known before he did.

But, hell. He was only Ava's father.

SHADOW SAT ON Grey's front steps. And waited.

She'd cried all the way here, trying to think of what to say. There were no easy words, and *I'm sorry* wouldn't cut it with Grey. And every time she glanced at the ground in front of the porch, the place where Jared had died, she was tempted to leave, to run away from that memory. She'd forced herself to come. She hadn't set foot on this ranch in ten years. Shadow eyed the long driveway that would take her to the crossroads then home. Thank goodness for one thing: Grey's father wasn't here.

He'd always been protective of Grey; protective of his daughter, Olivia, too. For that, she couldn't blame him. Everett Wilson expected big things of his children but he was also their fierce defender. After Jared was shot, Everett had done everything he could to clear Grey of suspicion. But he'd never approved of Grey's relationship with Shadow. Well, that didn't matter now, and she was prepared to take her licking. She didn't expect Grey to let her off the hook about seeing Ava for the first time under those circumstances, but she wanted to at least explain what had happened, that she hadn't intended to bring Ava back to Barren before he'd met her.

Heart thumping, she pressed her forehead to her knees, in part to block out the memory of her lost brother. At last, she heard the gate to the pasture shut with a grinding shriek of metal on metal, and the noise sent shivers down her spine. She didn't look up, even as the clip-clop of hooves came into the ranch yard. Shadow stayed where she was, half hoping it wasn't Grey but one of his men.

After a long moment, she heard Grey's

boot steps coming up the slight rise to the house. He must have seen her Mustang or glimpsed her sitting here at the base of the steps to the front porch, the site of the shooting neither of them would ever forget.

Grey stood in front of her until Shadow lifted her head.

"Well. Isn't this a surprise," he said. "Shadow Moran comes to Wilson Cattle. I know how much you like it here."

"I had to come. I want to explain, Grey."

His eyes were dark, his handsome mouth set in a hard line. Growing up, she'd always relied on him to remain cool and steady, unlike her father. If she and Grey had some argument back then, as they often did, by this point he would be ready to make up. They'd kiss and share whispered, heartfelt apologies and kiss some more.

Instead, he propped his hands on his hips, standing there like Finn Donovan over a suspect in some horrific crime. His voice stayed deadly quiet. Another bad omen, like the way he'd driven away from her house at a crawl. Of course he had. What else would she expect? But he seemed too tightly controlled.

"I thought I'd be prepared," he said. "I

mean, I already knew about her. Knew how old she is…but I *wasn't* prepared. Instead, there was your mother. And Ava."

"You were shocked," she said. "That was entirely my fault, Grey. I don't think you're ready to discuss this, but I thought I should come anyway. To tell you I care about having blindsided you like that. I wasn't planning on bringing her…home today. But then Jenna—"

"She's *my* child," he said. "Beautiful, like her mother, but hearing about her didn't begin to prepare me. What else is there to *understand*?"

"I know," she said, twisting her hands in her lap. "I should have told you long ago. I always meant to—"

"Yet you didn't."

"I know. I should have. But you went off to finish college and were running Wilson Cattle." She paused. "And there was always Jared to remember. It wasn't as if we could ever be together again, Grey. All those years we lived apart, leading separate lives—"

"Yes, and at Nick's party, I tried to change that, to talk to you."

But his nephew's seventh birthday party hadn't been the time or place for Shadow.

"How could we possibly talk then? With everyone around, and no privacy, the kids having fun, his mom even enjoying herself for once at the Circle H? I never thought I'd see that from Olivia."

"Shadow, you've been in Barren for a *year*. What changed your mind now?"

"I wanted—I was ready, at last—to bring Ava home. To our new house. I couldn't do that without telling you first."

"I take it you haven't told her—about me."

"I will," she promised. She explained about Jenna and David, and bringing Ava home sooner because her sister was upset. "Jenna needed time alone and with Ava there she'd only be exposed to Jenna's turmoil. Ava's not that pleased with me right now, but I had little choice. I couldn't leave her in such a tense situation."

His next questions seemed to be fired from a gun, so sharp and lightning fast Shadow imagined she could see the muzzle flash of a rifle. Another image of Jared crossed her mind. Grey wasn't calm now. "Did you think I wouldn't take responsibility? Even at twenty I would have done that, Shadow."

She looked away, then back again, forgetting that her eyes must be red and swollen from tears. "I wasn't sure then about the pregnancy. I only realized I was having a baby after Jared died. Before that, when you and I argued and I ran home, Jared heard me crying—" Her voice broke.

Thank God she hadn't been here then. She hadn't watched her brother die in this very spot. Shadow could barely stand to look at it. Briefly, she shut her eyes to block out the sight again. What if she *had* followed Jared then? What if she'd been able to stop him?

Grey's mouth tightened. "You didn't even warn me he was headed my way."

"I couldn't." Her father had been sitting in the recliner that night by the telephone. Shadow didn't have a cell then and she hadn't known about the gun, or where Jared could have gotten one. "I don't know what else to say. I can't begin to think how to fix this. I never meant for you to meet Ava like that. I meant to tell her about you first, then introduce you to each other..."

When she started to rise from the step, Grey reached out to help her up, an automatic politeness that made her want to cry all over again. From the instant he'd first seen Ava, she'd scarcely been able to stop the tears, and if he'd noticed the dried tracks on her cheeks, that didn't soften him now. "There's no way to fix it, is there?"

Grey stared at her for another long moment. She was tempted to tell him about the years she'd worked so hard to keep Ava with her, and her desperate decision to ask Jenna for help. But Shadow knew she couldn't redeem herself now. Bringing up the hardships of those years would only remind him of what he'd missed—what she'd stopped him from experiencing. Her voice quavered. "I'm sorry about tonight, Grey, and yes, I know it's too little, too late."

He had a right to feel shocked, angry, hurt. Now he must also feel betrayed again. "I've tried," she said, "to do the right thing—at least, for Ava." But the words didn't ring true. She had blocked him from their child's life, denied Ava the father she'd always longed for. "I should have done more—for both of you."

Head down, Shadow walked toward her car. She wouldn't—would not—think of Jared, of that terrible night or she would truly fall apart. With a shaking hand, she opened the door and turned back. Grey stood by the steps, a hard, unforgiving look in his eyes.

"About the wedding," she said, because how could they possibly be there together now? Grey probably wouldn't want to see her again. Ava, of course, was another matter; he hadn't touched on that subject yet. "I think it would be best if I don't take part."

He shook his head. "Don't even think about letting Logan and Blossom down. You've managed to hide my own kid from me for *ten years*. You can carry a bouquet down that aisle to the gazebo at the Circle H. You can live up to your obligations. Oh, and by the way, don't forget the wedding party weekend in KC. Be there." He took a few steps toward her. "And how's this for irony? My best friend will be marrying a woman who carries another man's child—and Logan can't wait to adopt Blossom's baby. You gave me no choice at all."

"Grey," she began, choking on his name.

"I'll be in touch," he said, then turned and went up the steps to the house.

The door banged behind him, shutting her out.

GREY STOOD WATCH on the hill that night.

It could indeed be a lonely business—boring, too—and he felt a bit guilty. Well before midnight Grey was already yawning. Maybe he shouldn't be so quick to judge Cody for falling asleep on the job.

Hours before, still churning inside after Shadow left, he'd decided to switch with Cody or one of his other men tonight, including his foreman, Dusty Malone, an ex-rodeo cowboy with slightly bowed legs in worn blue jeans. But all the while his mind was on Shadow. And Ava.

He could keep trying to hate Shadow for lying to him. He could sue her for full custody. Yet neither solution seemed right. He knew from Logan, who'd lost Nick temporarily, that nobody could really win that case. Even Grey's sister knew that now. Olivia and Logan had finally come to an agreement for the sake of their son.

Grey wasn't normally one to hold a grudge. He had a temper at times, usually for good reason, and he could be more than a little prideful, as Logan liked to point out. But this went beyond Grey wanting to prove himself innocent in Jared's death in part so Shadow could forgive him. It went even deeper than his love for this ranch.

Earlier, in the barn, he'd taken his mood out on Cody, who'd been running a hand along the stall bars as if he were strumming a guitar. "Cody, would you cut it out? Think you're Brad Paisley or something?"

The kid had shoved his hands back in his jeans pockets. "Sorry."

Grey would apologize tomorrow. Through his earbuds now came the soulful wail of the blues, which seemed a fitting complement to the soft, mournful lowing of cattle at the bottom of the hill. He tapped his fingers against the thighs of his jeans, keeping time to the tune. But the music wasn't distracting him from his thoughts as much as he'd hoped it would.

Despite all the nights he or one of his men had stayed out here until dawn, they hadn't caught the rustlers. At least the weather was warm, summer now, and Grey was doing something to try and preserve the ranch. He was more likely to do that than he was to find evidence about Jared's death that might clear—or convict—him. The stakes were higher than ever now. If he found proof that went against him, he wouldn't have to decide what to do about Ava, and Shadow would never forgive him. Grey wouldn't have to worry about Wilson Cattle then. He'd be in prison.

The thought depressed him.

He had to try harder, but how could he—

The sudden sound of an engine stopped him before he descended into self-pity, something Grey tried not to indulge even in his worst moments. A truck rolled into view, passing Grey's driveway and his silver truck. It edged up to the side of the road. The same white rig as before stopped, its trailer rattling as it shuddered to a halt.

This still didn't make sense. Why would these guys target him so many times?

After the first time, they'd left Logan's cattle alone, and Finn said there hadn't been any other thefts reported in the county.

It had to be personal.

On his feet, his rifle in hand, Grey crept down the hill. One man clipped the barbed wire fence and was in. Again. Grey kept going, circling past them in the dark, and cut across the land to his truck. Taking care not to make a sound, he propped the rifle on the floor against the passenger seat, shut the door, pushed the ignition button and eased out of the driveway.

He was almost on them before they saw him.

Grey heard shouts. "In the truck! Let's go!"

The three men scrambled. Doors slammed. The engine revved. The rig pulled out onto the road just in front of Grey and took off.

He stayed on the bumper of the stock trailer. Tempted to ram it, he couldn't take that chance. The rustlers hadn't loaded many cows, but there were at least three or four inside and they were his.

Seething, Grey called Finn and tailed them into town then onto a two-lane road that led toward Farrier. What to do? Force them off the road and maybe hurt, or kill, his cattle? Follow them to their destination? Three against one weren't odds he liked. And what if they had guns? Grey had a flash of memory: Jared Moran, lying in the dirt. No, he'd ease off the gas instead, let them go after he got their plate number.

Too bad his plan didn't quite work. In the dark, even in the glow from his headlights, he couldn't make out the whole license plate, though Grey did memorize a partial.

He swung onto the next side road then turned around.

And called Finn Donovan again.

CHAPTER TWELVE

SHADOW SHUT HERSELF in her office at Mother Comfort to make the calls she'd mentioned to her mother. The day after she'd gone to Grey's ranch, she was still heavy-lidded and hoarse from crying—not her usual way of dealing with a crisis. She was glad her mother had gone home after dinner; Shadow had spent the night on her living room sofa, head buried in her pillow so Ava wouldn't hear her, listening to the refrigerator motor click on and off in the stillness.

I'll be in touch, Grey had said. Shadow couldn't guess what his next move might be, but she suspected things were about to get even worse. Would Grey try to get full custody of Ava?

The door to her agency opened, the bell above it jingling and pulling Shadow from her ruminations. To her surprise, Jack Hancock walked in.

"I've been trying to reach you," she said,

schooling her features into a pleasant smile. "I called Bertie's place earlier but you weren't there. I think I have some good news."

"Me, too." Jack took the chair in front of her desk. "I was just over at the café. Did you know they're planning to offer a dinner service there? Breakfast and lunch don't bring in enough money. They're hoping for bigger checks later in the day. Six nights a week."

"I didn't know. That will be a nice option for people."

He grinned. "I got hired. For the time being, I'll be a sous chef, but if all goes well I could end up as executive chef—head chef, whatever they want to call it—in command of my own kitchen."

Shadow studied him. She couldn't get used to the change from weeks ago, when he'd gone to work as Sam Hunter's temporary caregiver and the ranch cook. Which hadn't ended well. "I know you weren't comfortable at the Circle H—"

"They weren't ready for haute cuisine," he murmured, although Shadow knew he'd actually quit after a fistfight with several of Logan's hired hands. She wondered what he'd done since then with his white chef's tunic and hat. Maybe he would wear them again in this new job.

With Jack's visit to the office, her spirits lifted a notch. Earlier, she'd found a caregiver for Ned Sutherland, who'd finally been released from rehab and gone back to his ranch. Maybe if she focused on Mother Comfort, and only that for now, she could get through this thing with Grey. Whatever happened. "I'm happy you got this job, Jack. And it's one you seem excited about."

His smile faded. "I'm still worried about Bertie, though. That's why I'm here. I mean, we need the money, but he can't be left on his own too long. You have a new applicant, maybe, since we talked before? It wouldn't be a live-in situation, 'cause Bertie and I don't have room for someone overnight. I won't be working full time yet, either..."

"All of my people currently have placements." Shadow straightened. Maybe she could help Bertie as she had Ned. "But, Jack, maybe I do have someone. My mother can't keep up her farm any longer, and I think another job would be good for her." Although she wasn't yet sure her mother would agree. At least Shadow had planted the seed. "As the mother of six children, she has lots of experience in caring for other people. Sick and well. And, as I told her, Bertie doesn't need specialized care, just someone to watch over him—even keep him company. What do you think?"

Jack was still smiling. "How old is she?"

Shadow wagged a finger at him. "I didn't hear that question. I don't need the government charging my agency with age discrimination." She paused. "I'm only half kidding, Jack. She must be close to you…"

"Still in her forties?"

"Yes. She was a teenage mom."

"Bertie does still need help sometimes getting up from his chair, so it wouldn't just be making meals and doing laundry, watching TV with him. She'd need to provide some minor physical support."

Shadow smiled. "I'm sure she can. She managed my father's care during his last illness and Bertie is in far better shape, from what she told me."

"Then I guess we've got a deal. If she agrees. I'll rely on your judgment." Jack got to his feet. "Two problems solved in one morning," he said.

"I'll speak to her later. Then you and I can talk again about terms." She paused, remembering the farm. "You don't have room for a small flock of chickens there, do you?"

"Egg layers?"

"Yes, but they're also like pets to her," she said, hoping Jack would take them. Shadow had to drive out to the farm soon to check on things—and help her mother pack again. The full attic and the rest of the house needed to be cleaned out before Finn served the eviction notice and the county took over. If Jack wouldn't house the chickens, or couldn't, she'd have to find some other arrangement for them. Shadow had thought of her backyard, but local zoning regulations prevented that.

After he left the office, she picked up the phone again. *Two problems solved in one morning*, Jack had said.

Maybe she could make it three.

Shadow phoned the rest of the numbers on her list, eliminating those that pertained to Jack Hancock. She would try to find something now for Derek. Once Finn served that notice, her brother would have to move out, like it or not, and the chickens would no longer be partly his responsibility.

Minutes later, she sat back in her chair. Conducting business, even some that didn't pertain to Mother Comfort, hadn't worked today. Because regardless of how many calls she made, she still had Ava to worry about, and mending their relationship wouldn't be easy. Neither would telling Ava about Grey.

Had she only been trying to avoid the real problems in her life? Her broken connection with her daughter? Her issues with Grey?

She made one last call.

For now, she would fix what she could.

JENNA ROAMED THE house in Shawnee Mission, taking inventory. Deciding what to take and what to leave for David—if he chose to keep anything at all, considering his move to Salt Lake and his need for such a big *change* in his life—took almost more energy than she had.

In the past week, sleepless nights had become the norm. She dreaded having to ask him about anything, for anything. In the space of those few minutes when he'd told her he wanted the divorce, he'd become a stranger. How had she not seen what was coming? Even their arguments in the past year hadn't raised any flags.

She couldn't seem to stop wondering what he was doing at any given moment, how he felt about the end of their marriage. David had never been as forthcoming as Jenna tended to be—witness her meltdown with Shadow about adopting Ava—but she'd thought little of that. Her father had kept his feelings under wraps, too, except for his occasional bouts of explosive anger. That was the only emotion she'd ever seen in him, really. David was more likely to withdraw into a newspaper.

She tidied a stack of them on the coffee table, and the simple rustling of papers crackled through the air.

The house was so quiet without Ava. Upstairs, Jenna stopped in her niece's bedroom. The Tim McGraw poster on the wall made her want to cry again, as she remembered Ava's expression when she'd come downstairs with her luggage. For a moment she'd clung to Jenna, then she'd gone out to Shadow's car without another word, not even goodbye.

She hadn't been this alone in years, and the silence seemed to reinforce that loneliness. Her inner panic, to be honest. At least the tears had finally dried up. For a while after Shadow left with Ava, she'd dissolved into a puddle of them, it seemed, every hour on the hour, unable to stop herself from sobbing aloud. She'd come close once or twice to full-blown hysteria.

What was she going to do? Where would she go?

Shadow had told her that their mother faced a similar move soon. Maybe they should get a new place together, Jenna thought, cracking a bitter smile. As if that would work. She needed her own space.

Downstairs again, in the doorway of David's home office, she hesitated. There was nothing in here she needed to take, or would want, or was entitled to—his books, the antique humidor he kept on the desk though he didn't smoke a pipe or cigars, another pile of financial magazines—so she quickly shut the door. Going in would only remind her of him, his clean scent, the sound of his voice. He'd already taken his laptop.

And still, she listened for his car in the drive, his footsteps in the front hall, like she was some teenage girl whose boyfriend had dumped her. But she wasn't a girl weeping over her first lost love. *Get a grip, Jenna.*

The thought made her straighten. Sure, she might cry again over Ava. She missed her terribly, but another emotion grabbed her by the throat now. She marched into the family room and gazed out the wide window wall at the pool. The underwater lights were on, giving the patio the kind of romantic appearance Jenna had always tried to maintain. Her beautiful home, the way she entertained, her annual Christmas open house. How she made it all seem effortless. Her clothes, always fashionable, always of the best quality. And all, all of it, shallow.

Like her almost-over marriage.

Shadow was right. Jenna had trusted David, relied on him. Too much. In their years together, she had too often deferred to him, allowed him to make their choices even when she didn't want to attend a certain party or go somewhere on vacation. She'd become a doormat. And all of that had led her here, alone and confused. Without the rudder she needed to change her own life.

What was it he'd said? *You should think about how to make yourself happy.* Jenna pushed out a sigh. She drew the draperies across the windows and toured the vaulted family room, turning on lights against the darkness, telling herself she would, indeed, be all right, if not happy just yet. Because she *would*.

Her grieving, like her marriage, was over.
Not that there wouldn't be more bad days
ahead, but never again would she collapse
in a heap in this chair or her bedroom or
lean against that front door, one hand on the
sleek wooden panel, as if begging him to
come back. She was stronger than that. Better than that. And she'd just tumbled into the
next phase.

She was angry.

WEARING HER GREEN camp shorts and shirt
with the community center logo on the
pocket, Ava stood, waiting. The half-sized
school bus that had brought her here from
her mother's new house had yet to arrive to
take her back. That morning, at the end of
the street, she'd been afraid the bus wouldn't
pick her up. She'd felt totally alone even
though her mom had waited with her. Ava
tapped one foot against the pavement, trying
not to look at the other kids who'd started
camp with her today, now gathered nearby
in a tight circle that excluded her.

This wasn't any fun at all.

She couldn't help remembering all the
mornings when her aunt Jenna had watched
from her porch or the front door to see her

off to school. Ava would trade this for a bagged lunch any day. This summer promised to be the worst in Ava's whole life.

She'd expected to attend the same camp in Shawnee Mission as she had for the last few years. She knew people there; she was part of a group of girls that included her best friend, Kaitlyn. A wave of homesickness ran through her, tightening her stomach, making her hands feel sweaty.

Everyone was staring.

So what? They obviously didn't like her, and she didn't like them. She sent them a weak wave anyway, to show she wasn't the stuck-up snob someone had accused her of being earlier in the day. Well, the girl hadn't said it out loud, but the way she'd eyed Ava's uniform—which was the same as everyone else's—and the shoes Aunt Jenna had paid the earth for, had said it all.

No one seemed friendly here, and all the activities—a morning hike through a sparse stand of trees behind the community center that never even disappeared from view, fishing for tadpoles in a creek with barely any water in it, an afternoon swim in the center's indoor pool and the baby stuff they called art projects here were just…stupid.

It was the only word she could come up with.

Ava looked around for the school bus but didn't see it coming. She tapped her foot again. The other girls glanced at her, as if she'd made some terrible noise. They murmured amongst themselves and a few of the girls giggled. Ava wanted to melt into the pavement and disappear.

Turning aside, shoulders hunched, she pulled out her cell phone.

To her relief, Kaitlyn answered on the first ring.

"Hi, it's me."

"Ava! How are you? Did you come home yet?"

"No," she said, feeling even more morose. "My mom won't let me. And my uncle David left Aunt Jenna." Then there was her mother. Who had that man at the door been? Ava wanted to know, but so far she hadn't asked her mom. She was trying to avoid talking to her as much as possible. "Everyone's all upset, and I... I miss you so much."

She pictured Kaitlyn, dark haired and with a pretty smile, perched on her bed while they talked. She lived two blocks from Ava and they usually saw each other every day. But that was in Shawnee Mission.

"I miss you, too," she said. "When can I see you, Ava?"

"Maybe my mom would drive me some day." She didn't hold out much hope for that. She told Kaitlyn about the new house, how small it was and that her mother had painted the bedroom where Ava slept pink.

"Ew," Kaitlyn agreed. "Gross."

"And she drives this old red car. It's embarrassing."

Ava caught the other girls at the bus stop looking at her again. One of them shook her head as if to say, *she's so weird.*

"I hate it here," she said. "I want to come home."

CHAPTER THIRTEEN

WITH HER HANDS tight on the Mustang's steering wheel, Shadow drove out to her parents' farm, hoping to talk to Derek. This was never her favorite thing to do, but she wanted to discuss a possible job she'd finally come up with for him.

She wouldn't stay long. Ava was attending her first day at the community center summer camp and she'd be home soon, though Jenna had called earlier to ask if she could spend the night with them and her voice had held a new bounce. Jenna would be there to greet Ava if Shadow was late getting home.

She turned into the gravel driveway and paused by the mailbox, tilted on its wooden post. To her relief, she found no more bills waiting inside.

At the house, a full garbage can spilled rotting food onto the front porch. Shadow had warned Derek about raccoons, but apparently he'd paid little attention, and her mother was gone for the day.

To Shadow's surprise, Wanda had taken the job at Bertie's, and Shadow had promised to check on her chickens when she came to see her brother.

She used her key to the house. "Derek," she called out in the darkened living room. She hadn't seen his car in the drive, and the drapes were pulled across the windows, another sign that he wasn't home. He liked light and space. Had he finally moved out before being ordered to by the court?

She strolled through the empty rooms, half tempted to set fire to the place. Amazed that Finn Donovan hadn't been here yet to serve the eviction notice, she plucked a musty afghan off the couch and stuffed it in the washing machine on her way to the bedrooms in the back. Her father had once tried to turn a hall closet into a laundry room, but it was barely big enough to turn around in.

At Derek's door, she gazed into the small room. Years ago, he and Jared had joked and scuffled and fought here. Strange to realize that, in one way or another, the whole family was gone, or scattered.

She walked back to the living room and

out the front door, locking it behind her. At least Derek hadn't left the house open.

She went to the chicken coop. And groaned. The hens were in the yard, clucking and pecking at each other, but when Shadow approached, they chose her as their target. She was far from their favorite human being. Their empty food bowls told Shadow they hadn't been fed.

"Derek, I'll…" She didn't finish the warning. Dire threats wouldn't help.

But to her surprise, there he was, coming across the yard, his dark hair rumpled. "Where were you? I looked through the whole house."

"Out back. My Chevy's in the shop. Calvin dropped me off a while ago, and Mama has me packing up the garage."

She pulled a paper from her pocket. "Here. I think I've found you a good job prospect. The hardware store needs another stock clerk. You'd be working with Calvin. Just call this number to set up an interview, but that's just a formality. I'm told the job is yours if you want it."

He stuffed the owner's name and contact information into his pocket with a shrug. "I'm not going back now. I was in town an hour ago. Could have talked to him then." At first she thought he sounded less than enthusiastic. Then she realized Derek was peeved about something. "Stopped by your house with a box of your things while I was there," he said.

Her pulse jumped. "My house?"

Derek hadn't been there before; he hadn't helped during her move. His tone sounded too casual yet cool. "I would have left the box on your porch, but Jenna was there." He waited a moment before going on. "Someone else was home."

He'd emphasized the word *home*, and her heart took a fast ride from her chest to her navy blue flats. The only other person there would be Ava.

He made a chiding sound. "Shame on you. You've been keeping secrets, Shadow. Who else knows about the girl? Or am I the only one who's been kept in the dark—for how many years?"

He'd seen Ava. Talked to Jenna.

"Nine years," she said. "Yes, she's my daughter, Derek."

He didn't hesitate. His blue gaze cooled. "Yours and Grey Wilson's." He must have seen the similarity in Ava's eyes to the blue-green of Grey's. Or maybe Jenna had told him. "The man who murdered our brother. Nice work."

Then he turned his back and stalked toward the house, his shoulders set.

"Derek," she called, but he didn't answer and he didn't stop.

Shadow wanted to get back in her car, race home and make sure he hadn't confronted Ava with his discovery. But she was shaking too hard to drive. Instead, she called home, where Jenna answered. She and Ava were baking chocolate chip cookies, but Shadow couldn't appreciate their enjoyment of the simple task. She started to ask Jenna about Derek's visit, but she heard Ava in the background. Jenna wouldn't be able to fill her in right now.

Taking a few minutes to clear her head before starting home, Shadow cleaned the henhouse, making sure there were no eggs left in their nests to spoil, then filled the automatic waterers and feed bowls. Satisfied that the chickens were in no danger of starving or dying of thirst on the increasingly warm summer days, she cast one last look at the house in the distance and drove away.

Grey wasn't the only one she should have told. Much sooner.

What would Derek do with the information?

SHADOW DROPPED HER keys on the kitchen table. Two trays of freshly baked cookies were cooling on the counter. With her thoughts still churning about Grey and Derek, she barely noticed the enticing aroma of chocolate chips in the air. She followed the sound of voices down the hall to her room, where Ava sat beside Jenna's open overnight bag on the bed, happily chattering away to a smiling Jenna. Shadow stopped just inside the door.

The suitcase contained several T-shirts, jeans, some lingerie and a pair of pajamas in a prancing deer print. Not at all her usual choices of clothing. If Shadow hadn't been so worried about her confrontation with Derek, she would have smiled. Her sister seemed to have a new outlook on her life.

Ava was saying, "I'm glad you came to stay with us tonight."

Jenna turned to Shadow. "You're sure you don't mind? I've spent too much time in that house by myself lately." Then she clamped her lips tight, presumably to avoid saying anything more about her situation with Ava in the room.

"Of course I don't. You look much better, Jenna."

"Can I go with you when you go home?" Ava asked, peering into the bag. "I don't want to stay here without you."

"You just started day camp," Jenna reasoned.

Ava's mouth set. "I don't like camp. I want to be with you."

Shadow and Jenna exchanged worried glances. "Sweetie, I know it's hard, leaving your friends, your room in Shawnee Mission, Aunt Jenna…" Shadow said, feeling helpless. How could she make things better for her daughter?

"You can come visit me anytime," Jenna said. "I know your mom will be fine with that." She looked to Shadow for agreement.

"Of course," she said.

"But why don't you give camp here a try first?" Jenna continued. "It can take time to settle in and feel at home in a new place."

Shadow wondered if Jenna was trying to convince herself, too.

"Once you and I repaint your room,"

Shadow added, "I hope you'll like it just as much as your one at Aunt Jenna's."

Ava thought that over. "Can I get another poster for the wall?"

Her tone was grudging. Ava was nowhere near to accepting this move, but Shadow took heart. This was a small step, but possibly an important one.

"You can have posters on all four walls if you like." Shadow gave Ava a quick hug then cleared her throat. "Ava, I think we deserve a treat. Would you get us all a plate of cookies, please? And a glass of milk for yourself. Thank you, sweetie."

She waited until Ava had drifted down the hall.

"I saw Derek at the farm, Jen."

"Oh, dear." But Jenna wasn't surprised. "He came by earlier. Ava got home right after he arrived—just as I was taking the box of your stuff he'd brought from the farm. I put that in your closet. And, by the way, that's some shoe collection you have."

"My one addiction," Shadow said. "He must have seen right away that Ava was my child. And with one look he knew she was Grey's child, too. Or did you tell him?"

Jenna rolled her eyes. "I did my best,

Shadow, but I could hardly hide her. She was
right here and full of stories about camp—
not all good, as you might have guessed. But
no, I didn't tell him. He just knew."

"I hope Derek doesn't try to hurt her in
some way—or hurt Grey."

Jenna tensed. "I hadn't thought of that.
This isn't good. You'd better warn him,"
Jenna said. "Derek was so broken when
Jared died—we all were—but he's never
gotten over that. He worshipped Jared."

"I think that has paralyzed him in a way.
Embittered him, too. He still blames Grey."

Jenna lifted an eyebrow. "Now he has another reason to dislike him."

"Hate would be a better word." Shadow
added, "Derek's angry with me, too."

"About Grey—you know I'm not his biggest fan and Mama isn't either—but what's
changed between you? Something has."

"It's gotten complicated. Now that he
knows about Ava, things are very…differ-
ent." Shadow told her sister about the night
Grey had come to the house. "We'll need to
find some balance between us for her well-
being."

Jenna glanced toward the hallway and laid
a finger across her lips. Then she couldn't

seem to help whispering, "What are you going to do?"

"Blossom and Logan have planned a weekend in Kansas City with the wedding party. I'll talk to Grey again then." Shadow put an arm around Jenna's shoulders. "What about you? How are you doing?"

"I'm not crying all the time," Jenna said. "I guess that's a good sign. Even better, Shadow, I could smack David. I'm as mad as a hornet whose nest has been disturbed."

THE WEDDING PARTY trip to Kansas City had loomed for Shadow like a bad appointment with the dentist. Now, a week after Jenna had stayed overnight, she dreaded it even more. Shadow had insisted on driving her Mustang to the hotel rather than riding with Logan and Blossom. But maybe, in order to talk with Grey, she should have gone with him. What would he make of Derek's discovery? What was he planning to do about Ava?

If this trip didn't go well, she would retrieve her car from valet parking and head home. As soon as she chose her dress she could make her escape, and besides, she wasn't in the mood for celebrating. Shadow was too worried about Ava's future, and Ava was still unhappy about her move from Shawnee Mission. Wanda had agreed to stay with her while Shadow was away, but what if Derek decided to stop by again?

When Shadow entered the soaring hotel lobby, Grey was the first person she saw. She hadn't talked to him since the night she'd gone to Wilson Cattle, and in this neutral location she studied him in a new light. Wearing black jeans and boots, a white shirt, and carrying his black Stetson, he was more than handsome. Grey's eyes homed in on her, as if he'd been waiting for her to arrive.

His gaze slid over her in a similar appraisal as he brandished his key card, and a rush of warmth flowed through her. He looked freshly shaved and had used the same woodsy scent she'd always liked. For a moment, better memories assailed her along with another wave of regret.

"Already checked in," he said. "I'm in room 1734." As if that night had never happened, Grey grabbed her suitcase and trailed her across the vast expanse of Oriental rugs and marble floors, past a huge round table in the center holding an enormous bouquet of flowers. He leaned against the reception desk, facing Shadow. "Unless you'll have company, drop in anytime to enjoy the view."

Shadow's pulse hitched. Apparently he was in a far different mood than that other night, and she abandoned the idea of speaking to him about Derek right now. "Company? What are you talking about?"

"Finn Donovan." As if that were clear and he'd been stewing about it.

Her cheeks turned hot. Shadow handed her credit card to the desk clerk, an attractive blonde wearing a stylish black suit.

"Why is Finn here?"

"Logan asked him to be a groomsman. Blossom's friend Tammy from Philadelphia will be a bridesmaid—at first she didn't think she could make it—so they needed another guy." Grey held her gaze. "He told me about your date."

Shadow lowered her voice, though she was certain the desk clerk could hear. "It wasn't a date and it never happened."

His brows lowered. "He'll probably try again."

What was this? He couldn't possibly be jealous.

"Grey. I'm trying to check in." With a forced smile, she took back her credit card and waited while the clerk activated her key card. She spotted Logan in another line. He sent her a quick smile then lifted an eyebrow in Grey's direction. "I'll see you at dinner tonight. Let's not mention Finn again."

"Finnegan?" he asked in an obviously teasing tone. "Like *Finnegan's Wake*?"

Her pulse thudding, she rolled her eyes. "Just what I need. A comedian." She turned back to the clerk. "Thank you. You've been very helpful."

"Enjoy your stay," the clerk said.

Shadow didn't miss her quick once-over of Grey from his shirt, jacket and boots to the black Stetson in his hand. She had to admit he made an impressive sight—enough, despite their problems, to make her heart race. With her key in hand, she marched toward the elevators. Grey walked just behind her into the waiting car. He punched the button for his floor. "Yours?"

She reached past him to push number ten. Unfortunately, they were the only two people in the elevator. She tried to focus on the old Hootie and the Blowfish tune piping through the speakers. It would probably remain in her head, an earworm for the whole weekend. She pressed as far back against the rear wall as she could, remembering other times when he'd teased her, made her laugh. He'd loved her then, and she'd certainly loved him back. "You should go down to the lobby again and work your charms on that woman at the desk."

He grinned, but it didn't reach his eyes this time. "You think?"

"She seemed to appreciate that you cleaned up well." Shadow abandoned any attempt at light banter. "Grey, what is this? Last time I saw you, we—"

"Didn't settle everything. We will," he said. "I haven't forgotten about Ava."

"I haven't forgotten Jared." *Or Derek*, she thought with a pang of alarm.

His gaze turned serious. "Let's declare a truce for now, at least until after dinner. Blossom and Logan want the evening to be special, and we owe them that." He gestured toward her pricey heels. "I like the shoes."

"Thank you. I like shoes in general."

She glanced at the ceiling, where both their images were reflected in the mirrored tiles. She looked again at the top of Grey's head, the cowlick in his light brown hair matted down by the black Stetson he held in his hands. To her discomfort, she suddenly wanted to run her fingers through that glossy hair.

The doors whooshed open at her floor—thank goodness—and she darted out into the hall, praying he wouldn't come after her. The elevator doors closed on Hootie and Grey. He called out, repeating her earlier words, "See you at dinner."

To Shadow, the mundane promise sounded more like a warning of the more serious, and necessary, discussion to come.

CHAPTER FOURTEEN

DINNER WAS NEARLY over and Shadow had choked down only a few bites. She sat beside Grey, trying to keep her mind on the lively conversation, but although he'd cleaned his plate of a monstrous steak, Grey wasn't taking part in the talk, either. Logan was across from her next to Blossom, and Finn, who had come by himself, had pulled up a chair from another table at the end of theirs. As soon as Finn appeared, Grey had guided Shadow to the chair beside his, but she avoided looking at him or Finn.

Shadow's stomach was in knots so tight they might never untangle.

"...and I'm so happy Tammy can be in the wedding," Blossom was saying, her hand tucked into Logan's on the tablecloth. "But she won't get here until the night before. Work stuff."

"Best friends?" Finn asked, shooting a look at Grey and Shadow.

"She was my rock when Ken was trying to find me."

Months ago, Blossom's abusive ex-fiancé had threatened her, then tried to intimidate Tammy into telling him Blossom's whereabouts, which had sent Blossom running from Pennsylvania straight into Logan's arms.

"I'm happy for you both," Finn said. Like Shadow, he knew that not long ago Logan had gone through a bad time with his ex-wife and had temporarily lost custody of his young son. Now all that was behind them, in part because Logan and Blossom had learned to rely on each other and their love. And Olivia, his ex, had softened her stance.

Shadow pushed back her chair. "I think I'll go upstairs. Long day," she added in a tone that, even to her, sounded unconvincing.

Grey tilted his head toward her plate. "Rainbow trout not to your liking?"

The lemon-butter sauce on the fish had congealed on the mostly full plate. "I wasn't hungry. You can have it if you want."

Blossom looked at her with concern. "Are you feeling okay? Nick's had a bad head cold this week. It's going around."

"I'm fine," she said, taking a step away from the table. "Good night, all. See you in the morning. I'll need help picking out my dress."

Unless she decided to get her Mustang from the valet tonight and head home, buy something local, instead—not that there'd be many choices in Barren.

She was halfway to the elevators when Grey stopped her. According to the numbers above the doors, the next car was on the twentieth floor but not moving.

His eyes a dark teal green, he gestured toward the hotel bar. "Let me buy you a drink to settle your nerves. And mine."

"I'm not nervous—except about you and Finn. You two were eyeing each other like Aaron Burr and Alexander Hamilton in a duel."

"At least neither of us died." When Shadow didn't respond to his weak attempt at humor, he sighed. "I didn't think it was that obvious."

"And practically forcing me to sit right next to you?"

Grey scoffed. "You and I just arrived first and took the available seats." He paused. "I let Finn get his own chair."

Grey steered her away from the elevators just as the next car arrived, and Shadow didn't resist. Maybe this was the best opportunity to talk to him. They went across to the bar, where he picked a corner booth away from the few other patrons then gestured at the bartender. When the man wandered over to take their orders, his eyes still on a baseball game on the television above the bar, Grey asked, "You, Shadow?"

"Sparkling water, please."

Grey chose an imported beer. He waited till their drinks came, then took a first sip before he set his bottle down with a distinct clink on the table. He ran a finger around the rim. "First, I owe you an apology. My trying to tease you in the lobby before was a clumsy lead-in when I should have just walked up to you and said straight out, 'I'm sorry.' I know you didn't mean for me to meet Ava like that—and on the very day you brought her to Barren. I know I should have called first, but I didn't. Guess I deserved to get shocked. Again, I apologize."

"I appreciate that," she said. "Apology accepted." Shadow reached into her bag and pulled out a small book with a quilted white cover. In pink across the album were the four letters, B-A-B-Y.

Grey stared at it. "Ava's baby book?"

As he took it, Shadow nodded. "Some of her first pictures. There are a lot more, and you can see them whenever you want, but I couldn't bring them all. If you like any of these, you can make copies."

He was already leafing through the book, stopping here and there. He ran a finger over an image of Ava at one month old. "She had fuzzy hair," he said, his voice hoarse. "Lighter than it is now. Like…mine. Mostly, though, she just looks like…herself."

Shadow's heart hurt. "Oh, Grey." She had deprived him of so many years, so much time and every milestone in Ava's life.

He couldn't seem to meet her eyes. "I already know about Doc, the Merritts, the adoption you'd planned for… Tell me why you didn't go through with that. Tell me about when she was born."

Shadow moved her water glass around on the table. "That wasn't easy," she admitted. "It started in the middle of the night." At first, she hadn't recognized the persistent ache down low in her back for what it was and had tried to go back to sleep. "I woke the Merritts and they drove me to Farrier General then came all the way to my room, when all I wanted was to be alone." Grey's gaze was still on the baby album, though he hadn't turned another page. "Once I got settled, they went to the waiting room, and I kept picturing them holding hands, anticipating the arrival of 'their' baby. That would be the most important day of their lives, Mrs. Merritt had told me. They would become parents at last, have the family they'd always longed for.

"The pains got worse, closer together, until there was hardly any time between them. The nurse kept telling me to breathe."

Grey had gone pale. "You shouldn't have been alone. I understand about the Merritts not being in the room, but..."

"That was hospital policy. That's not what you mean though, is it?" She caught his gaze. "I know, Grey. When it was happening, I cursed you for not being there, for not having any idea what I was going through. Even though I only had myself to blame for that." She paused, and when he didn't say anything, she went on. "Finally, it was time to push. By then the doctor had joined us. All at once, I raised my head, saw her hands cupped to receive a tiny body. And there was Ava."

Grey finally met her eyes. His gaze was somber, liquid. She wanted him to hear everything.

"I was exhausted but happy, and I watched the nurse wrap her in a blanket and put a pink knitted cap on her head. She had quite a lot of hair for a newborn, as you said. But I couldn't see her face. The nurse had turned away, started to leave. Then the baby started to cry, and I..." Shadow remembered that tug, deep inside of her. "I told her to wait. She stared at me for a moment, then asked if I wanted to see her, but her tone wasn't encouraging. The plan was for me to hand the baby to the Merritts right away. I even wished my own mother was there, but she wasn't. Neither were you. 'Holding her might not be the best idea,' the nurse said."

"What did you say?"

"I asked to hold her anyway. I needed to see her face, to cradle her close just once before I gave her up forever. The nurse came forward with what I saw as a disapproving look, and she held the baby out to me." For a second, Shadow couldn't go on. Reliving that precious moment when she'd taken her baby in her arms for the first time, felt the warmth of that sweet little body against hers. For what she thought, then, would be the last time.

"I looked into her eyes. They were blue and not very clear, but she seemed to focus on me. Grey, her look said, *Don't. Don't let me go.*"

"How could you," he murmured, his voice choked.

"That was when I named her. The name we'd chosen months ago. I knew then that I'd made the wrong choice about the Merritts." Shadow cleared her throat. "The nurse told me she'd better take her, but I couldn't let go. I laid my cheek, my tears, against the baby's head. Ava's little legs moved in the blanket. And, *Oh Grey*, I thought. *Look who we've made. Together.* Ava was all that was left of us. All that was good."

Grey reached for her hand. She could see tears in his eyes now.

"The nurse was staring at me, crying, too. I guessed she already knew what I would say. By law I had twenty-four hours to re-scind my decision. I hated to go back on my word, but giving birth, holding my baby, was so powerful, the most amazing thing ever. I couldn't leave her, and a big part of the reason was you," she said. "I still couldn't bear to tell you about this child, but I couldn't give up this part of you—of us, and the love we'd had."

Grey gently stroked her palm. He couldn't seem to say a word, and that was all right because she needed to tell him the rest.

"I decided that Ava and I would be a family. Somehow I would make it work. Caring for her, loving her, I knew, was the right thing to do." She turned her hand in Grey's, holding on at last to her baby's father. "When the nurse left us, I kept looking at Ava, thinking *I'm a mother.*" That same sense of wonder filled her all over again, but this time she wasn't alone. "Eventually, the nurse took her to the nursery while I talked with the Merritts. I hated to break their hearts, but I had to. *She's mine,* I thought. But she wasn't just mine, even then. She's ours, Grey."

WHEN SHE'D FINISHED, Grey just sat there. He wasn't sure he could say anything, but at least his anger over Ava had subsided, softened by the memories she'd handed him in their child's baby book and by her words about Ava's birth. He looked down at a photo of her wearing the little pink cap on her head.

"Maybe," he finally said, his voice still husky, "we can work from here, from that. Together. For Ava. After I find the rustlers who keep hitting my place, once I get some concrete answer about Jared's death…maybe we can have a second chance, Shadow."

"That's a lot of *ifs*." She pushed her glass of sparkling water aside. The ice cubes tinkled. His gaze caught hers, and held, in a way that showed how hurt he'd been by Jared's death, by their broken relationship. Was he right, and was it possible that they could try again with ten years of heartache between them?

"What if we hadn't split up like that then?" he asked. "If Jared hadn't gotten killed? You ever think of that? I know I do."

"Yes, I've thought of that." Shadow looked down at the table. "But we did break up and he did die."

Grey shifted on his seat. He took another swallow of his beer. "I've never told you my side of things. I'd like to tell you now."

When she didn't object, he began.

"The day we split, I felt mad—and hurt. I went home and spent the rest of that afternoon prowling around the ranch house, changing from one mood to the other, silently vowing to never see you again, then wondering what I would do without you. Around the time night fell, I grabbed my keys from the kitchen counter and thanked my lucky stars that my dad had gone out for the evening. No one else was home. I meant to drive over to your place, talk things out and, I hoped, start over." Grey hesitated. He couldn't hold back his feelings as he always had before. "I loved you, Shadow. I loved everything about you—your hair, your eyes, your smile. I loved your strength and how you handled a home life with your folks that wasn't exactly happy. You made the best of things. I loved how you could always make me laugh, especially at myself. I even loved our fights—and making up."

"That last argument was the worst by far," she said. "There was no making up."

She wasn't wrong. In their two years of dating, beginning to talk about marriage, even picking out baby names, he'd never seen her that angry or upset, her eyes blazing. Grey hadn't known what to do.

"I'd probably said all the wrong things earlier that day. But I didn't understand why you seemed so determined to take our relationship—already perfect in my mind—to that next level. I wanted to convince you we should wait."

Surely, there must be some middle ground, he'd thought.

"I hadn't left my house yet that night when I heard a vehicle coming up the drive. I thought it was my dad. He'd tried, hours before, to talk me out of going into town, pleading with you for another chance." Grey fiddled with the label on his beer bottle. "But the pickup was Jared's. I'd seen it a hundred times—when we were in the same class at school, every time I picked you up or dropped you off at your parents' farm. And I knew he and I were going to have it out. Right there."

"You shouldn't have answered the door."

"Maybe so, but I pushed through onto the porch. He stopped near the front steps, and I saw Derek in the passenger seat looking mad and scared, and Calvin Stern in the truck bed. I could tell by the set of Jared's mouth that he was loaded for bear."

Shadow was squeezing his hand. "What happened next?"

"Jared slammed the door and stormed

over to the bottom of the steps, glaring up at me. 'You made my sister cry,'" he said. I told him it was none of his business, and then I saw the gun. A big pistol, flashing blue-black in the dark. I swallowed, hard. Derek and Calvin had joined Jared, flanking him. I held up both hands and told them to take it easy. But that only inflamed Jared."

Shadow laid a hand on his arm, as if to stop him from saying more, but Grey went on. He had to. "He took a step, the gun held in front of him, and my mouth went dry. Jared's hand was shaking."

"Oh, Grey."

"'You don't want to do this,' I said, but he charged at me, the other guys moving right along with him. I met them at the bottom of the steps, told them to get going. That they were trespassing. I tried to tell Jared that I loved you. But he said, 'Shut your mouth! Don't mention her again.'"

Shadow looked horrified. He hated to put her through this, to make her revisit that night, but he couldn't stop now.

"Jared lunged. I blocked his arm but the gun was waving around. Someone was going to get hurt. I shoved Jared but he managed to stand his ground. He was bigger than me—and madder."

"What…did the others do?"

"Derek joined the tussle, kept telling Jared to get back, that your dad would tan their hides. He said Jared had promised nothing would happen, something about just teaching me a lesson." Grey freed his arm to take Shadow's hand again. "In the confusion I lost track of Calvin, but he's always claimed that he stepped back, scared."

Grey took a moment to try to settle his racing heart. For years he'd had nightmares about the shooting, and it was all coming back again. "I saw the muzzle of the gun pointed straight at my head. I don't remember clearly what happened then. I think I grabbed for the barrel to shove it aside. So did Derek, and for a second or two, the three of us wrestled for control."

Shadow put her free hand over her mouth. "My God, Grey."

He hadn't wanted to shock her. Yet after breaking his silence of ten years, he had to finish. "Then the damned gun went off."

SHADOW GLANCED DOWN at the open baby album showing a picture of Ava at her second birthday party with cake all over her face. She and Grey still held hands, and his warmth, his strength—emotional as well as physical—flowed from his skin to hers. She thought she could feel the steady beat of his pulse.

"Grey, I knew…but I guess I didn't know. Not from you."

"We were still kids then, Shadow. My dad didn't want to hear us talk about marriage when I wasn't even into my second year at college. He'd watched his relationship with my mom die a slow, hard death—and they'd gotten married as adults. He saw what that did to our family, to me and Olivia." He shook his head. "I can't blame him for that. Or even my mom, though we still don't get along. But there we were, you and I, picking out baby names. When you asked that day if we could elope before the end of summer, show everyone how wrong they were about us…"

Their fight had blown everything sky high. Yes, they were young, she'd tried to tell him, but they loved each other. They could make it. Grey would no longer feel torn between his parents, and Shadow could get away from her dad. But the argument had destroyed any hope of marriage. "You told me maybe your father was right."

Grey lifted his brows. "I changed my mind as soon as I cooled off. If I could have talked to you again that night, if Jared hadn't brought that gun..."

"Yet he did," she murmured. "I'm so sorry he did. Sorry for everything that's happened since." Her tears flowed freely now. "Grey."

His voice came out soft and low. "Shadow." He leaned closer, his gaze lingering on her mouth for a moment. He gently squeezed her fingers. And then, before she could guess what he meant to do, and as if he knew she wouldn't say no, he kissed her.

It was light and quick with the faintest brush of his lips against hers, but it sent a curl of flame through her anyway, made more intense by the exchange of tragic memories he'd shared about Jared, the heartfelt ones she'd offered about Ava. When she pulled back, she was shaking.

Her throat felt raw. For years she'd thought, like other people and especially her family, that Grey was guilty in Jared's death. Hearing his side of the story had changed that. She couldn't be sure, but she wanted to believe he was innocent. And the serious talk she'd expected, even wanted, wasn't over yet. Shadow drew her hand from his. "Derek knows about Ava."

Grey tensed. "How?"

Shadow told him about her visit to the farm and Grey shook his head. "I know how the Morans still feel about me. Especially him. But I'm more concerned about Ava." He plucked Shadow's unused straw off the table, opened it and pleated the wrapper. "If Derek knows, so could a lot of other people soon. What if he's already told his friends? Or someone else knocks at your door again one night? Or in town, you could run into a neighbor, Barney at the bank, the woman who runs the baby store, the pet shop owner…"

He was right. "We have to tell her, Grey. Before someone else lets that slip. Ava's going to day camp now. People will see you in her eyes, just as Derek did."

"Let's tell her together," he said. "It'll be our first act as coparents. We've already waited too long." Grey tried to smile. "Come out to the ranch, maybe. That might be good."

"Ava loves horses," Shadow agreed, de-

spite her own reluctance to visit Wilson
Cattle.

"We'll tell her there, then. As soon as we
get back."

CHAPTER FIFTEEN

GREY WATCHED SHADOW turn back and forth on a raised platform in front of a three-way mirror in the bridal shop near the hotel. He tried not to fidget. The blush pink carpet, the soothing music that played through the speakers, the fussy striped wallpaper and satin-seated chairs made him want to cut and run.

The room couldn't be more different from the ranch he was so afraid of losing, and Grey yearned for the wide-open spaces, the gentle lowing of cattle, the feel of a horse under him. And he couldn't seem to focus on anything but the talk they'd had last night.

Logan nudged his elbow. "What about this one?"

Grey balanced his Stetson on his knee. Shadow was standing still now, looking at Blossom, Logan, Finn Donovan and him in turn, asking for their vote on the dress she wore.

He said, "I liked the green one better."

Logan nodded. "Me, too."

"Too dark. I wish Tammy was here," Blossom said. "She has a good eye for fashion." She tapped her lip in thought. "Green isn't really your color, Shadow," she added in a soft tone that Grey supposed was meant not to offend her. "With your beautiful dusky skin and dark hair, I think this turquoise is a better choice. That would suit our Western wedding."

"I don't like the skirt," Shadow said. "It's too…" She couldn't seem to find a word.

"Poofy," Grey supplied, and she smiled, but it was as if she didn't want to. Or almost couldn't. She must be replaying all the things they'd said last night, too, their kisses.

"It makes my hips look a mile wide."

He spun his index finger so she would turn to show all sides again, just to be sure this wasn't the one. Her gaze caught his in the mirror and she folded her hands at her waist in a vain attempt to hide the dress she didn't like. Her shape looked fine to him, and the soft color on her lips reminded him of those kisses last night, but he knew she had to feel good in what she would be wearing. He offered his view.

"Nope. Not going to happen. What's next?" She'd already gone through at least a dozen dresses and Grey wanted to wind things up. For one thing, his right leg was already twitching, betraying his anxiety to get out of the bridal shop and making the hat on his knee appear to have Mexican jumping beans inside.

To make matters worse, he, Logan and Finn had been ordered to "dress for the occasion" and the lightweight wool of Grey's suit was beginning to itch. They'd all drawn the line at wearing shoes, but as a concession they had worn their best boots.

"Try the yellow," Blossom said when the turquoise dress didn't pass muster.

Grey sighed. The Stetson jiggled on his knee. He should be thinking about Wilson Cattle. If the ranch went under, he'd have nothing to offer Shadow for that second chance he wanted except the lifelong disappointment he would see in his father's eyes. And hers. No wife, no family, no kids to leave the ranch to... He should be home instead of hoping he didn't lose more cows while he was here.

Shadow emerged once more from the

dressing room down the hall. She swept into the showroom and Grey caught his breath. *You'd look real nice in a long white gown.* But this was even better. The simple style of the dress in a shade she called buttercup made her look slim, which she always did, and elegant…a word he'd never used in his life. Like *poofy.* The overhead lights shone on her bare shoulders.

"Wow," he said. He couldn't stop himself. Shadow at seventeen had been nothing like Shadow at twenty-seven.

Logan nodded again. "I like it."

"Works for me," Finn put in.

"I love it," Blossom agreed. "Shadow, that's the dress. What do you say?"

She hesitated only a second. "I say *yes.*"

Blossom grinned. "And that will be our accent color for the whole wedding, so the men can get their tuxedo fittings this afternoon. I'm thinking yellow cummerbunds."

Logan groaned. "Why not just go with pink?" He and Blossom, Grey knew, had had this sort of conversation before and Logan had lost. "Fancy onyx studs for our shirts, too, I bet. Blossom, we're getting married at the Circle H. Outdoors. It's a working ranch.

If I show up under that rose arbor you mean to put up for the ceremony, Tobias and Willy will laugh me off the property. I don't even want to think what Sam might say. I can already hear the horses snickering."

She ignored him. "We could have yellow roses, but no, white would be better. Humor me. I don't plan to get married more than once. I think you and Grey and Finn should stop complaining about those tuxedoes."

Grey almost grinned at his best friend's discomfort. But he didn't want to wear a monkey suit, either, even when he knew all women liked a man in a formal tux.

"I vote for casual," he said. "Let the ladies shine in their pretty gowns while we guys stay in the background looking like guys."

"What else would you look like, whatever you wear?" One hand across her stomach, Blossom shook her head. He liked her newfound confidence. "No, it's tuxedoes. Shadow?" she said. "Back me up here."

Shadow turned to the mirror, studying various angles of the strapless yellow dress, making its satiny yet subtle fabric shimmer. She glanced back at Grey as if she valued his opinion. Their eyes met and held for a second time today, as they had last night and so often when they were together and in love. He still was. He let his gaze linger until she said, "I vote for Blossom's wedding gown, this one for me—they're both simple—but somewhat more casual stuff for the guys." Grey blinked in surprise. It had been a long while since she'd actually taken his side, although they had agreed last night about Ava.

"Khakis," he said in a determined tone. "White shirts, no studs."

"Navy blue blazers," Logan put in, as if he'd had a sudden inspiration. "Except for our boots, we'll look like preppies from back East."

"Fancy boots." Grey grinned. "The fussiest boots we can buy."

Blossom's satisfied said she had won, if in a different way. "And yellow pocket squares."

Done, he thought in relief. Before Shadow disappeared into the back of the store for a dress fitting, changed into her own clothes, or paid for the yellow dress, Grey was on his feet. He clamped his hat on his head.

Maybe he and Shadow really could have something again. Beyond the fact that he still loved her, Ava gave them a special bond that would never be broken.

And he really liked that dress.

He just needed to put things right at Wilson Cattle.

SHADOW HAD SURVIVED the weekend in Kansas City, Grey's kisses in the hotel bar and their deep conversations about Ava and Jared.

No one knew better than she that she'd been unfair to Grey in keeping their child a secret from him for so long. But until recently, she'd always believed it was for the best. Because of Jared. *Maybe we can have another chance.* But could she trust Grey, even now? Or her feelings for him? His side of the story didn't prove he was blameless in her brother's death.

On Sunday morning, Shadow met Grey in the hotel lobby, where he was checking out, too.

After they paid their bills, he drew Shadow aside. This morning Grey looked far less serious than he had the other night, and he had a favor to ask.

"The thing is, I've offered to organize the rehearsal dinner for Logan and Blossom. It's not only because he's my best friend. According to Logan, it's usually the groom's parents who host the dinner."

"But his parents are gone," Shadow finished for him.

"Sam's not up for that, either, though he's going to walk Blossom down the aisle—or rather, from the house to the rose arbor. So, what do you say?"

"I don't know what you're asking."

Grey's gaze lifted to meet hers. Today he wore his usual blue jeans with a T-shirt that hugged his chest and showcased his biceps. She fought an urge to drown in his blue-green eyes. "I can't believe Blossom's parents said no to the wedding. They won't be here for her, Shadow, and that really hurt her. I wanted to do something, so I volunteered for the dinner." His gaze lingered on her mouth and he seemed to force himself to look away. "Would you help me with that? I'm a cowboy, not a social secretary. Or a wedding planner."

"Neither am I." Bringing people together was not her specialty, either. "What would this involve?"

His face brightened. "Not that much. We pick a menu, hire a caterer—I'm sure neither of us wants to cook—choose some nice wine to go with the meal, preside over things, I guess. Play host and hostess. I'll pay for everything."

"Where would it be held?" At first Shadow assumed he'd meant a restaurant, but he'd said *caterer*. "At the Circle H?"

"No, at my place," he said.

Shadow's pulse kicked up. "You know how I feel about Wilson Cattle." His story the other night had brought that back again in full force.

He obviously understood what she meant. "If I can live there, Shadow, walk down those porch steps every day, hear the sound of that gunshot over and over in my head…" He trailed off. "I suppose that's not a winning approach to convince you. Still, it's the truth."

"I've never thought of it that way." Like hearing his side of Jared's death. "Still, I'd rather we choose another venue."

Grey raised an eyebrow. "Are you offering your house?"

"I think we should find a restaurant or hall of some kind."

"Too expensive. And with my place hemorrhaging money? It'll be hard enough to pay for the dinner." Grey reached for her hand, as he had the other night. "I'm not asking you, really, to do *me* the favor. I'm asking for Logan and Blossom." He added, "It won't be that much work. But I'd really welcome your input. Your help."

Shadow took a deep breath and eased her hand from his, already missing his strength. "All right. For them." She said, "And you. I'll help."

His shoulders relaxed but his eyes remained serious. He obviously hadn't thought she would agree. "I'll call you to make plans," he said. "We can go from there. When you bring Ava to the ranch, we can look at the dining room. See if it works for the dinner."

She watched him for a moment, wondering how their joint announcement would go, then realized Ava and the rehearsal dinner weren't his only concerns. "I know that look," she said. "You're that worried about your ranch?"

"Yep. Unless you can find me some money, a no-interest loan, I'm in bigger trouble than I was with Barney at the Cattlemen's Bank." He glanced at the people milling around the front desk. "I've been trying to find out who's been stealing my cattle. Not long before we came to KC, the same white rig showed up again. Before I could confront them, it sped off into the night. Just like before. Only this time I trailed it long enough to get a partial read on the license plate." He glanced at her. "Finn ran that through the motor vehicle registrations."

"And Finn will follow up. Grey, I don't think you should take matters into your own hands—about Jared, either."

"By the time Finn gets around to checking out all those numbers, maybe I'll have found the guy myself."

She frowned. "Are you sure that's a good idea? It could be dangerous."

"My ranch, my responsibility." He smiled. "That your way of saying you care about me a little?"

"As Ava's father, yes. Don't fish for compliments." *As the man I used to love.* Shadow couldn't change his mind, even though Grey had opened up to her about their past and they'd shared those moments of closeness, those kisses.

She watched one of the hotel staff push a luggage cart past. "So, about the dinner. Some first thoughts. There'll be some toasts, one from you as best man, another from me as maid of honor, and I'm sure Blossom's friend Tammy will want to speak. Finn, too. That means having champagne on hand. You can get away with a chicken entrée for dinner, but I know how you are about beef, which usually means tenderloin, I've been told. That's not cheap—"

"I called over a dozen caterers this morning from my room. The café in Barren and Annabelle's Diner, too. I even spoke to someone at the fried chicken franchise between town and Farrier. Either their prices were too high or their menus didn't seem right for the occasion…" He trailed off again. "Any other ideas?"

"I don't know which places you called."

Grey pulled out a list and Shadow scanned it. "We—I could call the caterer here in KC who's doing Blossom's cake. She might have recommendations."

"I'd rather keep this local. Give my business to someone who needs it and not worry about some city outfit possibly messing this up."

Shadow thought for a moment. "Maybe I do know of someone else local." She told him about Jack Hancock's new job at the café. "What if Jack would cater the dinner? He's a very good cook—"

"If you like *coq au vin*," Grey said, his gaze following the bellhop's cart to the elevators. "According to Logan, all he serves is fancy French stuff."

"I'm sure he has more range than that. Do you have something against him?"

"Only by word of mouth. You should hear Tobias and Willy."

"Well, I'm not inclined to take the word of a couple of cowhands who don't know a thing about cooking—or weddings, for that matter."

He looked at Shadow again. "They'll be there, though. I don't want to see the event spoiled by another fistfight."

"I'm sure that won't be an issue. Let me talk to Jack. I can probably negotiate a good price, save us—you—some money."

Grey studied her. "Something else on your mind?" He must have noticed her growing sense of unease.

Shadow tensed. How could they be worrying about the rehearsal dinner when they still hadn't discussed the most important person, now, in both their lives? Going to Wilson Cattle was only a beginning.

"Ava," she said. "*How* do we let her know you're her father? What should we say?"

Grey had no answer for that, either.

And after Ava knew, where would they all be?

CHAPTER SIXTEEN

ON MONDAY MORNING Grey drove over to Farrier. Finn's help was more than welcome, but the sheriff's office, the long arm of the law in Stewart County, moved slowly at times and Grey didn't have time to waste.

Finn wasn't the one who'd lost so many cattle. When the sheriff had left his office for a minute, Grey had gotten a brief look at his list of registrations for white Ford trucks like the one the rustlers had used, and Grey had decided to check out the few he'd seen on the list in the nearby town. Whether Finn liked it or not—and it was more than likely not, given privacy issues and his reaction to Grey's "interview" with Calvin Stern—and in spite of Shadow's objections last weekend, he would talk to several people, see what he could come up with.

Grey had only one place left to visit when he headed for the Bar B&J ranch.

He hoped this wouldn't prove, like the others, to be a dead end.

Unfortunately, Fred Miller didn't cooperate.

He met Grey's truck before it even turned into the rutted driveway—which boasted a metal gate at the road. The gate was closed. Miller stood behind it, arms folded on his chest. He must have seen Grey approaching. With graying hair and hard blue eyes, he wasn't a tall man but he was broad and obviously fit.

"What can I do for you?"

Grey tipped his hat. "Name's Grey Wilson. My family owns Wilson Cattle."

"I know of it. I'm not in the market to buy cows—if that's why you're here."

Grey put the truck in Park then stepped out.

"Maybe you could open this gate, and we can talk."

"Maybe I won't," Miller said, standing his ground. "State your business."

Grey took off his Stetson then resettled it. "Some of my cattle have gone missing. Three guys with a white truck and stock trailer cut my fence and took off with them. Several times now. The other night I saw them again—and got their license plate number, or part of it."

Miller's gaze hardened. "What's that have to do with me? How'd you get my name?"

"Motor Vehicles tells me that a white truck fitting that description belongs to you."

Miller laughed. "And hundreds of other people in this state."

"Not that many in Stewart County with the partial plate numbers I have," Grey said. And none with the markings he was looking for. "How about letting me see it?" Maybe the truck or trailer would have dents to match the ones Grey had seen.

"Sorry, this is private property. You'd be trespassing."

"Not if you let me in."

Miller shook his head. "I own a white Ford, sure. That's all I can tell you." He turned away from the gate. "Unless the sheriff shows up here, I'm done."

Grey turned back to his truck, wishing now that he'd pursued the white rig to its destination, after all. Taken another chance on getting his head blown off.

Finn just might do that for him. He wouldn't be happy about this.

If Fred Miller had anything to do with the

rustlers, or was one of them himself, he'd probably get rid of that white truck—and any other evidence that would solve this thing.

JENNA WAITED FOR David in the hallway just outside his suite of high-floor offices in downtown Kansas City. Traffic on her way in had been stop and go, either wild or bumper-to-bumper, and her nerves were quaking. On the doors to the reception area a row of black, fancy letters outlined in gold announced the firm's name: The Regis/Mellon Group. Below, all the partners and their titles were listed. David's name was not among them.

Jenna could feel his pain at the snub he'd received, his sense of failure. A part of her still loved him, but she was also angry. Still boiling mad, in fact. She'd been as devoted to his career advancement as David was. But what had she been to him, after all? Just a convenience, someone who maintained their home, entertained his colleagues, always put him first?

That was her own fault, and now he was moving west, leaving her behind.

Yet she wasn't only mad at herself. She never had been, even when she'd first shifted from grief to anger. This was also

David's fault. He'd been so emotionally distant throughout their marriage, taken her for granted. He hadn't held up his end of the bargain.

She smoothed a hand, cool and moist, over the skirt of her navy blue suit. She'd softened the severe look with a white ruffled top and had worn her pearl earrings, an anniversary gift.

The light flashed above the elevator and the doors slid open. David stepped out, along with several other men. He touched the shoulder of his nearest colleague and gestured toward Jenna. "I'll be right in, Greg."

He waited until the others had disappeared through the glass doors and down a hallway to the left. David's office was there, too, Jenna remembered, although she hadn't been here in some time. Years ago they'd occasionally met for lunch or an after-hours dinner, a date night. But eventually he'd seemed to lose interest in being with her, and she'd stopped coming to the office. If she'd paid more attention to signs like that, maybe she wouldn't have been so blindsided by his departure.

He shifted his briefcase from one hand to the other. "What is it, Jenna?"

She squared her shoulders. Her days of prowling the house like a caged animal were over. David wasn't the only one who mattered. "I hoped we could talk—for as long as it takes."

"I have clients all afternoon. But I've been meaning to call you. I've retained Greg Sullivan—our newest *partner*—to handle the divorce. Do you have a lawyer?"

"No," she said. Until recently, she hadn't been able to do anything except mourn. Since her overnight stay with Shadow and Ava, she'd focused on getting herself together. She hadn't thought about lawyers—except the one who'd left her.

"I'm sorry, Jenna, but you need to hire someone. Maybe I was the only one to see that we were going wrong. Maybe I should have tried harder—or told you how unhappy I'd become. But if you're hoping we can reconcile…" He gazed at the receptionist's desk inside the glass then back at Jenna. "I've already moved out, and I don't want anything from the house. You should decide soon where you want to go. Once an agreement is reached, it will have to go on the market."

"I understand that, but—" Jenna caught his sleeve. "Is that all I was to you? Part of some agreement we'll both have to sign? Right now you're still my husband, I'm still your wife. I can't believe you've just stepped out of our life together—" Her voice shook, not with sorrow but with the hot anger she'd carried with her from Shawnee Mission. "How could you do that, David? I *loved* you."

In such a short time, it was as if there'd never been anything personal, or intimate, between them. She hardly recognized this man she'd married, had laughed and talked and shared friends with, dreamed of sharing a future with, a future far better than her unhappy past. A man she had loved with all her heart.

He looked at the floor. His voice sounded tight. "I love you, too, Jen, but our marriage is over. I'm not coming back."

She stiffened. "I don't want you back."

Until she said the words, Jenna hadn't known she wanted to say them, yet there they were, as if she'd rehearsed them. Those words were the reason she'd come here, cloaked in her righteous anger.

The receptionist was staring at them. David made a strangled sound. Jenna had finally gotten his attention, but that didn't seem to matter now. She studied him, his dark hair and gray-blue eyes, as he straightened his earnest tie, shot the cuffs of his custom dress shirt and walked through the door.

Without a qualm, Jenna watched him go, then summoned the elevator that would take her downstairs.

And left the building.

Left him.

"I WENT TO see David today." As Jenna told her, over dinner, about their conversation, Shadow saw a growing acceptance in her sister's eyes. She'd always thought Jenna had the best of all worlds: a loving husband, a beautiful home, financial security. Shadow had envied her. She hadn't realized something was missing. "I could hardly believe the words came from my own mouth," Jenna finished, "but in that one second I knew I wouldn't take him back if he begged me."

"Oh, Jen. I'm so glad you confronted him—had your say. I'm sure you'll be able to work things out with the divorce. I can see how much better you feel already—even better than the last time I saw you."

Jenna nodded. "I really do." She arched an eyebrow. "Now the question becomes—

what do I do next? I could look for another admin position like I had before, but that was so long ago. When I married David, we decided I shouldn't work outside the home because we wanted to have a baby." Her expression dimmed.

"I know how badly you wanted that."

"And I wanted to help him get ahead first. Once he made partner, I thought… But then there wasn't a baby, after all, and there's nothing else I know how to do except to run my home—the one I won't have for much longer."

"That's what Mama said." Shadow put her arms around her sister. She hugged her while Jenna struggled to control her emotions.

"You've been a great wife. And I know you would make a great mom—and you still can be. You did so well with Ava when we were there."

"That was my privilege. I loved having her with us, and you, too, but you were right to bring her home. You can forget the whole adoption thing. Now all we need to do is convince Ava that was the best decision for her."

"I'm hoping Grey will help with that." Shadow thought for another moment, but she wasn't ready to confide in her sister about Kansas City or the plan to tell Ava about her father. "Jen, remember when we were growing up and you always wanted to do something with art? You filled pages with drawings of elegant rooms, fashions... I always admired your talent."

"I wouldn't call that a talent. More like doodling."

"You're being too modest."

Jenna pulled away to meet her gaze. "I was never very good," she said. "Thanks for trying to support me, but no wonder I didn't follow up."

"But you did, Jen. Your home is gorgeous. You did that all by yourself."

"I did," she admitted. "I really like decorating, making things come together, choosing colors—adding those final touches with just the right accessories."

Shadow gauged her expression. Jenna's whole face had lit up as she spoke.

"And now David would sell the house you worked so hard on? Can't you keep it as part of your settlement?"

"I wouldn't be able to afford the mortgage, the maintenance. I'd have to let the pool service go, but I wouldn't want to deal with that myself. No, I need to be realistic. There's too much upkeep involved with that house. But you know what?" she said. "You were right. I'll be just fine. If I could face David, tell him exactly how I feel, I can do anything. You wouldn't want to help me look for a new place to live, would you?"

"Of course I will. Just let me know when you're ready." Shadow paused. "You can have fun creating a new home, but why not take that interest even further? Turn it into a new career."

"You mean become a decorator myself?" For another moment she looked doubtful before she suddenly smiled. "You know what? I just might."

Jenna had already grown from the frightened woman grieving for her broken marriage into someone who could look forward to the future—quite possibly a bright future—on her own. Shadow couldn't hold herself up as any kind of model, but she had already made her way in the world, was raising her daughter and had started Mother Comfort. She would never be dependent on someone else again, and she intended to shield Ava from the kind of poverty Shadow had known as a girl. And yet, something about the change in Jenna made Shadow wonder if something was missing in her own life, too…

HOLDING STORMY ON her lap the next day, Ava stared straight ahead as her mother drove under an archway of antlers with a sign that read Wilson Cattle Company. Ava's frown darkened. The dusty driveway seemed even longer than the trip from Barren and she wondered why they were here. Her mother hadn't said much except that they were going to visit someone and Ava didn't need to go to summer day camp that day. She looked nervous, too.

Ava clutched Stormy tighter to her. She had a growing knot in the pit of her stomach, and she didn't know why. She was happy to miss camp, and though she'd never been on a ranch before, that wasn't a bad thing; Ava loved animals, especially horses.

She spotted several on either side of the long driveway, grazing in the fields, and she wanted to stop and look at each one. She saw chocolate-brown bays, a lighter horse whose hide flashed golden in the sun, even a scattered few with spots everywhere. *Paints* one of her books called them. Yet the closer they came to the big ranch house, the more tense she got and the more pale her mother looked.

"Who are we coming to see?" Ava asked.

Her mother's voice trembled. "The man you saw at my house," she said and Ava's stomach fluttered. She'd wondered about him. "His name is Grey. Wilson," her mom added. It was the last name Ava had seen on that arch above the driveway. "He owns this place."

"Should I call him Mr. Wilson?"

Shadow hesitated. "We'll let him decide."

When they got close to the house, the man was already standing on the porch. Her mother slowed down but kept driving, past the front steps and around to the back where she parked. She didn't get out right away, and it looked like she was thinking really hard about something. Ava's stomach took another spin. After a moment or two, Grey Wilson came out the back door onto the smaller, rear porch.

Finally, her mom got out of the car and Ava followed. The man glanced down at her. "Welcome," he said, nodding at Ava and Stormy in her arms. "Who's your friend? He looks like one of my horses."

"Stormy." Her eyes focused on a point

just past his shoulder. He was tall with light brown hair but she couldn't see his eyes with the sun in her face. "I don't remember, but my grandma says she gave him to me when I was born."

"He's a nice start," Grey Wilson said, but Ava didn't know what he meant. He cleared his throat. "You two want to come inside? Or stay out here to…talk?"

Ava thought he looked as uneasy as her mother.

"Out here is fine. Oh, before we talk, did I tell you on the phone?" her mother asked. "Jack has agreed to cater the rehearsal dinner. He has all kinds of ideas, so we'll probably have to rein him in, but I like most of them. I don't know if you will." Her mom was talking too much, the way she always did when she was upset about something. She fished a piece of paper from her pocket, but he didn't take it. "This is what Jack came up with."

Her mom kept going. "He's trying out a new menu at the café right now, hoping to impress his boss. He hopes we'll like his suggestions, too." She smiled but it looked phony to Ava. "Actually, Mama seems to like working for him and Bertie. I may have detected a new spring in her step the other day when I went to help her pack up again at the farm."

A short silence followed. Was he mad? Or just wondering why her mom kept rambling about something so boring?

"Let's walk out to the barn." He glanced at Ava as he came down the steps. "You okay with that?"

She nodded, then held up Stormy as if to prove the point, but Ava had never been anywhere near a real horse before, not even at the Kansas State Fair every summer. She always begged her mother or Aunt Jenna to tour the horse barns, but then she'd chicken out. Their size was intimidating.

When they got close to the barn, she wrinkled her nose. "What's that?"

Grey Wilson laughed. "To me, nectar of the gods," he said. "Hay, horse flesh, oats and leather. Well, and manure. That's probably what you're reacting to." He led them to the nearby corral fence. "Once you get used to it, you'll probably love that smell, too." He pointed toward a full wheelbarrow of brown stuff with straw sticking up here and there. "Cody? Where are you? Come move this. Now!"

A younger guy with long legs loped out of the barn, blinking as if he'd been asleep. He tucked his plaid shirt into his jeans then tipped his straw hat at Ava and her mom. "Sorry, ma'am, miss. Meant to do this earlier."

They waited until he disappeared with the wheelbarrow around the side of the barn, muttering as he went. Then Grey Wilson said, "Well?" to her mother. "Who wants to go first?"

With a too-bright look in her eyes, Mom drew Ava close, as she used to do when they lived at the apartment. Ava remembered the day she'd told her they had to move—to Aunt Jenna's. That had been good news for Ava, except that she'd had to leave Hilga, her babysitter since she was born, yet her mom had acted as if she was trying to shield her from something bad. She hadn't tried to talk to Ava about anything that serious since she took her to the new house. But maybe that was about to change. Ava stiffened against her.

"Do you remember when you were little? And you always asked me—all the time— who your daddy was?"

"Yes," Ava said, her gaze darting from

her mom to Grey Wilson. Her heart started to pound. "You never told me. When I got bigger, I stopped asking but I still wondered—because I knew I must have one. Somewhere," she insisted. "Everybody does."

"I'm sorry for that, but I couldn't tell you then, sweetie. He and I weren't…together, and I thought we never would be. I didn't want you to feel bad because we wouldn't be able to see him."

Ava's stomach hurt even worse. "He didn't want me? You always said he would."

Grey Wilson hunkered down until they were level with each other to meet her eyes. "Of course he did." He touched her shoulder, his hand strong and warm even through her shirt. "Who wouldn't want you, Ava? But your mom is right. There were grown-up reasons that kept her from telling you about…" He paused and Ava kept looking into his eyes. They weren't in the sun now, so she could see them clearly. The same blue-green as her eyes. When he finally said "…me," the lone word wasn't necessary.

Neither was what her mother said next. "Grey is your father, Ava."

"Wow." She couldn't breathe. She pulled free from his light touch on her shoulder, turned her back on him—on her mother, too—and, forgetting her hesitation about the horses, ran inside the barn, dropping Stormy in the dirt behind her.

She didn't know what to make of this.

Or of the tears that clogged her throat and were running down her face.

I have a father. My dad is Grey Wilson.

CHAPTER SEVENTEEN

SHADOW AND GREY STOOD, looking after her. "Well, that was pretty ham-handed on both our parts," he said. "Guess there's no handbook for this kind of thing, is there?"

Or for telling you that Ava is your child.

"No, and I wish there had been some easier way. For you and her."

"She was crying," Grey added, his voice tight. "I kind of feel like crying myself." He turned toward Shadow and caught sight of the tears coursing down her own cheeks. Without hesitation, he drew her to him and they held each other, clinging as if through the closeness of their bodies they might find some better answer, some way to soften the reality for Ava. "I hope we didn't just traumatize her. Bringing her from Jenna's house to yours probably shook her up before. She hasn't had much time to make sense of that, either."

"I'll go to her in a minute," Shadow said.

"Let's leave her to take that in. She told you how she feels. She's wanted a daddy all her life, Grey. But I feel so guilty. It was me who kept her from you—and you from her."

"I didn't understand all your reasons until Kansas City, but…" The kitchen door banged shut in the distance, and his nephew, Nick, rushed out onto the porch.

"Are you done talking?" he yelled, racing down the steps.

Grey ruffled Nick's blondish hair, so similar to Grey's sister's. He had Logan's deep blue eyes. "We're done," he said, "but I think the little girl who came to see us might like to meet someone more her age. Nick, why don't you go into the barn? Her name is Ava. You can introduce her to Red and the others."

"And I could show her my horse—" Nick stopped. "Oh, I forgot he's not here. My other ones are, though." Nick edged away from Grey's side, obviously forgetting that the quarter horses at Wilson Cattle weren't really his. "We have carrots in the barn," Nick said as he ran off, then stopped to pick up Stormy from the ground before he disappeared into the barn. Nick called back, "We can feed 'em, right, Uncle Grey?"

"Just watch your fingers." Grey gazed after him. So did Shadow. Finally, hands on his hips, he said, "Leave it to the kids, huh? I hope she'll be all right with Nick. He comes on pretty strong sometimes, but maybe she shouldn't be alone just now."

Shadow managed a half smile. "Thanks for asking him over."

Grey shook his head. "I didn't. Logan dropped him off. He had to go into town with Blossom for her doctor's appointment, so I told them I'd watch Nick," he said. "That was after we set up a time for Ava to come here, but last-minute for them, and I didn't want to say no to Logan—he's taking Blossom out for lunch, too."

"No, I'm glad Nick's here. Ava hasn't made many—or, should I say, any—new friends yet."

Grey watched the doors to the barn. "We'd better supervise. There's no telling what two kids can get into in there." He turned back to her. "Before we do, I need to say this—when you first told *me* about Ava, I was shocked, yes, even angry that I'd been left out. And that's just for starters. When I actually saw her, I was stunned. Ever since, I've been thinking how to handle this. I've studied every picture of her in the baby book you lent me, learned a little bit of what her early life was like, but that's not enough. I want to play a role from now on—a big one—in Ava's life. I won't be shoved aside again."

Shadow held her breath. "What exactly does that mean?"

"I never saw her take her first steps, I never heard her speak for the first time, I never got to hear her say *dada* or learn who that little person was inside her head—all the opinions and interests, the favorite dolls, first storybooks, her love of horses. I never held her in my arms or took care of her when she was sick." He drew a harsh breath. "I'm her *father*. I always have been. I want to be the daddy she thought she never had, Shadow."

She blinked, not sure how to react. Her throat had gotten tight, and besides, what could she say? Grey was right. He was being so good with the children, so tender with Ava.

"I know," she said at last. "I want you to be part of Ava's life."

And mine, she thought.

Maybe they wouldn't need to go to court about custody. Grey hadn't even mentioned that, so Shadow decided the fear must have been in her mind.

Could they put Jared's death behind them and be together again? A family. She felt half-afraid to believe.

GREY STROLLED INTO the barn. The children were up ahead of him in the aisle. In a shaft of sun and dust motes, they walked along the row of stalls on the right-hand side, stopping at each one to greet the horse inside. Nick knew them all by name and several of them from the short rides Grey gave him whenever he came to visit. A year ago a quick walk around the outdoor corral with Grey holding the reins would have been enough to set Olivia off, but she now seemed resigned to the notion that her son was a little cowboy in the making—and didn't need to be overly protected.

Logan had been giving him lessons and Nick seemed to be a natural; he was already good at the trot and would soon learn how to canter the horse on his own. After that, Grey supposed he'd be galloping all over the Circle H and Wilson Cattle.

"Look at this one!" Ava drew Nick to the next stall. "He's got yellow hair."

Ava was several inches taller than Nick and was two years older, yet their age difference didn't seem to matter. They were already bonding through their mutual love of horses.

Grey smiled. He didn't know what Nick had first said to Ava, but whatever it was, her tears were now drying on her cheeks.

"That's Bucky, for buckskin," Nick told her, obviously the expert. "Be careful. You shouldn't run or you'll scare them. And he bites. So does my daddy's horse—I mean, Grandpa Sam's. Cyclone doesn't have any manners," Nick said, which was true. The young black colt at the Circle H did need to be properly trained.

Grey glanced at Shadow, who had followed him in. Resenting her for the ten-year silence about Ava hadn't gotten him anywhere. Maybe he should take a page from the children's book.

"Nick, the carrots are in the tack room fridge. If you guys do a good job, you can ride later."

"We'll be right outside," Shadow said, not seeming too comfortable with his suggestion.

He hastened to reassure her. "I know Ava

hasn't ridden before. I won't let anything happen to her. If she had a bad experience the first time—"

"That wouldn't be good."

"No it wouldn't. She'll be fine, Shadow. I promise."

Satisfied that the kids would be safe in the barn, he walked her out again into the sunlight. Grey propped one booted foot on a lower board of the corral fence. "So," he said, "what exactly are we going to do?"

"I wish I knew. We have to do what's right, but figuring that out isn't easy."

Grey gazed at the corral where Nick and Ava would ride that afternoon. Something inside him had settled but he wasn't as sure about Shadow.

"I've dreamed of this," he said. "Having kids, seeing them run all over this ranch the way Logan and his brother Sawyer and I did when we were growing up. Like Nick, we were always either here or at the Circle H."

"Little cowboys," she murmured.

He cleared his throat. "Now Ava's here— and she's mine. I can't tell you how that feels, seeing her at Wilson Cattle. My home, and my family's. I want to see her enjoy this place. Not only today, but just like I did then. Like I still do."

"I understand. But, Grey, being here is so hard for me. It makes me remember—"

"Jared."

"Yes, and my father too. Wilson Cattle paid our bills—that is, whenever he was working." She frowned. "He must have been hired and fired a dozen times. I can still hear my mother crying about that, long before we lost Jared here."

"Sure, our fathers went back and forth for years," Grey said. "But you know why your dad got fired. He didn't show up. Or he went home early. His work ethic wasn't the best, to put it mildly." Which reminded him of Cody. Grey was still trying to re-educate him. "He sat on his— He was lazy, Shadow. You were well aware of that."

"That's true, and I'm also aware that your father always took him back. We were grateful." Shadow paused. "That was very nice of him, Grey. But it's still painful."

Grey nodded. "He felt sorry for your mother. For all you kids." He traded one foot for the other on the rail. "I hate to say this, but your dad also took money from the ranch office. He sold a new saddle that wasn't his for cash once, then claimed he'd never seen it. And still, my father gave him another chance. For your sake, too. He liked you, Shadow. He would have come around, about us, but not until we were older." Grey's mouth tightened. "I want Ava to grow up— the rest of the way—without the turmoil I had, with a better role model than you had. I hope you'll agree that's me."

"I want to, Grey. I do, except—"

His spirits sank. "It always comes back to that, doesn't it? It thought the trip to Kansas City helped. Our talk about the shooting, about Ava's birth. I kissed you," Grey reminded her. "You kissed me back. I'd hoped we were closing in on the truth about Jared."

"But what if you never find that?"

Grey sighed. "Even if I don't, we'll still have Ava to consider."

Nick and Ava chose that instant to burst out of the barn. "Uncle Grey! You gotta see how much Nugget likes Ava. I already brushed Cinders. Can we ride now?"

His mind still half in the hotel bar where he'd thought they were getting somewhere at last, Grey stepped away from the fence. So this was what it would be like to have Ava here and friends with Nick. To be a real dad.

A good ride always cleared his head. As a boy, that had kept him away from his parents' constant tug-of-war. He didn't want to go back there with Shadow. Still, he knew how she felt about the ranch. No matter how he and Shadow managed this, he vowed he wouldn't go to that same place with Ava.

"Sure, you can ride," he said. "I'll saddle up for you." Nick started to protest but Grey held up a hand. "My place, my rules." He tried not to look at Shadow. "We'll give Ava her first lesson. Next time you can both learn to tack up your horses."

Today he would let Ava use the old, worn and well-loved saddle Grey had first owned. He kept a newer, child-sized rig here for Nick. As soon as he figured things out with the rustling that threatened his ranch, he'd buy Ava a saddle that custom-fit her, think about getting her a gentle mare, a first gift from him as her father.

He had a lot of time to make up for.

He wouldn't let Shadow stand in his way.

AFTER THE KIDS finished their ride—Ava's very first!—they were hungry. Starving, they both claimed. Grey took them up to the house with Shadow lagging behind.

Watching Ava on Nugget being led around the corral by Grey while Shadow "baby-sat" Stormy had eased her fears for Ava's safety and brought tears to Shadow's eyes. How often in the past ten years had she thought of a scene like that? Of her and Grey, married and being parents together? She'd told him as much in Kansas City. They both wanted the best for Ava. And yet, for Shadow there was still Jared, the memory of his death here. Because of that tragedy, she might never be able to try out the fantasy even when she yearned for that second chance with Grey.

In the kitchen she hung back, letting Grey prepare the meal. He moved about the room with the ease and familiarity of someone who had always lived at the ranch. Like hers, his upbringing had been fraught with conflict, yet this was the house he'd shared with his father, learning Everett Wilson's management style, always knowing he was part of this place. That it was his legacy, his to inherit one day. And unlike Shadow with her family's farm, he'd always wanted it to be.

Jared had never expected, or hoped, to take over the farm. Neither had Derek, although he still lived there—or, at least, he would until the eviction. She was surprised she hadn't heard from him since he'd first seen Ava.

At the kitchen table she nursed the cup of fresh coffee Grey had put in front of her. For the kids he made chocolate milk and quickly grilled hot dogs. He offered to fix Shadow a hamburger, but she wasn't hungry so Grey put both sizzling patties on his plate. Their earlier talk obviously hadn't put a dent in his appetite, although she knew he'd been hurt by her lack of trust.

After they ate, the kids sprawled on pillows on the family room floor to watch TV, and Grey showed Shadow the dining room, which looked just as she remembered it from the days when she and Grey were together and she'd sometimes come to the ranch for Sunday dinner.

"This table can seat a dozen people," he said, "but by my count we could have twice that many guests." Logan and Blossom hadn't wanted to exclude anyone. This event would not be just for the wedding party, small as it was. Friends were invited, too. Neighbors would come to the reception after the ceremony. The entire casual weekend would include everybody close to them and even some not-so-close newer acquaintances who'd recently moved into Barren.

From the doorway beside him, Shadow took stock of the room, trying to force her mind from her concern for Ava. If they stuck to this topic, maybe Jared wouldn't come up again. "Why not move the kitchen table in here, then? If you shift the big one over, they would both fit, and all you'd need would be more chairs."

"I think there are extras stored in the attic. My mother left her family china here when she moved out, so we won't have to buy or rent any, and there's plenty of flatware. What else?"

"Table linens. A centerpiece for each table. Candles."

Grey winced. His shoulder brushed hers, spreading warmth through her body. "I'll leave all that to you. I could handle a cookout, man the grill and fill a cooler with ice and drinks, but whatever you want is fine, as long as it's not fussy."

Shadow sent him an arch look. "Really?"

Grey's expression quickly changed from teasing to shuttered. Shadow couldn't fool herself. He was hurt again, and she didn't know what would come of that with Ava.

Always, because of Jared, she had a sense of unease at this ranch that sent shivers down her spine, as if he might pull up again at the front steps with that gun in his hand.

Through the archway from the dining room, past the family room and a front parlor that no one used, was the porch… Shadow shivered again. She'd come to the ranch twice now in recent weeks, but the sight of those steps never failed to rouse the memory of losing her brother in such a violent manner.

"I'll spend some time on Pinterest tonight," she finally said. "That should give me more ideas for table settings and so on."

"Then you'll let me see them?"

"Of course."

Shadow would have left then, but Ava and Nick's episode wasn't over and the children didn't want the day to end. Shadow was exhausted from everything that had passed between her and Grey, but for Ava's sake, she could stay awhile longer. Ava was enjoying her new friend, sharing the sofa with him, laughing at their show. The whole scene lulled Shadow into a false sense of belonging here, something she hadn't allowed herself to think about, or want, in years.

A fresh wave of guilt coursed through her. How could she deny Grey this new opportunity to be with Ava as often as he wished? To let their daughter live her own fantasy on this very ranch? She would be tearing her child apart, just as Grey's parents had fought over him and Olivia.

But how could she suppress her own feelings for the ranch? Force herself to come here over and over again?

Maybe, since telling Grey about Ava's birth, she could at least explain tonight about the years when she'd tried to care for Ava without him. Maybe then he would be able to understand her concerns.

"Grey, can we talk outside?"

"Sure."

On the front porch, Shadow tried not to look at the foot of the stairs. She put her back to the driveway, leaned against the railing and folded her arms—as if that could protect her from his somber gaze.

"You know about my decision to keep Ava—in large part because of you—but I'd like to tell you about the years after that. They weren't easy, either, not that I expected them to be, but I never regretted my decision. The only thing I regret now is that I didn't tell you."

"Go ahead," he said with a glance at the lighted rooms inside. "The kids have another twenty minutes or so before their show ends."

"When Ava was a newborn, I left the Merritts' home—of course—and moved with her to Kansas City, where we had a small apartment. So small I could reach almost everything without taking many steps. The best thing I could say about it was that, however shabby it appeared, it was clean.

"After Ava was asleep, I would lay out the bills on the coffee table and try to figure which ones I could pay. I was working as an aide at a nursing home, and I'd met this amazing woman named Hilga Olsen who took care of Ava for practically nothing because she reminded her of her grandchildren who lived far away. Hilga was too proud to admit she couldn't afford the trip to upstate New York to see them."

Her elderly neighbor across the hall had become Ava's unofficial nanny from the day they'd moved in. Hilga wouldn't hear of her leaving the baby with anyone else, and certainly Shadow couldn't afford day care. Hilga had been a lifesaver, the grandmother to Ava that Shadow's mother was not then, a stable, kindly presence whom Shadow couldn't possibly replace.

"You *still* didn't ask your parents for help?" She was grateful he didn't add, "Or me."

"No, but by the time Ava was five and a half, I wondered how much longer we could hold on. We were still together, and that was all that really mattered to me. But the bills kept piling up. I'd taken night courses to complete my GED, but there was no way I could do more than that. And I was relying on Hilga far too much already.

"I considered asking for extra hours at the nursing home, but I wouldn't gain that much at my pay rate. At times I even wondered if I'd made the right choice, not in keeping Ava but in moving away from Barren, from any possible family support. I was almost done paying back the Merritts for my prenatal care, at least, but I needed to further my education, take some courses toward an associate's degree so I could move up into management. I really liked the work, liked helping people Hilga's age, although my patients were mostly in far worse shape."

Grey's expression softened. "That experience prepared you to open your agency here. I have to admire your grit, Shadow."

She gave him a sad smile and continued. "Then I got behind in rent and found out the building was being sold. We needed a new place anyway—Ava and I were sharing my double bed at that point—but downtown Kansas City isn't exactly affordable."

"Not very comfortable," Grey muttered, "for either of you."

"She was a restless sleeper, too. She had quite a kick," Shadow said. "Anyway, I ended up suggesting to Hilga that we try to find an apartment for all three of us. Splitting rent, we might have even been able to find something in a nice neighborhood with a good school nearby. Though Hilga's finances weren't much of an improvement over mine."

"So, what happened?"

"One night, Hilga knocked at my door. I was still hopeful that maybe we would work things out."

"From your tone, I take it you didn't."

"As soon as she walked in, I could tell something was wrong. Her hands were knotted together, and she told me her son and

his wife had invited her to live with them."
Shadow swallowed. "She would have her
own room and bath in Utica, and be with her
grandchildren. How could I compete with
that? With family? She'd had some health
problems, too. She would rely on her son and
his wife. 'No matter how good friends are,'
she said, 'they eventually turn away. They
have to think of themselves.'" She paused.
"Hilga told me I needed to think of Ava. It
wasn't a criticism—and I knew how much
she loved her—but I was heartbroken."

"That must have been hard," Grey said.

"That was the only time I thought of calling my mother—when Hilga left. I wanted
to find out if she, at least, had changed her
mind about me, about Ava. I wanted to
beg. But my father was still there, probably sitting in his recliner watching reruns. I
couldn't ask for their help."

"You could have called me then, Shadow."

"That didn't seem possible, either. Not
with Jared still between us. But Hilga's comment about family stuck with me. That's
when I turned to Jenna. If she were willing to help with Ava, even for a little while,
I could get on my feet. Ava loved her occasional visits with her, and if Jenna's husband

would agree, Ava could begin first grade, not in a good school but a great one. I took a deep breath. And dialed their number."

Without a word, Grey walked toward her and took her in his arms. "You had a rougher time than I might have imagined. That was my fault, too, Shadow. I should have been there. I should have known, somehow."

"I don't blame you, Grey."

"Not for that," he said, but he drew her closer.

Shadow's head dropped like a wilted flower onto his shoulder as if she couldn't hold herself upright any longer. She couldn't move. All the years of being alone, of caring for Ava without him, seemed to condense into this moment, Grey's lips on her hair. He brushed it aside, his other hand on her shoulder, then slowly, sweetly, he kissed his way down her cheek to the line of her jaw and then to the corner of her mouth.

"I'm sorry," he whispered. "You shouldn't have had full responsibility for Ava—struggled like that—but you did a great job, Shadow. She's a wonderful little girl. And somehow, we'll make this work. For her," he murmured. "And for us."

Shadow wanted to make it work, too. But

there was still Jared. And, in that moment, she hoped Grey did find proof that he was not to blame. That he could somehow prove his innocence. Then, in the next instant, she stopped thinking at all.

Grey's mouth took hers, not light and quick this time. He kissed her with the gulf of years between them breached at last, with that intense, soul-reaching passion she had never forgotten. Neither had he, she knew, as she let him take her deeper, then farther still, as if in the joining of their mouths they might find forgiveness. For each other. Find love again.

CHAPTER EIGHTEEN

GREY WAS LIKE most men. When something troubled him, he took action. A suburban guy might mow the lawn or tinker with his car, but as always, Grey went riding. Tonight, he had a purpose. And he needed to let his thoughts settle about Ava's first visit to the ranch, his impasse with Shadow earlier and the way he'd kissed her as if his very life hung in the balance. After that, she certainly knew how he still felt about her.

He could only hope she'd soon change her view of him regarding Jared. Clearing his name had become even more important, and not only to prove he was innocent in the shooting. If he was guilty, he'd have nothing to offer her or Ava except a tainted family background. A father who might become a convicted felon. Which would be far worse than losing the ranch. He didn't want that to happen, either.

He nudged Big Red through the last of

the thick brush at the top of the ridge. From below, he heard the familiar, soft lowing of cattle, the shifting of hooves and the far-off munching of rich grass. Dismounting, he tied Red to the nearest tree, then lay down on his belly a few feet away, binoculars in hand.

As he swept the area, a sudden movement caught his attention. Over the milling sounds of the herd, a dark shape appeared and another horse ambled through the cows and calves to the fence line. There, the man in the saddle climbed off the horse—which looked oddly familiar, even in the dark— and snipped the wire. Not in the same spot as before, but close.

Grey swore under his breath. He hadn't lost any more cattle—yet—but he also hadn't recovered the others. Now, clearly, he was about to lose more. In his mind he was already doing the new calculations. If he didn't put an end to the rustling—no real thanks to Finn, thus far—and never mind any necessary loans Grey needed, the ranch would be even deeper in the red, for sure.

Like Shadow in Kansas City years ago, Grey had barely managed to pay most of the bills last month, and he was in danger of just hanging on until he couldn't any longer.

When his father and stepmother came for Logan and Blossom's wedding, Grey would have to admit he'd failed.

And what about Ava? The ranch should be hers to inherit one day—assuming Wilson Cattle still existed.

The guy was through the fence now. Grey jumped to his feet. Catching Red's bridle, he untied the horse from the tree, swung up into the saddle and cantered down the hill. There wasn't a stock trailer or a white truck in sight, but someone, he saw, was ready for the others.

In a flash Grey recognized him, as well as the horse he rode. All along, had this been not only personal but an inside job?

Grey didn't call to him until he'd reached the bottom of the hill. Then his voice rang out. "Cody!"

He rode up to the fence, reined Red to a halt and leaned over the pommel. The ranch hand's gaze flew to his.

"Hey, boss." Even in the dark Grey could see his startled expression, but Cody could be brazen as well as careless, and he made an attempt at an alibi. "Where'd you come from? I was on my way back to the barn when I noticed this piece of broken fence here. Stopped to mend it till tomorrow when I'll do the job proper-like."

"I just watched you cut this fence. Why?"

Grey knew—he was obviously one of the rustlers—but he wanted to hear Cody say it, to confirm his own sense of betrayal. Cody's head jerked around, and he scanned the road. He had run out of words.

His jaw tight, Grey said, "I've treated you like a kid brother. Put up with your less-than-stellar skills on the job. I've forgiven your lapses in feeding horses, fixing this fence how many times…and this is how you repay me? Stealing the source of my livelihood? And yours," he added, "although I guess this might be more lucrative." In the distance, Grey heard the roar of an engine. Within minutes, what he imagined must be the borrowed truck and trailer would be here again.

Cody hung his head, perhaps hoping Grey would take pity on him.

"Don't move. For starters, you're fired."

He had his rifle out of the scabbard on his saddle and pulled his cell phone from his shirt pocket to call Finn. Suddenly, Cody ducked under the fence where Grey and his horse had penned him in, then broke and

ran. Grey had underestimated him again.
Grey shouted after him but Cody grabbed
Nugget's reins and was on the horse before
Grey could move.

In the few seconds it took to kick Red
into a gallop, Cody was already far ahead
of him. Grey had never seen the horse run
that fast. She was normally bomb proof and
easygoing, and she'd taken good care of Ava
that afternoon, as horses tended to do with
kids, but—he saw now—she hadn't been
spurred in the sides by Cody's metal rowels
that glinted in the night.

Grey cursed again, this time aloud. In minutes he'd exhausted his already tired horse
and lost Cody over the hill, but he wasn't
running straight for the barn as Grey expected. First a cattle rustler and now a horse
thief. He had no doubt the other men with the
stock trailer would pick him up at some pre-
arranged meeting point in case things went
wrong. Which they definitely had.

Still, Grey was glad to have a lead on his
missing cattle, if not in the mystery of Jared
Moran's death.

AVA'S MOTHER WAS trying to tuck her in for
the night, but she wasn't sleepy. She was ex-

cited after their visit to Wilson Cattle and her first horseback ride—not to mention the fact that she'd learned Grey was her father. For the first time since Ava had come to the house, she almost felt as if she belonged here. She'd rather live at the ranch, though. Maybe there she'd have a bigger room.

She eyed the bedcovers then glanced at the Hello Kitty decals on the walls. She looked at the desk that matched her bed and bureau. And had to smile.

"This was quite the day, wasn't it?" her mother asked. She had a strange look on her face. "I mean, with meeting your dad, and—"

"Know something?" Ava cut in. "I used to imagine Tim McGraw was my dad. I liked that idea—because he looks like a cowboy." She picked Stormy up off the blanket. He smelled like dust, which Ava thought was a great smell. She had to agree with Grey… her father. Maybe the adults thought she'd freak out when they told her, and at first Ava hadn't known how to feel, but this was really cool. Amazing, in fact. "Grey is, like, the most cowboy guy I could think of, even better than Tim McGraw because he's real and he's here. Do you remember when I was little and I loved that one book?"

Her mom smiled. "*Janie Wants to Be a Cowgirl*. Yes, I remember that very well. We probably read it a thousand times—and always more than once at night before you'd go to bed. You couldn't sleep without Janie," she said, "Or Stormy."

Ava wrinkled her nose. "Even after I learned to read, I liked to have you read it to me. I loved Janie! She had pink boots."

Her mother drew her close, and Ava let her. After today, she felt okay to talk again about things they'd done together. She hoped they'd do even more things with Grey Wilson. She snuggled against her mom, inhaling the scent of shampoo and a lingering trace of the same dust from the ranch yard. Grey—Dad—had said she would like all the other smells there one day, too. They were related.

"You were the most affectionate little girl I've ever known," her mom said. "My sisters never wanted to cuddle when they were small. I loved reading to you."

"I could read to *you* now."

"Yes, you could," she agreed, then her expression got serious. "Are you okay with this? Your dad and I would have told you in a more…well, better, way, but we couldn't think how. Except to say it."

"I'm okay," Ava said. "You guys did fine." She nestled closer, leaning her head against her mother's shoulder.

"Do you know how many times, since that early morning in the hospital when I first held you in my arms, I've tiptoed into your bedroom to watch you sleep?" Her voice sounded thick, and Ava felt her mother swallow. "In our apartment, then Aunt Jenna's house and now here? I always say a little prayer, Ava, because you're such a blessing to me. I love you so much, sweetie." And Ava's whole being seemed to settle into the bed, into this house, where her mother wanted her to live.

"I was mad at you for a while, but I love you too, Mom." She sat back. "Can we ask Kaitlyn to come visit sometime?" Maybe she could go with Ava one day to camp and together they could talk to those other girls, try to make friends. She hadn't tried at all before.

"Of course we can. She can stay over and we'll make pizza. We'll watch movies all night—and maybe we'll even read about Janie again. For old times' sake."

Ava giggled. "Kaitlyn would laugh at me. She thinks Stormy is a little kid's toy. She doesn't know he was my very first horse." She grinned to show she knew that was just pretend. "Grandma even picked him out for me. I like her."

Ava's lids were drooping. In a nightly ritual that had been theirs ever since she could remember, and that Ava had refused like a brat until tonight in this house, her mother kissed the top of her head, then each cheek in turn and, finally, planted a light peck on her lips. As she tucked Stormy beside Ava, she said, "Time to sleep, baby. 'Night."

But Ava opened her eyes again, and she looked around the pink and white and black room. "You did this for me. Didn't you?"

Her mom sent her a rueful smile. "I tried, yes."

"It's okay. Can we paint it, though, before Kaitlyn comes here?"

"That's a deal."

Holding Stormy, Ava relaxed into her pillows, warm and cozy under her blankets. She had a whole new life to dream about.

And Tim McGraw wasn't in it.

Amazed at the sweet moments they had shared, Shadow left Ava's room. As she tiptoed down the hall, she heard the front door open. All thought of the afternoon, of Ava learning Grey was her father, Shadow's conversation with him to explain her past struggles, even their kisses, flew out of her head as she hurried to greet her mother.

Wanda smiled. "A good day, over-all." She gestured at several boxes she'd left in the front hall. "The last of your things from my house. Most of them are just old school papers and such."

Just when Shadow thought she was asleep, Ava called out, "Good-night, Grandma."

"Good-night, Ava. Sweet dreams."

Shadow blinked. The two hadn't exactly become the best of friends, but Ava seemed to be riding high on her first visit to Wilson Cattle. To her father. After all, a dream of hers had come true—never mind Shadow's doubts about her relationship with Grey— and even Shadow's mother seemed upbeat tonight.

"I had the boxes in the car all day. I would have come sooner, but I stayed for dinner at Bertie's house. Jack can really cook." Her mother's cheeks looked strangely pink. "And would you believe, that child has actually taken to me a bit?"

"And you've taken to her," Shadow pointed out. Somehow, she'd missed that transition, but the few times she'd asked her mother to babysit, including the weekend she'd gone to Kansas City, had obviously been positive for both of them. "I'm glad you're through blaming her for being Grey's child."

"I never blamed her." She glanced at Shadow. "I blame him. Where does that leave you?"

Shadow shook her head. "I took Ava to the ranch today. Grey and I agreed beforehand that we should tell her he's her father, but I should have guessed. She and Grey bonded over horses. As you must have heard in her voice, she's excited. I wonder if she'll be able to sleep at all." Shadow smiled sadly. "Ava already loves that ranch, the very place that represents everything painful to me." She didn't have to tell her mother it was the place where her father had failed their family, where her brother had died, possibly at Grey's hand, and where she'd suffered heartbreak.

She gestured at the house she'd saved and

worked so hard for. "I'm worried Ava will want to live at Wilson Cattle."

"She hardly knows him, Shadow."

"But she will. I can hardly keep them from getting to know each other—and I wouldn't." She rubbed a stubborn knot of tension between her brows. "I hope we'll take things slow. And I have to get through Blossom and Logan's wedding—and the rehearsal dinner before that. Then I guess Grey and I will have to come up with a solid plan."

Her mother searched through her bag for her car keys. When she looked up at Shadow, it seemed clear she wanted to change the subject. "Now that I have a paycheck, I'll be able to afford a new dress. That," she said, "and some other nice things I've never had. I may even get a cell phone."

"I'm glad you like your job, Mama."

That was one worry off her mind.

Her mother's unmistakable infatuation with Jack might well be another.

JENNA HAD MADE enough mistakes in her life, the biggest one being David Collier, as it turned out, and their confrontation in his office days ago was still on her mind. Thankfully, her mood had changed from shock and grief about their broken marriage to anger and, most recently, to acceptance, to a growing interest in her future without him. Her talk with Shadow had helped.

For David, she'd given up her college education. Marrying a handsome, charming lawyer on his way up at the firm, buying the house in Shawnee Mission, spending all that effort and money to overcome her infertility had seemed the wisest course at the time, her way out of the poverty in which she and Shadow had grown up.

But she'd been wrong.

With Shadow beside her today, she parked her SUV in front of an apartment complex on the outskirts of Barren. The reality of what was happening had finally penetrated the fog in which she'd been living ever since David announced he was moving to Salt Lake City. Her visit to his office still surprised her; it had been like cleaning out the attic of her mind.

She and David had agreed that the house she had loved, the house that had taken her from her parents' farm to an upscale neighborhood, would go on the market tomorrow. Jenna would have to watch strangers drift through the rooms she had decorated, hear their criticisms of her taste. Maybe, as her Realtor strongly advised, she should leave during the showings.

"Let's do this," she said to Shadow, who went with her up the walk to the new, two-story apartment building with neat hedges and flowers in front. Honestly, she had to admire her sister. Shadow had never waited for a man to come home late for dinner or not at all, never begged for the family Jenna wished for. Even in difficult times, Shadow had made her own way. Now, so would she.

Jenna's Realtor answered her knock with a broad smile. "Come in, look around. You're going to love this place."

Jenna hesitated. Would she? Her first instinct, even after the brave self-talk she'd given herself, was to turn around and go back to her car, but the high-end model wouldn't be hers much longer, either. David had leased it for her—but in his name. Maybe, after the settlement, she would buy a sporty BMW or, if that cost too much, a sedan that would truly be hers.

Shadow squeezed her arm in support and they stepped into the apartment. Light and airy, Jenna noted. The window wall at the end of the living room looked out onto a pretty, leafy view and there was a working gas fireplace along another wall. As she wandered through the other rooms, her spirits rose.

"Two bedrooms," she said, exploring further. "I didn't expect this much space." Maybe she wouldn't miss the four bedrooms she'd had to maintain in Shawnee Mission, two of which were now empty without Shadow and Ava there.

"There's another bath for guests," Shadow pointed out. "The master has its own en suite plus the same view as you'd have from the living room. This developer does nice work."

The Realtor said, "He calls these *apartment homes*."

Would she feel at home here? There were two balconies, one off the main room and a smaller one for the master. She wouldn't feel cramped, as she'd feared.

Though small, the kitchen was well designed with stainless steel appliances. "I like this eat-in breakfast area by the windows. I'll need a new table and chairs. Maybe something retro would be fun. There should be enough space for my dining room furniture—part of it, anyway—in that corner of the living room." She pointed out a simple but pretty chandelier. She paused. "What about a pool?"

"You have the complex pool here, complete with hot tub. Gym facilities, too," the Realtor said.

Shadow took her hand. "Really, Jenna, you won't be giving up that much."

"Most people don't use what they have in a large home," the Realtor agreed. "You won't be that far from good shopping and you can always go into Kansas City."

"I'll be closer to Barren here," she heard herself say when, for years, like Shadow, she'd wanted to be the farthest she could get from her hometown.

Shadow said, "Closer to Mama, to me and Ava."

A good point. She didn't want to lose touch with her niece.

In the living room again, she lingered near the door. With a hand on the knob, ready to open it and leave, she stopped. Tons of ideas raced through her mind. She would make a home here to suit herself, and… "Shadow. Remember what you said about my 'art'?"

"You were wrong. You were very good."

"Yes. I think I was. And you were right. I

did a great job of making our house a comfortable, cozy place."

"Without a doubt," Shadow said, beginning to smile.

"I'll have to take some courses, maybe get licensed or certified—I don't even know what I'd need yet—but I think I'll make a good interior decorator."

Shadow hugged her. "I'd hoped you would make this decision. This is amazing, Jen."

"That's not to say I won't have times when I still feel down in the dumps or regretful about my marriage, but I'm not going to tumble down a hole and hide from what I might become."

The Realtor was smiling, too, and all three women high-fived each other. They walked through the apartment once more, the empty rooms echoing but filled with a promise she hadn't expected to feel. Here, Jenna could work on restoring her relationships with her family. She could begin to restore herself.

"Thanks, Shadow, for coming with me. Thanks for showing me this place," she told the Realtor. "I'll take it."

CHAPTER NINETEEN

SHADOW LOOKED AROUND the family room at Wilson Cattle, making sure the guests all had drinks and food. The few changes she'd been able to make here in the past two weeks—bright throw pillows for the sofas, clean windows, a quick coat of fresh paint for the dining room, which she'd done with Grey one night—made the old ranch house sparkle.

In the far corner of the room, Blossom stood with Nick and Logan, Logan's arm around her. As they chatted with friends, she gazed up at him with love in her warm brown eyes. She had a definite glow, in part because of her baby-to-be. Finn was here, too, but he'd spent most of his time talking to Grey, the two of them in a huddle, their faces serious. They must be discussing his missing cattle and the ranch hand who'd betrayed him.

In the archway to the dining room, Logan's

ranch hands, Tobias and Willy, stood shoulder to shoulder, eyeing the first course—a tandoori-style shrimp appetizer that was one of Jack's new specialties. She and Grey had used his mother's best china and sterling silver flatware at each place. Centerpieces of white daisies tucked among lavender hydrangeas and greenery were low enough not to prevent conversation across both tables. The dual arrangement worked out well.

The evening promised to come off without a hitch—except for Shadow. She couldn't seem to take pleasure in the coming dinner. Since their talk about Shadow's first years with Ava, and then their kisses on the front porch, she'd felt unsettled. She and Grey had been polite, even comfortable, with each other, but as they'd finalized the plans and worked together on the house to prepare for tonight, neither of them had mentioned what would come next—for Ava or for them.

Ava wasn't here tonight. Jenna was staying with her.

Shadow was just glad Derek hadn't come.

She glanced toward Grey, who was talking now with Dusty Malone, his foreman, and some other ranch hands. Grey looked even more handsome than usual in his white shirt, pressed jeans and best boots. For the occasion he'd added a gray herringbone blazer that highlighted his broad shoulders. For someone who'd said he knew little about events like this, he was doing just fine.

Outdoors, Grey had smoothly dealt with the improvised parking lot, using several of his men as valets. Inside, there were candles everywhere, shimmering and glowing as softly, as romantically, as Blossom did in her flowing cream-colored pants and glitzy top. As she sent Blossom a smile, Shadow's mother joined her, wearing a flattering new blue dress.

"That shade suits you, Mama. You look pretty."

Jack was moving through the room in his white tunic and chef's hat, carrying a tray of hot hors d'oeuvres. He turned to smile at her mother, then sidled over to them. "Mrs. Moran, may I suggest the stuffed mushroom caps?" he said smoothly, as if he served at such functions every day.

Her mother took a bite, her eyes on Jack. "Delicious." Shadow had never seen her eat a mushroom before. Mama reached next for a tiny quiche, then seemed to think better of it. "I'll stop with one before your cooking turns into ten pounds I don't need."

In front of everyone, including Shadow, Jack leaned down to kiss her cheek. "You are beautiful. To me," he murmured, adding, *"Mon petit choux."*

She blushed. "When you speak French, I just melt."

Shadow gaped at their flirtatious exchange. *Really?* Jack just grinned. He hoisted the tray a bit higher. Shadow wanted to smile at the return of what she and Blossom termed his French phase. Her mother and Jack—or Jacques—Hancock?

As soon as he moved on with his tray, Shadow said, "You're seeing him, Mama? I mean, other than when you're at Bertie's?"

Her mother's expression was all but smug. "Jack likes me and I like him. We're not that different in age," she said. "A few years, is all. Bertie says I'm the best caregiver he could ask for," she said with pride. "Since Jack's working dinners at the café every night, I'll be spending more time there."

"Mama, what is going on?"

She ignored the question and continued. "Bertie even has room for my chickens." Her gaze followed Jack across the room. "At first

Jack didn't take to them, but Bertie swayed him to our side. Jack will have all the fresh eggs he could want, and he's going to pay me for them. An added attraction, he said, for the menu at the café." She grinned. "Locally sourced food is quite the thing now."

Shadow couldn't remember the last time she'd seen her mother smile like that. "Well."

"Jack says we can probably build a good henhouse."

Shadow blinked. For the first time in a long time her mother looked excited for the future, like Jenna, so maybe Jack was that man. She could never have predicted this match, but it worked.

"Mama, I'm happy for you," she said.

Her mother waited until Jack went into the kitchen with his empty tray. She lowered her voice. "What did he mean when he called me that?"

Shadow had taken one semester of French, but she thought she had this right. "*Mon petit choux*? He called you his little cabbage, I think. A Brussels sprout."

Her mother's cheeks turned an even brighter shade of pink. Clucking as if to chide Jack for teasing, which she clearly liked, she wandered off just as dinner was being served.

After the shrimp dish, there would be Wilson Cattle filet mignon, grilled over an open mesquite fire. For those who didn't prefer beef, there was chicken Marsala. Jack had surprised them with the menu, elegant enough for the rehearsal dinner, yet suitable for the simple ranching community gathered here. As her mother might say, "We don't do fancy."

Her mother didn't speak to Grey all evening, but she did manage to hide her animosity toward him. Several times Shadow caught her giving Grey an appraising look, as if she might see him in a different light, but with a stab of guilt, she realized she should be focusing on her own relationship with Grey, not her mother's.

At the end of the meal, Jack's cool, smooth dessert stuck in her throat. Shadow excused herself to refill her water glass in the kitchen.

Jack swept in, concerned. "Too much sugar in my blueberry panacotta?"

She stood with her back to him at the sink. "No, something went down the wrong way. I'll be fine."

"If I may say this, you don't seem fine." With a hand at her shoulder, he gently turned her around. "There's pain in your eyes."

Her heart stalled. Was she that obvious? Could others see, too?

"I am an observant person," he continued. "In earlier times I worked in restaurants, yes, but I also tended bar, an environment in which people tend to bare their souls to a perfect stranger. Your mother is worried about you. Is it because of us? You do not approve?"

"I do," she said. "I wish you both well."

"If Bertie can come back from the rehab center to do well again at home with your mother's care, if she can find happiness for what I think must be the first time in her life, then nothing is impossible." Before Jack had finished speaking, the dining room door opened again.

Grey said, "Your dinner was a hit, Jack. People want to thank you for an excellent meal." His gaze shifted between them, a clear signal for Jack to leave the kitchen. When he did, resettling his chef's hat as Grey often did his Stetson, Grey's eyes locked onto hers. He briefly touched Shadow's arm, sending a wave of warmth through her. "What was that?"

She shrugged. "He's smitten with my

mother. An old-fashioned term, I know, yet it suits them."

Grey's shoulders relaxed. "I doubt Tobias and Willy would agree, even after that magnificent dinner, but Jack's a great guy. She's a good woman, Shadow. If only she felt more inclined to like me."

Shadow didn't want to talk about that. She didn't want to think about tomorrow and the wedding, being surrounded by love and celebration and so many hopes for the future when she couldn't begin to know where she and Grey would end up. Being here tonight, in his home, seemed to make that worse— as if she really could belong here, and they could be together again, this time forever. Yet everything was still up in the air.

She looked away. Grey's obvious pride that the dinner had gone so well made him all but glow like Blossom. "People are starting to leave. We should get back out there," she said.

Half an hour later only one car remained. Jack had been the first to arrive for the party because he'd been cooking; now he was the last to leave.

"Good-night, Jack," Shadow said, rising up on tiptoes to kiss his cheek. "The dinner—

your food—was amazing. I wish Blossom had used you for the reception tomorrow."

"Mais oui." Starting toward his car, he patted the check in his pocket that Grey had written. "Food is my passion." He winked over his shoulder. "Blossom had hired another caterer before you thought of me. But I will enjoy sitting next to your mother tomorrow at the wedding. And I may be able to help here and there. Now I must get home." Her mother had already left in her own car.

"Thank you," Shadow said, "for being so good to her."

"It is easy. And will continue to be."

With the house quiet, she and Grey cleared the last of the coffee cups and dessert plates then went out onto the back porch.

"I missed Ava being here tonight," he said.

Shadow had told him about their mother-daughter conversation after Ava's first visit to the ranch. Busy with Grey and the rehearsal dinner plans, though, they hadn't found time for her to ride again. Or was Shadow avoiding that? "She would have liked seeing Nick, but Jenna offered to take her, and I wasn't about to tell a room full of friends and neighbors that you're her father. Would you have told everyone tonight?"

"No," he said. "This was Blossom and Logan's night. They know," he added. "Does anyone else?"

"Not that I'm aware of." Shadow thought of Derek and their encounter weeks ago at the farm. "My brother worries me, though. I wonder what he might do. He still thinks you killed Jared."

Shadow didn't say that her mother did, too. She cleared her throat. She looked down at the strappy, heeled sandals she'd worn tonight. They were among her favorites, but she didn't have many occasions to wear them. When she'd bought the shoes to add to her collection, a poignant thought had crossed her mind. *I could wear these to my own wedding.* The man she imagined at the altar was Grey.

"We're going to have to tell people that she's our child," she said. "It's not fair to Ava, as if we're trying to keep her hidden. Tonight wasn't the right time, but after that—" She glanced up. "How are we going to manage this, Grey?"

A short silence followed. He dug the toe of his boot into the dirt. He jammed his hands in the rear pockets of his dress pants then rocked on his heels. His gaze didn't quite meet hers. "So. What if we…for Ava's sake…what if we…try again? For that second chance?"

Her pulse tripped.

"It could be the perfect solution," he insisted. "I have some stuff to clean up first, but Ava would have both of her parents. She wouldn't be shuttled back and forth between us, always trying to please each side like I did. We're the adults here, we're responsible. You love her," he said, "and though I've only known her a short time, so do I. How can we do less for her than give her the whole family she's always wanted?" His gaze warmed. "We both know the spark's still there, Shadow—for us, I mean. For me, it never even flickered."

"I care about you, Grey. But to…what would we do? Live together?"

"More than that," he said. "I want her to have my name. I want you to have my name."

Shadow stared at him. "Are you proposing?"

"That's how it sounds, yeah." He moved closer to her.

She'd never expected that. "I don't know

what to think—or say. If we do something so impulsive, what happens if it doesn't work?"

"We'll make it work. And it's not impulsive."

"I know how you feel about your parents, but that's not reason enough to—"

He quoted her words from weeks ago at the diner. "Hitch ourselves together like a team of oxen?" He was smiling. "Come on, Shadow."

"I've never thought of marrying." That was a lie, but she went on. "For the last ten years I've devoted myself to Ava. We struggled, yes, but we did survive—in no small part because Jenna helped when I needed her most. That's a debt I can never repay, but I fought hard for my independence. I can support us myself—"

"That's all material," he said, "and I know this ranch isn't exactly profitable right now, and that I haven't proven anything about my involvement that night with Jared. But I'm talking about something more important."

He didn't have to say the word *love*. She'd felt it in his kiss several times before. Unable to speak, Shadow framed his face in her hands. And like the night in Kansas City, Grey just kept looking into her eyes until she tilted her head, and he did too, and they angled their mouths, their lips meeting at last in a new whisper of a kiss.

She let the kiss go on, and so did he, until it became more than the mere brush of their mouths, deepening, as if neither of them would end it. Nothing had changed between them in that regard. She still wanted Grey. But with the past hanging over them, could love be enough?

Not wanting to leave the shelter of his arms, she drew away. "I don't know," she murmured. "I can't afford to make another... mistake." The wrong choice. "I don't mean to hurt you, Grey, but I need to do the right thing for Ava. Every time."

Grey's shoulders sagged. "I do, too. I get it, though. You mean because of Jared. But if I don't ever learn what really happened, and you say no to my proposal, awkward as it was, you and I will have lost our last, best chance with each other. Ava will have lost something, too."

She glanced toward the front of the house. Ten years, she thought, and the tragedy of her brother's death was still keeping them apart.

"Oh, Grey."

"Shadow." He drew her close once more, breathing the words—old and new—against her mouth and said, "Even our names go together."

Like ashes and smoke, she thought. Then he kissed her again.

"I HAVE TO PICK Dad and Liza up in KC before noon," Grey said. Shadow sat next to him in the passenger seat of his pickup. "So we'll have to make this quick. I'll have time on the drive home to tell him I've messed up with the ranch. And that Cody Jones is still on the loose." Tight-lipped this morning, he didn't mention their talk, or his proposal, the night before. Grey had insisted on going with Shadow to her mother's farm. He didn't like the idea of Derek being there, possibly confronting her again about Ava.

She felt sorry for Grey. She had little fondness for Wilson Cattle—her worst memories still lived there—but for Grey to lose his legacy ranch? She had never, in her darkest moments, wished him ill.

"Your father believes in you, Grey. He wouldn't have turned Wilson Cattle over to you if he didn't." She waited a moment before going on. "Maybe it's really you who doesn't believe in yourself."

"Could be, but he deserves to hear from me in person."

She admired him for shouldering that responsibility, as he was willing—no, eager— to do with Ava now. "I know how hard you've tried—not only to find proof about the shooting, but to try and stop the rustlers."

It was hard to imagine the legendary ranch in bankruptcy and Grey losing the heritage that was all-important to him. Now he could be ruined, and he would lose everything. She didn't envy his task with his father.

As they drove out to the farm, she was glad Jenna was still with Ava at Shadow's house. Her sister would bring Ava to the wedding later.

Shadow would be at the farm only long enough to move the hens and rooster to Bertie's ranch for her mother. A last visit, she hoped, to the place where she'd grown up. Her belongings were now in her attic and closets. She still wondered where her mother would move. They needed to talk about that. Maybe Shadow could help her find a place, as she had helped Jenna.

By the henhouse, Grey stopped his silver

truck. It had more room than her Mustang or her mother's aging compact sedan for all the animal cages that would fill the truck's bed. Shadow cast a quick look toward the main house and was thankful not to see Derek's car. She'd rather avoid another confrontation, especially with Grey here.

Grey stared off into the distance, obviously still worried about his own troubles. At least they weren't discussing Jared now.

"Have you made any progress? With the rustlers, I mean?" Shadow asked, hoping to draw him out of his silence.

He shook his head. "Finn has finished talking to people with motor vehicle registrations on the other half of that list, but no white-truck owner has turned up with any link to Cody. I spoke to a bunch of people myself—I know you didn't think that was a good idea—but I found nothing, either. Not with Fred Miller or anyone else on the list."

"Fred's a mean old guy."

"How do you know him?"

"I don't, really. I've only met him once or twice, with Derek." She ran through her memory then came up with a connection. "I remember. He's Calvin Stern's uncle on his mother's side."

Grey's expression changed, as if a light bulb had come on. "Thanks, Shadow. Calvin may have been the key all along, but not in the way I expected. I was looking at him because of Jared."

While Grey called Finn about the owner of the Bar B&J, she hurried from the truck, not wanting to keep him long before his drive to the airport. Most of the flock was in the yard, scratching at the bare ground for some stray kernels of corn. At the door to the chicken coop, she paused. "Grey, there's not room in here for both of us. Would you unload the crates?"

"Sure."

Inside the coop, Shadow put a hand to her chest. The hens had food and water this time, but as a girl she'd hated to collect eggs, one of her daily chores. Whenever she failed to do so, avoiding the hens' pecking at her hands and legs, she'd had her father's anger over the waste to deal with and her mother's disappointment in her. Now, perhaps because of Derek, half a dozen neglected eggs in the nests were already turning into chicks. From past experience she could tell these had been here for some time, but before she could deal with them, she heard Grey call out.

"Shadow, come see this!"

She ran out to the yard, where he dashed from here to there, trying to catch a live yellow chick that had already hatched. He was laughing at the chase. The sound gladdened her heart; she hadn't known how to cheer him up. He scooped the chick into his hand then darted off after another. "I could use some help here," he said.

A little bird ran under the coop. For years there'd been a hole between the now-dry earth and the floor of the henhouse above that provided enough room for a chick to scoot through the gap into darkness—and safety. A red hen ran next to the hole, clucking like the worried mother she probably was. "Oh, dear," Shadow said. She bent down by the hole. *You were never good with my chickens*, she could almost hear her mother say. Good thing she wasn't here.

Shadow dropped onto all fours and lay flat to push one arm through the hole, blindly fishing for the missing chick. A warm fluff ball grazed her fingers then scampered off again into the black hole, cheeping in outrage.

A feather floated past Shadow's nose, making her sneeze before she tried again to reach the chick. And failed. "Grey," she called.

Counting to ten for patience, she reached in even deeper, but she couldn't grasp anything but dank air. Then Grey was there, a hand at her shoulder. Chicks fluttered all around them.

"I've got most of them in the crates now, but let me try. My reach is longer."

Lying flat, he pushed his right arm and shoulder into the hole. After a moment, he handed Shadow the escaped chick covered in dirt, but then he reached back into the gap under the henhouse. "There's something else in here. Did your folks store things under this coop?"

"No." She crooned to the chick she held. With its fluffy yellow feathers and dark eyes, it was actually cute.

Grey shoved his arm deeper and groped around. A second later, groaning at the apparent strain to his shoulder, he pulled out a brittle plastic bag, its clear surface clouded, and stood up. Whatever it contained must have been there a long time.

She and Grey stared down at the package in his hands. The layers of newspaper inside couldn't disguise the obvious shape of a handgun, and Shadow's heart beat faster. She hadn't looked at a firearm since Jared died. It took another moment before the significance of Grey's find fully registered. If she didn't miss her guess, he was holding the missing weapon that had killed her brother.

Shadow was stunned. Grey looked shocked, too.

"We shouldn't open this," he said, swallowing hard. "Fingerprints."

She still couldn't quite believe it. "The cops searched every inch of this farm after Jared died."

"Well, they missed a spot—not an obvious one—and this gun must have been here all along."

"This is potential proof of whoever pulled that trigger," she said. "Assuming it's the same gun that killed Jared."

This was what Grey had tried so hard to find.

Would the gun prove him innocent? Or guilty?

She wanted to believe in him, and she almost did, yet in that moment their past loomed over her. Shadow reached out for the plastic bag and, hating herself for not being able to trust Grey, she thought, *I can't.*

As she took the bag from him, their fingers brushed and she watched his eyes dim even as the warmth of his hand went through her. She had tried, but he could see that she had failed.

She couldn't love him the way she did before, the way she wanted to now.

The way I still do.

CHAPTER TWENTY

GREY MET HIS father and Liza at the Kansas City airport. On their way home he told his dad about the gun he and Shadow had found under the henhouse. She'd promised to take the bag to Finn Donovan for him, and Grey had wondered for a second if she didn't even trust him to deliver it.

If there were still viable fingerprints, Finn would compare them with Grey's, which were still on file from ten years ago, yet he couldn't overlook Shadow's first reaction. Like him, she'd been shocked. Then he'd seen another expression cross her features, one she probably didn't even realize she had. He could only call it fear that the missing gun would prove him guilty in her brother's death.

Grey tried not to fault her for the lack of trust. Perhaps because of him, Shadow had lost her brother, which was hard enough for her to bear. He could understand that—because of Ava. If anyone tried to hurt her, or his sister Olivia, he'd have a hard time opening his heart to them.

If the ballistics report confirmed this was the gun that killed Jared, and Grey's fingerprints were found on the trigger Shadow would never join him for the last gasp of Wilson Cattle or anything else. A hundred years plus of prosperity, Grey thought, and under his watch he'd managed, all right, to lose everything. Now he might have lost his freedom, too. And, worst of all, Shadow and Ava.

He glanced over to see the familiar set of his father's face. He sat on the passenger seat, and Grey's stepmother was in the back seat of the extended cab.

His father didn't respond to Grey's story of the plastic bag or even to what he'd told him about the ranch. "Logan's wedding still on for today?" was all he said.

"Yep." Grey wasn't in the mood to take part, though he would. All he could think of was that gun and the match that might be made of his fingerprints, assuming they were there. His and who else's? There were only four possibilities: Grey, Jared, Derek and Calvin. But Calvin claimed he'd never been near the gun.

"Dad, I'm sorry. I let you down. I promised I wouldn't, but when you go over the ranch accounts, you'll see. I was already having trouble for the past six months. Then after the bank denied me a loan, the rustlers struck. I've lost too many cattle—assets that are now in the red column. Without a big influx of cash, there's no way I can rebuild the herd. I'm a bad judge of character, too," he added. "Cody Jones was nothing but a plant for whoever else rustled those cows."

His father made a sound of disgust. "People have been stealing cattle and horses since man first domesticated the animals. They probably always will. The crime is just more high-tech these days—normally. Doesn't sound so in this case, from what you've told me." He shifted in the suit Grey had never seen him wear before. "Stop feeling sorry for yourself. While I'm here we'll talk to Barney again, tell him he'd better negotiate a loan, or I'll pull every cent I have in other accounts out of that bank."

But Grey wouldn't let his dad make up his losses. "Handing Wilson Cattle to me was a mistake."

His father straightened his tie. "Who am I talking to here? Grey, listen to yourself. I don't recognize my own son. I 'handed' this ranch to you for one reason—because I knew you could do the job. Sure, I challenged you last time we spoke. Wilson Cattle is—was—my heritage, too."

He hesitated. "You can save it for your children one day. Don't turn your back on my help now just because you're too proud." He tugged at the tie again. "I didn't plan to tell you until after Logan's wedding, but Liza and I want Wilson Cattle to be yours. That's official. At this point in my life I'd rather take it easy, travel some more, spend time with the woman I love. Frankly, I like the excitement in Dallas, the good restaurants. We even saw a play and a couple of operas last season. Liza is in charge of my cultural re-education."

Grey glanced at Liza in the rearview mirror. His stepmother sent him a smile.

"She's good for you, Dad. You're good for her."

"After all that hoopla with your mother? Always vying for your attention, making Olivia prove her loyalty. I'd say so." He shook his head. "I wish your mother nothing but happiness—that new husband of hers, too—but I'm a far happier man than I used to be." He hesitated again. "So. You going to take care of business or give up when the going gets tough?"

Grey cracked a smile. "You trust me? But why, when I haven't proven myself, after all. And Jared Moran's death still hangs over me." And prevented any future with Shadow. Maybe finding the gun this morning had only made that more certain in her mind. But why would she think he'd hidden the gun there? Whether or not it had been Grey's finger on the trigger, he hadn't been the one to hide the gun. He knew that much.

His dad sat back with a sigh. "Jared's death shook us all pretty badly. And at nineteen, that was a hard road for you to travel. I admit the shooting set plenty of people in this town against me for a while, as well, just for it having happened on my property. I've always believed in your innocence, Grey. If they're still looking sideways at you, that's their problem. I don't need to know what Finn learns from that gun."

"Unless my prints are there."

Despite his worry about the gun, Grey tried to take in his father's words. His trust in him. *Maybe it's you who doesn't believe in yourself*, Shadow had said. His dad might be the only one who did believe, and Grey wouldn't give up. If the gun couldn't prove his innocence, and if Shadow never forgave him, he would summon some of his determination to trust in himself—which would require setting aside some of his stubborn pride.

As he turned in to the driveway at Wilson Cattle and felt the same sense of homecoming he always did, Grey knew he wasn't done yet. Except, quite possibly, with Shadow.

He glanced at his father. "Then it looks like we're going to keep this ranch."

"You are," his father said. "I'm just here to observe."

AT THE CIRCLE H, Shadow studied Blossom in the bedroom mirror. "Almost done. Quit fidgeting." She tucked a strand of Blossom's russet hair back into the sleek topknot she'd worn today with tendrils that framed her pretty face and showcased her lace veil. In a yellow dress that matched Shadow's, Blossom's friend Tammy held the bridal bouquet. "This gown is perfect on you," she said.

"A beautiful bride," Shadow agreed.

Blossom hugged them. "I'm so nervous. But I can't wait for Logan to see me."

Her ivory wedding dress had lace across her shoulders and down the elbow-length sleeves. Underneath that feminine overlay the strapless bodice boasted an empire waistline above a skirt that fell in a fluid column to her heeled sandals, highlighting her pregnancy at the same time it appeared to disguise that change in her shape. A satin sash completed the look.

Shadow could hear the first strains of wedding music begin to play from the yard. It was time, and she had to put that morning's trip to the farm out of her mind, the quick surge of distrust she'd felt toward Grey.

She and Blossom walked with Tammy through the house to the front door, and Shadow felt a few nervous twinges. She hadn't seen him since they'd found the missing gun.

When she'd handed it to Finn, he'd told her he might be late for the wedding. And for Finn, Logan and Blossom had adjusted the start time, but he still wasn't here. They would have to begin without him.

At the top of the porch stairs, she and Tammy stood in front of Blossom and Logan's grandfather, Sam. With his leg cast off, he was ready to walk Blossom down the makeshift aisle to the rose arbor where Logan was waiting, fussing with his yellow tie. Shadow flicked a glance at Grey. Standing next to Logan, he looked more handsome than ever in his white shirt, navy blazer and tan khakis, his hair combed and shining, his face newly shaved. Hoping his somber expression was due to the ceremony that was about to begin, she glanced at the new boots he wore. Then, with the change of tune that was her signal, she began her walk.

A minute later, with the first notes of "Here Comes the Bride," Blossom and Sam stepped out with only a slight hitch in his gait, her arm looped through his. Shadow watched from her place in the arbor adorned with white roses. She swallowed her regret.

If things had worked out years ago, she and Grey might have gotten married in a similar way, starting their lives as one, like Blossom and Logan were doing now. Instead, they'd spent ten years apart. Last night, and Grey's proposal, had given Shadow a glimpse of what they could have, but this morning, as if potential happiness couldn't last any longer than that, they'd found the gun.

She studied the assembled guests, including Grey's father and stepmother, Willy and Tobias, and her mother and Jack. They were all seated on white chairs and looking misty-eyed as the bride came down the aisle beside a beaming Sam. Or was Shadow seeing them through a blur? Weddings always brought tears.

Swallowing her emotions, she watched Nick, the ring bearer, who held a satin pillow and was grinning at his father the whole way to the arbor.

She scarcely heard the vows. At the last second, Finn had slid into his place beside Grey at the altar. She kept blinking, remembering better times with Grey, wishing… And then trying to read Finn's face for any sign that he'd discovered the truth about the gun.

When the service ended with a first kiss between the new husband and wife, Shadow looked away from the tender meeting of their lips. She found herself staring into Grey's eyes, remembering last night and the kisses they'd shared, deeper than in the Kansas City hotel bar or at his ranch the day they'd told Ava he was her father. If she wasn't wrong, he was thinking of those kisses, too.

As soon as the applause died down and the joyful recessional ended, people rose from their chairs, gathering in small groups to laugh and talk. Shadow bypassed them all with a wave, stopping only for a moment when Logan stepped into her path. "Congratulations," she said, giving him, then Blossom, a kiss, "Best wishes, my friend."

"Thanks for your part in making this a perfect day," Logan said, returning her hug. "Except for one thing." His gaze briefly clouded. "I wish my brother could have been here."

Shadow thought the same about Jared, although, like Derek, he probably wouldn't have been invited. And she thought again of Grey.

They hadn't said a word to each other during their walk up the aisle together after the ceremony. All she knew was that they'd found the missing gun. Together. She didn't know whose prints might be on it. But did that really matter now?

If she couldn't believe in him, even without that proof, what chance did they have? She owed Grey more than that.

She hurried off to find him. To tell him she believed. But Grey was gone.

GREY WALKED DOWN the drive with Finn. Halfway to the road, Grey stopped to peer inside a Stewart County cruiser, greeting one of Finn's deputies at the wheel with a nod. In the rear seat, to his utter surprise, sat Derek Moran.

"What's happened, Finn?"

"I'll let him tell you. I've already taken his statement—a new one." He nodded at Derek. "Start talking. Grey deserves to hear this straight from you."

Derek cleared his throat, his gaze fixed on his hands in his lap. "The night of the shooting, Jared said we'd go out to Wilson Cattle, raise some hell after you broke up with Shadow. I could go with him if I kept out of his way. You'd hurt Shadow, but you wouldn't hurt her again."

"I know all that," Grey said.

"I didn't realize he had a gun, I swear."

"When I came out of the house," Grey said, "you all went for me."

Derek glanced at Finn, as if for his approval to keep talking. When he got a nod, he continued. "Everybody grappled for the gun at the same time—your daddy's gun."

"How do you know that? It was gone long before that shooting."

Derek shrugged. "My dad stole it, Jared told me. The last time he'd been canned at Wilson Cattle, he'd gotten really mad. Guess he figured your father owed him, figured he'd sell it somewhere to get money. Or maybe he kept it as a trophy."

"Why didn't you say something before?" Grey said. "Jared could have killed me with it—or you." Instead, it was Jared who'd died at the foot of the front porch steps. "I shouldn't have tried to wrestle the gun from him but I lost track of who was where. We were all one ball of fury."

Finn said, "Tell him, Derek."

Grey could barely hear him speak. "In the scuffle the barrel got turned toward Jared's belly. I don't know how, but then me and Jared were fighting over the gun. Calvin had already backed off and you were still yelling at us to cut it out." His voice quavered. "Everything happened so fast—the gun just went off."

"And afterward, the gun went missing," Grey said.

"Calvin split before the sheriff could get there. He took it—for me. He was plenty scared, too, but I couldn't let the police have that gun or they'd learn who pulled the trigger. Calvin gave it back to me later, after he made his statement to the sheriff. And we buried it under the henhouse at the farm."

Finn shifted. "There are two sets of prints on that pistol, Grey. Not in very good shape after all this time, but still there. Jared had had a few scrapes with the law—a couple of DUIs and some minor vandalism at a party—so his prints were on file. So were Derek's, from the night of the shooting." He paused. "Both of their prints are on and near the trigger. Not yours. Not Calvin's."

Grey couldn't seem to process what was being said. He still remembered shoving the barrel away from him, but after that…another blur.

Derek was crying now, his face buried in his hands. He kept saying, "I was only fifteen."

Grey's mouth tightened. "You're not a kid anymore. Why try to blame me?"

"I figured your daddy would get you off with all that Wilson Cattle money if it ever came to that. Then, when nobody was charged, some people said he lied to protect you and that kind of protected me."

Grey couldn't speak. He was in shock, but as the words sank in he also felt a jolt of exhilaration. Those same people would soon know he wasn't guilty. *Innocent*, he thought. *I didn't do it*.

"That's not all, Grey," Finn murmured. "While I was looking into your old case, I was also trying to get a handle on those rustlers." He tipped his head toward Derek, and Grey realized what Finn was saying.

"*You* stole my cattle?" Grey said. "You and Cody?"

"And Calvin," Derek murmured.

Grey had known Calvin's uncle was involved, but… "All *three* of you?"

Finn broke in. "Your cows are at the Bar B&J. After you called I went over there. Fred Miller had lent his white rig to Derek and his friends. Several times. Miller runs a small operation, but his fields looked mighty full. Cattle everywhere. He'd had them mostly hidden away in a pasture on the far side of his ranch, but one of my other deputies and I recognized your brand right away."

Amid his relief that he would get his cattle back and his anger at Derek, Grey felt a rush of pity for the younger man. "Why did you do this?" he asked.

"To punish you," Derek muttered, his gaze still on his hands. "If it hadn't been for you,

Jared would have stayed home that night. When Shadow came back to Barren, she made people remember again, and I could see how you still felt about her. I thought if I could drive you out of business, she'd have nothing more to do with you. She always hated being poor. And then I found out she had a kid—*your* kid—" His voice hitched. "I did it all for Jared," he finished.

In seeking revenge for the brother he had loved, Derek had squandered his own life from fifteen to twenty-five. Ten years. In a way, that was like a prison sentence. He'd been locked inside himself.

Finn looked at Grey. "I don't think these boys intended to sell those cows at auction. Their theft was an attempt to bring you down. You can go get your cattle any time. By the way, we picked up Cody Jones. He's at the station now making his statement and singing like the old canary. He's obviously clear in Jared's death—wasn't involved—and so is Calvin. He's been cooperating, too."

"You may as well add horse thievery to the charges against Cody Jones." Nugget had finally come back to the barn that other night, her sides heaving and her muzzle flecked with foam. She must have covered the entire ranch in the time she'd been running free. Once she'd been cooled down, Grey had given her an extra ration of grain and plenty of hay, but he was still mad. The horse could have been injured.

Derek began to whimper. "They can't send me to prison for life, can they?"

"I'm no lawyer, but you're in deep trouble about the cattle. In Jared's case—" Finn began.

Derek cut him off as he met Grey's eyes. "I had to blame you. How could I ever tell Mama, my daddy or anyone else? Shadow? If it was me," he said, sobbing, "who killed my own brother."

CHAPTER TWENTY-ONE

SHADOW WATCHED AN apparently shaken Grey walk from the patrol car back up the driveway to the bridal party now gathered with the photographer.

"Don't know if I can smile after that," he murmured. He told Shadow what he'd learned. "I almost feel bad for Derek, except it's the first time in his life he's ever admitted to anything. And what an admission it was." He added, "Finn's not sure it can ever be proved that Derek actually pulled that trigger. Jared might well have shot himself, but Derek's going to have to live with that the rest of his life. I'm sorry, Shadow."

The news about her brother wasn't easy to take. Shadow didn't know how she could smile during the picture taking, either, but she did. Inside, her heart was breaking—for her mother, mostly.

After the wedding party had posed for pictures—a few of them taken of Shadow standing with Grey, his arm around her waist as if they still could be a couple—the others drifted toward the house. Jack met them with a tray of champagne glasses and another of hors d'oeuvres. Today, as he'd indicated he might, he'd offered to help the Kansas City caterer serve at the reception. Shadow and Grey stayed behind. It was dusk, and the lights strung in the trees were coming on.

Shadow didn't know how to begin her apology to Grey, and she searched for the right words, if there were any.

"I'm sad about Derek—devastated, really." Her voice shook. "No matter what, he's still my baby brother, but I'm so glad for you, Grey." She paused, ashamed that she'd turned her back on him only that morning. He looked past her now at someone who approached. The rest of her apology would have to wait.

"Grey. Hard luck with those cows," one of his neighbors said, laying a hand on his shoulder. "My men and I will be over to help tomorrow."

A second man left a group of people arriving for the reception. He glanced at Shadow, then Grey. "Count me in, too. In a community like Barren, we stick together."

Grey nodded, but his eyes showed confusion. Another four or five people weighed in, all offering support. They tipped their hats to Shadow. "Been quite a while," the last man said, "since we've had an old-fashioned roundup. We'll bring all those cows home in no time. My trailer can hold quite a few. We'll all get it done."

When he and Shadow were alone again, Grey said, "What was that? I don't remember asking any of those guys—" He broke off.

"You're not going to refuse their offer?"

He shook his head. "No, I think there's a limit to my pride. I'll be grateful for their help."

Shadow touched his arm. "I want to help, too, if I can," she told him. "Grey, I owe you an apology but that's not enough. In my heart I think I always believed you were innocent— but it was my head that couldn't trust in you all the way. Until today. I knew that before Finn came, and Derek."

"I don't care when you knew or even why that all happened." He waited another beat before saying, "I'm fine now…fine about everything tonight…as long as you'll forgive me, Shadow."

She blinked. "For something you didn't do?"

Grey rested his forehead against hers, a

faint smile in his voice. "That's all I've ever wanted," he said. "I forgive you, too."

Shadow lifted her head. "For keeping Ava from you? No, Grey. It's more than that. My secret was worse—far worse, it turns out—than your possible guilt about Jared. Even if you had pulled the trigger, it was an accident. I made a choice."

She caught sight of her mother coming toward them. Shadow sighed. "Mama, I'll see you later. We're trying to talk."

Wanda smiled. "I know you are, but I'll be out of the way soon. I just wanted to tell you that you don't need to worry about me moving in with you or where else I'll go. Ava needs her room, and I already have a place. I'm moving into Bertie's," she announced, sounding thrilled. "Jack just asked me. There's not much extra space, but the three of us will make do."

Shadow stared at her for a long moment before her mother continued. "I've been managing since I was a mother for the first time at eighteen. If you think your daddy ruled the roost, so to speak, and told me what to do, you're wrong. He didn't always win our scrambles."

Shadow hugged her, but her mother wasn't through.

"I want to say this, too. That one time I was wrong, Shadow. When you needed us, I let him have his say—and you left home. It wasn't until he passed away that I realized how wrong I'd really been. That's my one regret, baby—except for losing Jared." She let out a shaky sigh. "I don't know how to feel yet about Derek. I made a mistake with him, that's for sure, but maybe he's already paying the price."

"Mama, we'll handle Derek. Together," Shadow said.

And still her mother stood there. "I'm not sure about you yet, Grey Wilson, even after knowing what my Derek did." Apparently the news had spread through the reception like wildfire. "I'll work on that." She paused with another glance at Shadow. "I made my worst mistake years ago. I hope you won't make another one now."

Shadow hugged her for another moment. "We all made mistakes, Mama."

"No kidding," Grey said, before her mother went back to Jack, who was waiting for her. He was still staring after her when Shadow spied her sister and Ava coming across the lawn from the parking area. This would be the biggest part of her apology to Grey. Before she and Jenna reached them, Ava ran off with Nick.

"Thanks, Jenna," Shadow said.

"You're more than welcome." Her sister glanced at Grey, then at Shadow. "Before I join the party, too, I should tell you how excited I am about my apartment. And becoming an interior designer. I'm really going to do it. Who knows? Maybe someday I'll even try to adopt a child." She turned to Grey. "I'm sorry for my brother's actions, but I'm…glad for you."

"Thanks, Jenna," Grey said.

With a light touch to Shadow's shoulder and a smile, if a tentative one, for Grey, she went off to wish Blossom and Logan well. They'd just turned back to each other when Finn loped up to them. Shadow began to despair of ever being able to talk to Grey.

He must have agreed. "What is this? Grand Central Station?"

Finn paused. "This won't take long. About these charges, your cattle—"

"I don't want to press charges."

Finn stared at him. "Why not? I've busted my—"

Grey put an arm around Shadow's shoulders. "And I appreciate it, Finn. I know I mentioned adding horse theft to those charges. But I've changed my mind. About all of them. Shadow's had enough. So have I. Mrs. Moran, too. Let this end with Jared. As long as I get my cattle back, I won't see Derek—or the others—go to prison."

"Guess I'll leave you two to work things out then," Finn said, but he was smiling. Still shaking his head, he walked away.

"About that, Shadow began, but before she could mention Ava, Grey grinned.

"Let's do it now," he said.

In the distance the band was tuning up and Shadow began to hope at last, to believe, in a new future for her and Grey. But first, she turned toward the guests at the reception. Spotting Ava in the crowd, she waved her over.

For a second Ava hesitated, as if she wanted to stay where she was. Then she ran toward Shadow and Grey, stopping short in a swirl of her party dress's skirts. She looked like an angel to Shadow.

"What do you want, Mom?" Ava glanced at Logan's son, who was wildly waving for her to rejoin him. "Nick and I are going to the barn to feed the horses. They don't like wedding cake."

"Sweetie, Grey and I have something to tell everyone," Shadow said, unsure how Ava would take this announcement. Hopefully, she thought, just as she'd accepted Grey as her father."

"Before someone else does," he murmured.

Shadow agreed. Everyone was looking at them, and she'd always wondered how this might play out, but the right thing—the most right thing she'd ever done for Ava—was now. With Grey.

He took Ava's hand. Together, he and Shadow led her toward the center of the group. Grey raised his voice for attention then said, "Folks, we don't want to interrupt this great party for long, but we want to share with you—"

Shadow finished for him. "Our daughter. Please say hello to Ava… Wilson."

Ava's face showed a sudden mix of emotions. She was a smart girl, with Grey's sharp mind and Shadow's ability to problem solve. "I'm going to change my name?"

"Yep," Grey said. "If you want to."

"Yay!" She flung herself into Grey's arms

and he caught her to him, as Shadow had always imagined—hoped—he would. Her throat tightened. To the cheers and claps of everyone around them, they hugged for a long moment, all three of them, before Ava pulled back. "Can I have a horse of my own?"

Grey laughed. "You can have a whole barn full."

As the guests at the reception, family and friends and neighbors all, looked on, Ava wrapped her arms around Shadow, squeezed once then turned and ran back across the lawn.

"Nick!" she shouted. "I'm Ava Moran Wilson! Beat you to the barn!" Everyone at the party laughed and applauded.

Jack made a sign with his fingers held up in a circle and Shadow's mother broke into a grin. It would take time for her to fully accept Grey, but Shadow had no doubt she would come around. She'd never given her mother enough credit.

From the center of the lawn Logan put his hands on his hips and nodded his approval. Blinking, Blossom laid a hand over her heart.

"No more secrets," Grey murmured.

"None," she said. It was her promise to him. After the noise died down, the band began to play the first tune, a slow, tender ballad, and Logan and Blossom walked onto the wooden stage for their first dance as a married couple. Grey led Shadow away, deeper into the trees, and took her in his arms. "You know, our daughter really needs this family together. What do you say, Shadow?"

She thought of everything that had happened today, her disappointment in Derek coupled with her happiness for Grey. With more clarity about Jared's death, and a newfound belief in Grey, her memories, all of them, could be laid to rest. She didn't need to make her childhood poverty or her parents' rejection the focal points of her life.

She could have gone back to her mom and dad the morning after she'd talked to Doc, begged them to change their view, as she'd felt tempted to do five years later. Or maybe she couldn't have. Either way, she was confident that she had always tried her best for Ava. Now, she would do that for herself and Grey.

She let her gaze drift from the Circle H toward the boundary of his ranch, then made another decision. She had no idea how he might respond, but it was more than time for her to show him she believed.

"I say my house in town is too small for the three of us. If it's all right with you, Ava and I will move to Wilson Cattle."

"That's where the horses are." He framed her face in his hands and took a deep breath. "But are you sure? I know how you feel about the ranch."

"How I felt," she said. Her treasured independence no longer seemed as important as it had for the past ten years. And with today's revelations, her connection to this place could finally begin to heal. Still, what Grey said next stunned her.

"Maybe you have too many bad memories there. I'll sell Wilson Cattle if that's what you need. We can buy a bigger house in town. You and Ava are more important to me than a piece of land."

"It's more than land. It's your family's heritage," Shadow said, shocked—but touched—that he would make that offer. "It will be Ava's, too." He had truly set aside his pride, yet she couldn't ask that of him. "I'll always remember Jared died there and I'm sorry that may have been because of Derek—if it was, it was an accident. But I want to make new memories. You love the ranch, Grey. So does

Ava, and that will help me to heal. I'd do anything for you and our daughter."

Afraid her emotions would get the best of her, she tried to lighten the mood. "How could I deprive her of her horses?" With that, Shadow had no more doubts. "I'll warn you, though. I have plans for that house. It hasn't changed since the day your mother left. It's time to freshen things up."

"That's what Liza always says." Grey grinned. "You can do whatever you want. As long as you're with me."

He nodded toward the band and the wooden floor in the middle of the Circle H lawn, where Logan and Blossom were ending their first dance in a loud flourish of sound. "One good thing about a ranch—there's plenty of space. The neighbors won't complain about the noise." He added in a too casual tone, "You know, we did pretty well with the rehearsal dinner. And this wedding makes me think of…weddings. How'd you like to plan another?" He took a deep breath. "I love you, Shadow. I know I asked before, but you didn't answer. Will you marry me?"

"Finally," she said and gazed into his eyes, giving him her trust and all of herself at last. "Yes. I love you, Grey. I never stopped." She smiled a little, enough to let him know she was teasing even when her next words were true. "You're still the cowboy of my dreams."

He kissed her, and then once more, his kiss warm and just as true, before he led her from the trees out onto the dance floor and into his arms for another song.

Their friends' wedding reception was in full swing, but Grey and Shadow were just beginning.

All over again.

* * * * *

If you enjoyed this Heartwarming story by Leigh Riker, you'll also love THE RELUCTANT RANCHER, the first installment in her KANSAS COWBOYS miniseries, and MAN OF THE FAMILY, a touching romance featuring a single dad. Find all of Leigh's books on Harlequin.com.

Get 2 Free Books,
Plus 2 Free Gifts—
just for trying the Reader Service!

LI17R

Get 2 Free Books,
Plus 2 Free Gifts—
just for trying the
Reader Service!

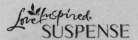

HOMETOWN HEARTS ♥

YES! Please send me **The Hometown Hearts Collection** in Larger Print. This collection begins with 3 FREE books and 2 FREE gifts in the first shipment. Along with my 3 free books, I'll also get the next 4 books from the Hometown Hearts Collection, in LARGER PRINT, which I may either return and owe nothing, or keep for the low price of $4.99 U.S./ $5.89 CDN each plus $2.99 for shipping and handling per shipment*. If I decide to continue, about once a month for 8 months I will get 6 or 7 more books, but will only need to pay for 4. That means 2 or 3 books in every shipment will be FREE! If I decide to keep the entire collection, I'll have paid for only 32 books because 19 books are FREE! I understand that accepting the 3 free books and gifts places me under no obligation to buy anything. I can always return a shipment and cancel at any time. My free books and gifts are mine to keep no matter what I decide.

262 HCN 3432 462 HCN 3432

Name	(PLEASE PRINT)	

Address		Apt. #

City	State/Prov.	Zip/Postal Code

Signature (if under 18, a parent or guardian must sign)

Mail to the **Reader Service:**

IN U.S.A.: P.O. Box 1867, Buffalo, NY. 14240-1867
IN CANADA: P.O. Box 609, Fort Erie, Ontario L2A 5X3

* Terms and prices subject to change without notice. Prices do not include applicable taxes. Sales tax applicable in NY. Canadian residents will be charged applicable taxes. This offer is limited to one order per household. All orders subject to approval. Credit or debit balances in a customer's account(s) may be offset by any other outstanding balance owed by or to the customer. Please allow 4 to 6 weeks for delivery. Offer available while quantities last. Offer not available to Quebec residents.

Get 2 Free Books,
Plus 2 Free Gifts—
just for trying the Reader Service!